PRAISE

"A Grand Guignol haunted house story. Don't turn the lights off."
—Silvia Moreno-Garcia author of *Mexican Gothic*

"Masterful. Jessup understands the humanity that beats at the heart of horror, and never flinches from the flaws that lurk at the core of every family."
—Jonathan Wood, author of *Broken Hero*

"One of the most gorgeous haunted house stories I've ever read."
—Bonnie Jo Stufflebeam, author of *Glorious Fiends*

"A family experiences an immediate, unsettling attachment to their new home, a house rife with occult secrets. We've been here before, but as horror fans know, it isn't the trope an author chooses, that gives the story a kick. It's all in the execution. The classic premise here has been sharpened by Paul Jessup's keen use of the vernacular, characters who are damaged in fascinating ways, and some mind-blowing yet plausible family history. A dizzying concoction of suspense and supernatural horror, served on ice."
— S. P. Miskowski, author of the collection *Strange Is the Night*

"Paul Jessup's prose is as psychedelic as the dead hippie cultists haunting the Glass House. This book slams together your traditional haunted house story with something far more cosmic and eerie, and then dowses the entire mix with frenetic energy. Powerful, weird, and sexy: I've never read anything quite like it."
—Wendy N. Wagner, author of *The Secret Skin* and *The Deer Kings*

GLASS
HOUSE

by

PAUL JESSUP

Aunt Val –
enjoy my spooky
books

Underland Press

This book is published by Underland Press, which is part of Firebird Creative, LLC (Clackamas, OR).

What do you have to be afraid of . . . ?

Edited by Darin Bradley
Book Design and Layout by Firebird Creative

This Underland Press trade edition has an ISBN of 978-1-63023-075-3.

Underland Press
www.underlandpress.com

GLASS HOUSE

For my Aunt Dar, who opened the doors of horror to me at such a young age.

-1-

The real estate agent said *these are good bones,* and Dana just had to agree. So strong, so beautiful, so rigid beneath the skin. And there was so much to love about the flesh of it, too. The crown molding, the lattice windows, the ivy and cracks and cobwebs and everything. The whole place just left her so breathless and electric. She was in love, yes she was. She was in love with every inch of this house.

Next, they moved through the spacious living room. Walls dotted with Corinthian columns and a cathedral ceiling spotted with mildew. Archways like the legs of giants straddled the rooms, coated in tarnished vine mosaics. Her daughters played between the arches, calling out to each other, tagging one another, laughing. Lily and Rae, her darling things, her lovely little ones.

Now eight and ten, they were only two years apart, practically twins. She touched her stomach, the place where they'd once grown inside of her, and felt a connection with this house. *You understand me,* she thought. After all, we both contained bodies and wombs and life. This house knew the loss of those that left the womb, of having someone outside of you who was once inside, feeding on you, listening to you, sharing your heartbeat.

Breathe it all in, an invigorating incense. Rotted vegetation and raw soil and things growing in the dark. Intoxicating. Her hand on her stomach again, that empty womb tingled. A connection between the two of them. This room like a shrine, like a temple. There was an echo of frescoes along the walls, and she wanted to peel them back, and uncover their hidden secrets. Her trembling palms pushed flat against that wall. Humid and sweating on her hand. How could a wall sweat like this? It seemed impossible. And yet, it did. Like an echo of her skin: *the flesh of this house sweats.*

A heat grew inside her with each breath. To undress the walls of this house, to suck in the pheromones it gave off. Oh, the promises it would give her. It understood her, deep in bone, deep in flesh, deep in every aspect of *herself*, in a way no one else ever could.

"It's beautiful," she whispered, so calm, "Lucas, honey, don't you think so? Don't you think it's beautiful?"

Lucas Glass, that rugged man she'd married ages ago. Handsome in a brutalist architecture sort of way, with a constant five o'clock shadow and carved stone features. His black hair curled raven feathers with a touch of gray. Lucas. Her gothic film director. Obsessed with creating artistic documentaries on the macabre. Once upon a time he read old poetry to her and sang off-key love songs on a boat on a river. Now that was all past and muted and sepia-toned. They were almost strangers now, weren't they? How did that even happen . . .

She reached over and clasped his hand. Her pulse raced quick and heavy and full of excitement, as he sighed that frustrated Lucas sigh. A slow, burning, sigh: the sigh of an impatient director. "I don't know, I mean. I really don't know. I love the atmosphere of it all, but can we even get it up to code? Will it even pass inspection?"

The real estate agent twitched her freckled nose and pushed her wire thin glasses up her face. "I'll email you the documents, but it's already passed inspection as of last year. We had another buyer back then who bowed out at the last minute, but I can assure you, that the electric is up to code, same for the plumbing and everything else as well. But never mind that! I have so much more to show you. The best of the best is yet to come." Her voice was cheerful and chirpy and rounded out with a subtle accent. Hungarian? Maybes. German? No, not quite. Swedish? Not even close. Something European, that was for certain. Almost like a feminine Peter Lorre, or Bela Lugosi, but not quite.

"Wait until you see the upstairs, the downstairs, the garden out back. Oh, wait until you see *the crypt*."

And the agent darted ahead of them. So quick! A whirlwind of a tiny body. Black and grey hair piled up on her scalp in a neat little bun, stray strands curling down on her cheeks, as she moved in rapid movements. A rabbit in fright, a hunted prey of a thing. What do you have to be scared of, agent rabbit? What hunts you in the dark hallows of *our beautiful house*?

Oh! Did Dana just think it? Did she call it *our* house already? Lucas hadn't even a chance to say yes. And yet, she knew that it was true.

A thrill, and a scream of joy inside!
Our beautiful new house.

-2-

Dana's hand grasped the banister, her fingers a rude circle of skin against thick wood. She felt it breathe against her palm, sweaty and subtly flexing against flesh. It was a living thing, this house. The railing was like a lover's spine arching against her hand. She wanted to kiss the wood, to lick it, to feel it grow against her lips. Lucas had left her so lonely, so empty. This house would fill her, and she would fill it.

Agent rabbit thumped up the stairs ahead of them, the world moving in slow motion, their bodies accented by stray sunbeams and crowded with dust motes. Lucas between the two of them like an ancient statue of a shattered god. A dream, a dream, everything moved like a dream. Shadows pierced by the knife of sunlight, cutting through the fog of dust and dirt. Hard to breathe. Breathless. Constricted by the weight of the air. She felt dizzy. Touched her forehead. Wiped away that sweat. Her two little girls right behind her, dancing barefoot on the floorboards. When had they taken their shoes off? Should she yell at them to put them back on? She felt feverish, unsettled, off-kilter.

Did this house ache like she ached? The need swelled between them, as her daughters laughed as they played. The staircase grand and overpowering. It could fit them all and have room to spare.

And ahead Lucas gasped as he stepped onto the second floor, his body disappearing into the summer haze.

"What? What is this? Dana, honey, come here, come quick. Does this hallway feel familiar to you? It feels so familiar to me, but I, I, I just can't place it."

Oh, almost there, not far behind him now, as she stepped up that last stair, and saw what Lucas saw before her:

A hallway so distinct, surrounded by doors leading to bedrooms. And over that? A stained-glass dome, all loosely decorated and delicate. It looked like a religious mural, maybe, or a tarot card, possibly, or wait . . . an album cover? Lucas was right, she had seen it before, she recognized it, but she couldn't put her finger on what it was, exactly.

"Come on, tell me! Tell me if you feel what I feel. It's familiar, isn't it? But in a lazy hazy way, you know, like a faded memory?"

Her whole body sang in recognition as she stared up, goosebumps dotting her arms. A skull with a keyhole in the stained-glass dome, eyes on a hand, a crown of candles, drops of blood, a chalice and a sword. In the center of it all stood three women and one little boy. There was an implication of violence in this mural, an implication of sacrifice, of mutilations to come. This whole thing felt like a promise, a whisper: déjà vu. So beautifully gothic it hurt her heart.

"I recognize it," her voice all gravel and hoarse, "But I don't know where. Did we dream this place? Is that it? A shared dream that we brought into existence? I feel like it's an album cover, if that makes sense, like it's an old record. Why do I know this?"

Lucas shook his head. "No, more like . . . like some lost childhood memory rediscovered later in life."

And she touched the walls, feeling every bit of it. Rough things, covered in a patina of dirt and filth and tattered wallpaper. It would take hours upon hours to scrub these clean, yet she still felt pulled towards it. A desire to take care of this house, to scour it and bathe it and love it. All of the imperfections called out to her and she swooned in the heat of the hallway.

"There is something here, a memory, maybe?" Lucas said. "Something lost inside of me, something that needs to be found . . ."

She knew exactly what he meant. The girls jumped up the steps behind her, and she moved further, further down the hallway. Agent rabbit pointed at each room, listing off the sizes and what work needed to be done in each one. The strangeness of it all crept around inside of her as a fog entered Dana's thoughts. Was she dreaming now? It felt like it, the haze, the fog in her mind, the way the world seemed to move in slow motion. Lucas stood right there, right in front of her. His body was obscured in the haze of dirt and dust and shadows, his face beatific and outlined by a stray sunbeam.

What was this? What a strange portent. As if to see him decapitated, beheaded, his expression one of saintly rapture. Like all those images of her Catholic school youth, a mixture of reverie and horror all at once. This, this wasn't right. She was beside herself with sorrow and loss, and she ran over to him and grabbed his tattooed hand, their sweaty palms meeting and sliding fingers against palms against fingers. Yes, he was still solid and real in the mist. Why had the house shown her this? Was the house a jealous house?

He smiled at her and looked at her so savagely. "You okay?"

There was no way to respond to that.

Rae called out from behind them, her words masking a squeal of pure joy. "This one is mine!" And she ran into one of the larger rooms, opening the closets and windows, filling the house with sounds of wood creaking and rusty hinges groaning. Her sister laughed, ran about, searching for a room of her own to claim, as Dana watched on. There were more than enough rooms in this house for all of them. Huge, sprawling, beautiful thing it was. A monstrous house that could fit several families, easily. A house she loved, and a house that loved her back.

-3-

At the bottom of the hill rambled a garden all overgrown and beautiful. It contained massive weeds as tall as Lucas, blowing lazily in the strong summer wind. She touched one, and it felt all velvety. Leaf like human skin, buds like human faces, the path now overgrown and dappled with cracked stones. Grasshoppers leapt about, hunting, as birds watched with hungry eyes from the tree branches. Gnarled things, protective things, those trees. Do not go beyond this point. Do not travel deeper into the place behind the house. You do not want to know what lives there.

It feeds on light.

She gripped Lucas's hands tighter, tighter. He turned to her, smiled some nervous smile. "You all right?" It was half a whisper, barely audible to the rest. And she nodded, and yes, she was all right, oh so very all right. Her pulse faster now, faster. What he probably read as fear was something else. Something far more powerful than fear. It rose all hot inside of her and threatened to erupt.

"I, I, this place, it's, I can't explain how it's *affecting* me."

And he smiled that Lucas smile. A smirk, oh so mysterious, always hiding his true feelings. They passed beneath a large weeping willow tree, with branches drooped down and dangling over their heads. Leaves brushed their hair like the hands of lost children, as the spindly boughs rattled like bones.

She watched calmly as their daughters played between the branches, picked them up, moved them about. She felt some odd sense of foreboding as they danced with them in a primal, brutal ballet, whomping each other and laughing. The tree shifted around them. The noises it made sounded like a living thing, an ancient thing. A thing that felt pain and laughter and hate. She should stop them, before the tree makes things *worse, and releases some of its pent up ancient anger.* "Girls, girls! Maybe you should quit playing with the tree, okay?"

And Lucas shot her *his look, a* disappointed, burning hate of a look. She pulled her hand back, as he tried to grasp it again, missing and frustrated as she kept her hand away. Not now, no, maybe later, but not right after that look. "Just let them play with the tree," he said.

But she would not feel silly.

"No," and she glared at him, returning his own sour look. Let's see how he likes it, to be belittled by a simple stare. No response? Good. That would show him. To think that maybe somehow they could patch things up so simply. The house might be a first step, but it also might be the last step in their marriage. She glanced back over at Lily and Rae, and saw that her girls didn't even seem to care. They were kicking rocks now, and drawing spirals in the dirt with sticks. She turned again and looked toward that mammoth, ancient, tree.

And what was this? What was this, here? A book harshly nailed to the trunk, its spine straight with the cover peeled back like wings. Paper feathers floated downward, coating the roots below them with words. *Step forward, Dana. Step forward. Reach out, fingers grasping, and touch the rain-ruined leather binding.* It twitched a bit. From the wind, from her touch. And she pulled that hand back, placed those quivering fingers to her lips, and closed her eyes. Why was this book placed here? A sacrifice, yes. It felt like a sacrifice.

Rapture, rupture, seismic, orgasmic, eruption.

"What could it mean? What could this book mean?"

Agent rabbit grew impatient. Her face scowled, her lips tightly pursed in anger.

"It doesn't matter, you can do whatever you want with it when you own this place. Tear down the sentinel books! Put up more! Just do whatever you damn well please! But only if you buy, buy, buy! But before we get to that," and her nose twitched again, and her lip peeled back to reveal her two front teeth, "we need to get to know this place *intimately*. Come, we've got one more thing I need to show you both. It is the most important piece of this entire house, and you will simply love it. Just, simply love it to pieces, I promise you."

Did she just say sentinel books? Dana needed to ask more, to pry into what she meant by this and get to the bottom of everything. But no, too late, too slow, agent rabbit was already running up toward the house, her legs stomping a rhythm like a march hare against the ground. She should follow, the house called to her, promised such beautiful indiscretions. It was better inside, far away from that tree, and the wicked sentience that crept between the branches.

-4-

A black door in the side of the hill, guarded by two decrepit stone owls and random dandelions. Chthonic things, those owls, the size of large dogs or maybe even small horses. That door made of thick oak with dents and chunks taken out of it, chained shut with rusted links and chunky padlocks. The house watched her from the top of the hill, not quite sane, the windows staring as the storm clouds rushed toward them. The humidity would break soon, and the rain would pour down with thunder and lightning and everything else. You could taste it in the air, like pennies or the sea ripe on your tongue.

She reached out and touched the left owl, as the stone feathers brushed against the tips of her fingers. What was it called in Japanese? Wabi-sabi? No, that couldn't be right. Mono no aware? No, maybe not that either. She couldn't remember. It wasn't important. The beauty of decay, of broken things glued back together, there was some word for it, some perfect word that described this feeling she felt right now. That was this *house*, and that was what was important.

Breathless now. There was a promise of something horribly wonderful about to happen. Feel that sweat slide down her back? Drip, drip, drip. The real estate agent unlocked the door and swung it open, a wave of cold air whispering against Dana's cheek. It smelled tangy, a savagely sweet smell. So familiar, yet not at the same time. Blood? No. That wasn't the smell of blood. Was it?

"Wait until you guys see this, I know you're just going to love it, just adore it. When I saw the two of you, oh, I just knew this would be the house for you, and you would simply *love this*."

Lucas tried to grab her hand again and she let him this time. They were working on it, they were working on it, they were working on it. The rhythm of his heart raced against her palm, sweat mingling between the two of them, connecting them together, trading fluids through the

pores of their skin. Was this okay? Was it okay to hold hands? Why
did it feel so strange, so foreign, so wrong? Each time it felt even more
wrong. Could they ever breach these walls between them?

Never mind that now. She would try, she would have to try. That
was the promise of this house. They walked forward together, following agent rabbit, deep into the inky black darkness beyond that door.
Wooden stairs whispered under their weight, as the ceiling above
erupted to the sound of child's play. Her girls had gone upstairs (*too
dangerous down here*), laughing and running through the entire first
floor. All while the adults explored this strange cellar world inside the
hill, beneath the house.

Lucas's free hand lifted his phone high up and used it as a makeshift flashlight. It cast a strange, eerie blue light. One that carved long
shadows in the dark.

"Welcome, welcome, may I present to you the family crypt."

Lucas's hand tensed around hers. Something changed between
them. This didn't feel so weird any longer. The crypt came sharply into
view before them, his cellphone light dimming erratically, the battery
weak and almost dead. Shadows of stone coffins, dirt floors, bones set
into the walls themselves. Skulls in alcoves. And the air smelled like
a butcher shop. She'd been right before, hadn't she? Blood, blood, it
was thick with the raw scent of blood. How long have they been dead
down here? It all smelled so *fresh*.

Her hand trembled against Lucas's hand, a vibration of flesh against
flesh. The crypt felt like a secret place, a vulnerable place, the inner-
most raw underskin muscle of the house. Oh, it wanted her to see this,
it needed her to see the house like this, all wide open with all of the
secrets exposed. Lucas's hands gripped hers tighter and tighter and
tighter, an intense circle of skin against her knuckles. He seemed to
swoon and breathe heavily and she had to hold him steady. Had he
felt the house like she felt the house? All yearning need and desperate
whispers?

"Do you know whose skulls these are, whose coffins? My god, why
are there so many . . ."

Agent rabbit perked up at this and smiled her lupine smile and
twitched her freckled nose. "Didn't you google the address? Didn't
you do any research at all? I thought that's *why* you chose this house

in the first place, out of all the houses I've offered to show you. Don't you know where you are standing?"

And Lucas sighed that Lucas sigh yet again. Long, slow, burning.

"Pretend I don't know and illuminate me, okay? Go ahead and shine a little light on my darkness."

"This is the Gemini House. *The* Gemini House, for the real, honest-to-god Sunshine Family."

A gasp. He grabbed Dana's hand tighter and she smiled a soft, sweet, crooked little smile. Oh. She knew it now, knew it in the bones and her blood and her beating heart. This was their house after all. It was always their house, would always be their house, forever and ever and ever, amen. Lucas was obsessed with the Sunshine Family, and he'd introduced her to them when they first started dating. How long ago was it now? At least a decade and a half.

Back then he'd played her their records non-stop. And even though they could stream the songs he said he preferred the old vinyl. That they reminded him of a time before he was born, a time he felt connected to, somehow. The music on the records gave way to long, rambling, crazed speeches about life and the environment and the things beyond the dark and the stars. This was the enigmatic, enthralling voice of their leader, their master, the Father of the Sunshine Family. Deep and gravelly, a voice like grave dirt and stones sliding against stones. *What walks in the pines? Where does it go? What walks in the pines? What sings in the snow? And who, who, who will devour the light when we're gone?*

"No, you're kidding, right? How the hell did we not realize this? I thought I recognized that hallway! It's the cover to their last album, *Apocalypse Heart*. And why the hell is this place so damned cheap, then? I mean, if it's *their* house, that historical *Gemini House*? Then there must be like a billion offers, especially after the suicides, and everything else . . . and, oh, man. Oh, man! This house has some history to it. I thought I recognized it, and oh, man. I thought I did! We lucked out, oh, we lucked out. Man, oh man. This is so awesome."

Agent rabbit licked her lips and smiled a hungry smile. "From the moment I saw you I knew that you would be perfect here. It takes a special kind of person to love the Gemini House," and for some reason she blushed, her face turning scarlet in the dark, "it's best if we talk about the rest this upstairs, all right? There a few conditions to owning a house like this, a reason it's so cheap and so few people even care about owning it, even as a curiosity."

Lucas nodded and Dana grinned a big ear-to-ear true love falling through the crust of the world *grin*. This was kismet. Karma. Destiny. This would be their house, and it would fix everything.

-5-

What a strange and unreal car ride back home. The house disappeared behind them in a vague whisper, and the trees along the road dotted outside their windows in Morse Code. *Dot dot dash. Tree, tree, pole.* All while Dana stared off in silence, her hand on that cold glass. Was that even real? How could such a thing exist in this world? It all seemed like it happened in a hazy, half remembered dream.

For so long she dreamt of living in ruined old houses, the kind with cobwebs and the whisper of ghosts. It made her estranged and lonely as a child growing up in the suburbs. All the other kids played war and family and war some more. But not her, no. She was a strange child, with her dollhouses coated in fake spider webs and haunted by hand-painted *papier-mâché* ghosts. Tiny, detailed murder scenes disturbed her immediate families, while at night she played out love stories replete with monsters and flickering candle flames. What gave other children nightmares gave her a thrilling, almost-religious sensation.

The minivan's AC pumped frosty air directly into her face, cooling away the sweat from earlier, as she turned around and glanced in the backseat. There they were. Her perfect little ones, fast asleep against the cracked vinyl. Those frayed seatbelts strapping them in. Safety, always safe, keep them safe even now, even in this rolling death machine. The sun set behind their heads, casting halos and painting the interior of the car an unnatural ochre hue.

She touched Lily's cheek, and moved a curl of black hair from her sleeping eyes. No, no, stir a little, but don't wake, not yet. This silence felt like a meditation, and Dana needed that silence, that meditation. There was a lot to take in. Everything felt different, everything felt the same. Reality had altered for a tiny bit, and now slowly righted itself, creating a new normal out of the detritus of the old.

"Did we really just do that? Did we really just sign papers for the house? The Gemini House!"

Lucas kept his eyes on the road. His face didn't change at all. No emotion registering. "I can't believe it either."

"Everything is signed," she said, "Do you think I'm being silly? I don't think I am. It feels too right, too good to be true. I can't believe it's real."

And he coughed in his hand, never once taking his eyes off the road.

"I think, I think I might have something here. I think this is more than a house to live in, I think there is a work of art waiting to be made. I'm already starting to take notes, gather ideas . . ."

Oh, no. What did he mean by that? Did he want something more from this house? Wasn't it enough that the Gemini House would be their family home? They both loved all things gothic and macabre, why did it have to involve something *else*. Something like work.

Damn it. They were working on it.

"What is it, Lucas? Just tell me."

A nervous tilt of his head, glancing at her with his peripheral vision. Sides of his eyes staring, briefly.

"I'm picturing a documentary, right? The house, the history, the whole suicide cult? Everything. Can't you picture it? I could film it all while we restore the house and our lives living with all of that history, showing everything we discover, every secret we uncover. The house wants to be on camera, it needs to be on camera. Can't you feel it? This house contains the weight of our destiny, all our lives leading up to this moment, now. I've already made a call to my agent. Netflix might even be interested, especially from a cult true crime documentary . . . they'd never seen anything like this one. They told me, man, oh, man, get this, they said it makes all the others look boring and trite and menial."

Silence. Not sure how to take this, not sure how to approach this at all. She turned, looked out the window, avoided his eyes. There was no way she was going to let him see the anger swirling around in her own gaze. Her hands clenched tight into minifists, knotting up her shirt. She remembered his last documentary. It won lots of awards, but it tore them apart. What he put them through, hell, what he'd put *Lily* through! His own daughter, of all people. She said she would never let that happen again, never, ever, ever.

Between them, inside of her. Something broke.

"I don't know, Lucas, I don't know . . ."

After such a wonderful day and now this. He'd promised her, and what was that promise even worth anymore? Nothing it seemed. He would just do whatever he wanted to, damn the consequences.

"No, no, not like that. It'll be about them, you know? The Sunshine Family. All that's happened to them, and so much more, right? Like, I want to get all meta about it, dig in deeper to it. I want to explore the emotions of the place, yanno? Those haunted feelings it gives off. Oh, it would be so beautiful, this could be my life's work, my magnum opus. The Sunshine Family! Just. Man, oh, man. I've spent so much of my life thinking about them, reading about them, about the Gemini House. How could I *not* do this? And I promise, *I promise*, it will not involve either of the children. Okay? Please say it's okay."

She turned her gaze from his and glanced behind at her darling little ones once more. So peaceful. Rae tossed a bit, turned a bit. The night sky now blared down at them, coating their faces in stars. The sun had set when she wasn't even paying attention. How sudden. How abrupt.

"All right, as long as you keep them out of it," and she touched Lily's cheek, gently, a whisper of a touch, "I don't want this to be another *Hour of Smiles* scenario, okay? That wasn't something they needed, not ever. I still worry about the nights when she has her episodes . . . we can't fix what you broke, all in the name of your stupid movie."

He paused longer than she wanted. Could she still trust him, or even trust a pause like that? It had taken her so long to let that last incident slide. If it had happened more than once? She and the girls would be gone, bam. Just like that. But. It was only the once, she kept telling herself, only the one time a year or two ago. He would never do that again. He promised, and she trusted him. Against all odds, she trusted him.

"Of course, of course. Nobody wants that, especially not me. You have to understand, I hate myself for that. Even in the end, it wasn't worth the awards, nor all the accolades, or even the money. If I could go back in time . . ."

She turned and let her eyes meet his eyes, just so he could see the soft fires blazing inside of them. She needed him to see this, to see her anger, and understand. They wouldn't be working on this anymore if he did that again. "But you can't go back in time, what's done is done."

And he nodded, solemnly, without words.

-6-

Daddy once taught Lily what it was like to die. She still thought about it a lot, and sometimes woke up in the middle of the night (like tonight) and thought back to the *Hour of Smiles*, as she promised him she would be a good little girl, the best little girl in the world. Even after he closed the coffin lid.

Think about it now, while everyone else was asleep in the living room. They were all draped over couches and rolled out sleeping bags on the floor. The last of their items all boxed up around them, getting ready for the big move. But Lily couldn't think about the big move, no, all she could think about was the sound of the hammer driving the nails into her coffin. She wanted to scream, but she was a good little girl. The best little girl. The most wonderful little girl in the world. She bit that scream back down. Teeth against the inside of her cheek. Eyes bugging out in a bit of pain. But no, don't cry out perfect girl, Daddy counted on you for his movie, for his perfect film, oh, you would be a star, oh, you would be a bright shining star . . .

She remembered what he told her to think about in that moment. The worms. The rot and decay of her body. He showed her pictures, showed her what happened each moment, each day, how the body transforms after death. She thought about these things, thought about how it might feel. To be trapped in her body as it liquefied, intestines turning into thick goop. Something inside of her squirmed. The worms, the maggots, something inside of her screamed.

Was there a ghost inside of her? A floating ghost waiting to be freed once the body rots? Would it feel everything? Fingernails pushing out, skin receding back? Death was not a gentle thing. It ripped and tore and left everything mangled and broken.

Remember, remember, the leathery faces on the pictures, the teeth all long and gums short and small. *We are all vampires when we're dead.*

No, she should stop thinking about this. She should stop remembering this. She needed to sleep! There was so much to do tomorrow. And yet, she couldn't turn it off. Her mind kept going back there, back into the darkness. Sleeping in the sleeping bag was just like it was in the coffin. Surrounded by darkness, closed in, zipped-up tight. Be a good girl, don't scream, don't howl, don't punch through the wood of the coffin. It was a Halloween decoration repurposed for daddy's movie, yes. Though for a bit he had toyed with the idea of buying her a real child's coffin, to add to the authenticity of the experience.

But that must have been too much for him, poor daddy. She remembered walking around those showrooms. Touching the beautiful marble, the insides lined with velvet. So soft. "I want this one daddy, or maybe this one?"

And he coughed and turned green and they left so quickly.

No, stop thinking about this, thinking about this will bring back the other one, that other thing, that dead little boy who sings. You won't be able to sleep until dawn if you remember him. Don't go this far back, don't see him, don't even speak his name...

But it was too late, wasn't it? The memory came clear and sharp and pointed. Stabbing her in the gut. Remember the sound of flies? All that buzzing, and at first she thought it was bees, but no, no. It wasn't bees at all. Flies, fluttering inside of her coffin. What was daddy doing? This wasn't part of the plan.

Something inside ached and flopped and almost vomited. Didn't want to remember this anymore, didn't want to think about it all, no. No. No.

She was a good girl, the best girl ever, until she saw something moving in the dark of the coffin. Eyes slammed shut, and yet, something moved in the shadows. Something was there in the coffin with her. Was there enough room? How could there be enough room for her and the little boy with the bandaged face? Yet, there he was, wrapped up around her, moving in the dark with her. His lips blackened and burnt, and his eyelids gone and eyes bugging out. His bones rattled beneath the bandages, and he reached out and tried to hug her, tried to embrace her, and he smelled like cinders and smoke and burning flesh, and he whispered in her ear, his voice like flies buzzing, so hard for him to speak through burnt lips, yet he did, he did, and each time she remembered this, he said something different, always something different . . .

Don't go there, he said this time, stay. Stay. Don't go there. The Gemini House is dangerous.

And even right now, even in her living room, on the floor, the memory brought it out of her again. She couldn't help it. Her body began to flail about uncontrollably, her limbs mechanical things, her mind racing, her mouth frothing. She wailed, and it wasn't right, that sound from her mouth. That wailing was the wrong sound.

Oh, and this would be *so embarrassing* later. She was too old for this, ten years old was way too old for this. And yet? Uncontrollable. It happened without even a single thought. She wet herself. A slow warm trickle against her leg as mommy ran up and over to her, and held her sobbing against her chest. Soothing her, over and over again. Her mother comforted her, helped her, encased her in skin and hair. While Lily said over and over again, in a voice unlike her own, "The Rattling Boy doesn't want us to go, mommy, the Rattling Boy doesn't want us to go."

Her mother held her tight and made comforting, cooing noises over and over again. "It was just a dream my darling one, just a dream and nothing else. You love our new house, remember? We all love our new house."

She could not be comforted, she could not be consoled. They stayed awake the rest of the night, bodies entwined together, giving each other such meager peace in the morning hours, while the sun rose up and painted the world with a cold, blue light. Still sobbing, even though she was unable to produce tears any longer.

-7-

Oh, Lily, oh, Lily, oh, little zombie girl. Oh, Lily, oh, Lily, oh, sleepless, stumble-down girl with circles under her eyes. Books now clutched close to her chest in the backseat of their minivan. She was surrounded by loose boxes as they followed Daddy and Rae in the U-Haul in front of them. The boxes rattled next to her, threatening to topple over and crush her in the backseat.

Mommy wanted all the girls in the same car, but Rae kept looking at Lily strangely, and kept moving away from her touch, as if Lily was infected by some unseen ghost disease. It hurts, yes, to see Rae act like that toward her. But sisters were sisters, and causing each other emotional and physical pain was just the nature of the sibling beast.

So, it was just the two of them, in the dark cave of the van, with Lily nodding off here and there. Her dreams slipped about in her mind, and before she knew it, she walked in an echo of their new house. Of course, this was a dream version of the house, everything was backwards and nice and clean. And someone new waited for her upstairs, a stranger. A woman dressed all in pale clothes, walking in a strange, jerky fashion. The stranger's arms at weird angles, as if posing, her hands at either side of her face, her fingers wiggling like spider legs. Elbows jutted out.

A ripped black rag draped over the stranger's face, a whisper of a thing, an empty mask, all blank and haunted. Why did the rag make her uneasy? That same feeling as finding maggots in her fruit. And, and, and what did this stranger want? With her? With little zombie girl, little coffin girl? What did this stranger want?

And each time she saw the stranger, Lily forced herself awake. Jerking, crying, trying hard not to scream. Mommy's eyes glanced back in the rearview mirror, the sky all cloudless and hungry out of the front window. Green eyes filled with concern, her lips parting briefly and saying, "Lily, dear, my darling, my sweet, are you okay? It's not that dream again, not the one from last night, is it?"

Oh, and shake her head no, no, no. It wasn't the same dream. This one was different. This was a *true nightmare*, while last night was a memory and a vision and that little bandaged boy who was scary but only trying to protect her and keep her safe. Unlike that woman in the nightmare, she seemed ominous and sharp and hateful Who was this woman in pale clothes? Just some random dream person? She felt real, she felt sinister, she felt like someone Lily had met before. Was this what the bandaged boy warned her about last night? Couldn't be sure, maybe didn't even want to know. Maybe this should stay a mystery.

"I'm just having trouble sleeping mommy," and then a smile, yes, she forced a smile. *See? See? I am sweet and lovely and amazing.* "That's all, I think. Maybe the move is making me all wonky, I don't know. Maybe."

"Oh, okay then, my love, my sweet, my beautiful lovely girl. If there is anything wrong, anything bothering you at all," and Mommy chewed her lower lip, and Lily knew that nervous, anxious gesture, "You can tell me. You know that, right? You can tell me anything, I would never betray your trust."

But could she? Could she tell her? The way Mommy yelled and screamed when Daddy pried her free from the coffin was a terrifying thing. She had been a good girl, and wasn't even teary-eyed or anything. Maybe her eyes bugged out, maybe, and maybe her lips were pursed shut, maybe, and maybe her hands were clenched tight into fists, maybe. That didn't matter, what mattered was Mommy's rage and her hitting Daddy and Daddy just taking it and apologizing over and over again. *She could've suffocated, she could've died!*

"I'm okay, Mommy," she spoke so calmly, her Daddy would be so proud, "Honest. If it was something really bad or scary, I would tell you."

Oh, that memory, that last bit with the bandaged boy still rolling about in her mind.

And Daddy, oh, Daddy, strong Daddy. He praised her for being a good girl, for everything being all okay. He told her how she was going to be a star, and, oh, our little girl wants to be a star, doesn't she? But . . .

She wasn't so sure about that. Stars were small and sharp and covered in lights that cut you, light that burned your eyes. She wanted to be the dark between the stars, maybe even the dark in the coffin.

Something inside her died in that coffin and came back to the light all changed and different. Ghosts now, ghosts everywhere. Ghosts following her, ghosts whispering to her. The ghosts loved the dark, and she was the darkness now, all of the darkness all of the time.

And then she nodded off again, and the crazy woman was gone, and instead there was the smell of ash and fire and nothing else. Maybe the sounds of distant screams. A little boy burning up like a torch and crying out in pain. She sat in her dream and listened and wasn't terrified, no, no. She was something else. Something calm and a bit sad, but not terrified.

-8-

That night they all slept in the living room. The ceiling was lined with gold and white Christmas lights powered by a portable generator. Daddy said no electricity yet, not for a few more days still. And for some reason, that gave Lily a strange sort of comfort. No computers, no tablets, no blaring artificial light to hide her parents from her.

Dad reached over, sighed, and placed the needle on the record player. Scratch, fuzz, and then a pop or two as haunted sounds began to play. A voice yawped through a megaphone, masculine, slow and building. The voice preached of the world around them and the coming ages of death. It had been a long time since Daddy played this record, she was so little, yet she remembered all of it so clearly, she could almost speak along with it and not miss a beat.

Light was an abomination, the voice said. *The universe is housed in darkness, in the void between stars. We came through this horrible light and are tainted with it, burning up from the inside. And someday, someday,* that voice growled, *we'll shed it all and return to the void once again, covered in the ashes of our lives. We need to do something important with what time we have left on this melting meat rock. Something sacred. Even in death we can be tiny miracles, healing the world with our light. Your ghosts will be our sentinels, guardians of the doors closed and the mothers that lay behind the stars . . .*

"Do we have to listen to this right now?" Mommy said, and leaned her head against the living room wall. Her face was outlined with a halo of Christmas lights, making her the most beautiful woman in the world. Daddy should listen to her, Lily didn't like this record, either. "I think I've had enough Sunshine Family for one day. I mean, we *own their house,* right? We own it now, they don't, not anymore. Not if we don't let them."

And Daddy hummed along, and his voice was all deep and bellowing. He seemed to be completely ignoring what Mommy had said, and that made Lily angry and frustrated. "Man, oh, man—it's been a long great while since I heard these records, not since your girls were tiny and just barely out of your cribs. You remember that hon? The way they would sing along with the songs, and even Rae would repeat back all the crazy stuff in these spoken word sections. Amazing how little of this has changed over the years . . . so little entropy wearing on the record itself. Listen to how clean it sounds. Do you hear that? So clean."

And before Mommy could complain and Daddy would have to shut the record off, the Sunshine Family started singing Lily's favorite song! Oh, Daddy was right—she remembered it now, barely a fog of a memory with her coloring in her favorite coloring book pictures of medusa and mermaids, singing along. This sensation made her feel sad and happy all at once, like discovering a lost part of herself she didn't even know was missing. She couldn't help it, she had to sing along!

It's such a shame
When the dead sing your name
And you won't have any ears
To hear them with . . .
Oh, it's such a shame . . .

And the chorus was like the crash of ocean waves. Rolling in and out, in and out. It swept you up and filled you full of all this wonderland sound. The instruments! So many instruments playing along. A violin, yes, but also a few trumpets and a French horn and a guitar and bongos blasting out, and oh, oh, a pan flute! And oh, oh, listen to that! What was that even? A hollow blaring horn sound. What was that?

Her eyes circled closed and drifted off, and there was a calmness, her parents both singing along. Mommy no longer complaining about the record, just letting the Sunshine Family take them in and keep them. And then. And then. And then. Oh, no. The disconnect came back.

Even here, even in this moment, surrounded by love and family and music, she felt so *lonely*. The suffocating kind of loneliness, like she was outside of everything reaching in. She stopped singing, everything felt so far away and out of reach. She hated these moments of bright sadness. They came to her at the worst possible times, when she felt her most happy and joyful.

She opened her eyes again, just briefly, and saw Rae curled up in her sleeping bag, moving about, trying to get whatever sleep she could get. And so. And so. Lily reached out. Tried to communicate through the communion of flesh. To push beyond loneliness into something else. She still couldn't find it in her heart to sing, even though she badly wanted to feel that feeling again, to have that community of music between the record, Mommy, Daddy and herself? But the sadness was too great. Maybe this would help, hand on sister's hand, knuckles grazed against knuckles, as she held her breath.

Rae's hand jerked back. "Cut it out—I'm trying to sleep. I saw something behind the pines today, out in the garden, and it freaked me out."

And then her sister wiggled the silver sleeping bag further away. She looked like the maggots that had lined the bathroom ceiling when they first arrived. Remember? Mommy screamed and bleached the whole damn thing before anyone could use it. That's what she thought of, the way the silver sleeping bag moved. Like a larval thing crawling across the ceiling.

And of course, this brought on that horrible, sinking feeling. Even as her favorite song wrapped her up in that lovely chorus. All those voices singing, all those people playing. How she wanted to join them, how she wanted to be a part of the Sunshine Family right now. She saw the appeal, and why Daddy loved them. They sound so together, so happy, never being pulled apart. And for a moment, a brief moment, she wondered what happened to all of them? She would have to ask daddy that in the morning. He would know the answer for sure—he always knew the answers to everything. Maybe she would feel better then, less lonely then.

Though she doubted it.

-9-

Rae knew a secret, shhh, don't tell, that this house was a musical house. She could play it like a piano and play it like a violin and yeah, play it like a big brass band! Trumpet sounds on the stairs all *bwah bwah bwah,* and the French horn of the creaking doors, and the saxophone slide of the oven starting up.

And like all good musical child prodigies, she had perfect pitch. No, really! She really did, she's not just telling you nice stories. See, watch this! Any time she heard any song she would whistle it right back atcha. Even if she'd only heard it just the once! Just the *once.* She was proud of this ability. It felt magical, like a gift. Even now, when she ran through the hallways of the second floor. Bang, bang, timple tinny bang! She played music that spun around inside her head. A constant soup of all the everything she's ever heard.

And because of this, her mad genius mind thrummed with millions of rainbow sparkling thoughts of music. Watch these thoughts buzz on through! No one had thoughts like these. Not even bad staid boring grownups. They all had gray thoughts and rainwater thoughts. Jealous of the Rae thoughts.

Still, though, still, her dad buried Lily and not her and he rose her from the dead and not Rae and he tried to give Lily the gift of second sight and Rae just wasn't even considered, was she? No, Mommy put a stop to all of that and now Lily was broken and cared for and Rae was lesser. Because. Because. Because. Rae was the younger . . . the unburied, the un-resurrected. Her daddy didn't care enough about Rae to nail her in a coffin and throw dirt on her face.

No. Stop. Don't think about that. No! You're a genius, Rae. Super mad crazy awesome rainbow spitting genius! Stand right there, arms akimbo, underneath the stained-glass dome. Her head tilted up: super hero pose! The house was her instrument, not Lily's. And that made her brilliant important amazing special.

And to prove it, she would use her special talent, that prodigy musical talent of amazingness. She would play a song she'd heard just once, only once, last night during Mommy and Daddy's late-night record album binge.

And she would use that house to play it now, right now! Oh, ha ha, that will show them all. Look at her genius! Weep at her prodigy! It would be a bit tricky, yes, don't get her wrong about that. It was mostly violins and drums and that was it, no singing even. So, she would have to get creative to hit those right notes on the second floor, using the stomp stomp for the drums and the whispering violin glide of the windows. But she could do it, don't you doubt that at all, if anything Rae was re-source-ful.

She conducted all of it. Everything around her a carefully constructed orchestra. This was a dance and a rhythm that became a tiny childhood trance. Completely lost and caught up in all of it. A glaze of her eyes, the world a dizzy blur. Until, until, until she lost wind and the exhaustion of it all caught up with her.

And she bowed. Thank you, thank you, thank you. The applause of bird wings rattle bang against the windows of the house, her adoring crowd. Thank you, thank you, thank you. She almost didn't even notice the new stranger that appeared. Oho, and this stranger was very strange, indeed. Though, Rae thought *recognized* this strange stranger somehow, like a distant sad memory. How could that be? Was it a dream that she'd forgotten? Wouldn't be the first time she'd dreamt of someone before meeting them in real life! Probably wouldn't be the last time, either. Rae had just that kind of luck.

She paused for a moment, and looked up and realized, oh. That was where she'd recognized her! This strange stranger was one of the ladies illustrated on the stained-glass dome. That was her! Except no longer stained glass. Wow, Rae wondered how she did that? That must be a neat trick, to walk right of a stained-glass window like it was nothing.

She turned around and looked at that strange stranger again, just to make sure she wasn't seeing anything, and yup! That was her, the same woman on the dome, she was certain of it. She felt like she should be scared, that this sort of thing shouldn't happen in the daylight, and that should make it even scarier? But it wasn't, somehow. Rae felt calm, and a little bit excited, and wondered if her music summoned the woman from the glass? And if so, wow. That would be really cool.

The stranger walked a little closer, with a mechanical jerking motion, her body cloaked in black wasps. Sad little things, writhing all over her bone-thin body. And her face was scarred with spiral scars, the flesh raised up all red and sore. One of her eyes gone *(left eye)* a gaping hole of muscle and tissue and glinting white porcelain bone. Her head completely shaved bald and coated with more spiral scars. Her fingers like long skinny spider knives.

And of course, Rae waved and shouted, "Hiya!"

She would not be deterred by this strange stranger. Mommy and Daddy acted like strangers were dangerous things, but pfft. What did they know? Their heads were full of boring fluff, like the clouds of cotton shoved into the heart of stuffed animals. They didn't even see the pure unbridled genius of Rae! No, no, no. And they buried Lily instead of her and what, just what. Didn't they know anything at all? No! They knew nothing. Rae knew everything. And she knew that a stranger was just a friend she hadn't met yet. Ipso facto this must be a new friend. See? She knew Latin. How many other little girls knew such good things as Latin?

And this new friend was a rude new friend. They would have to discuss *manners* after this, yes indeedy. A nice, long talk about manners and friendships and not just showing up and being all rude and unspeaking. "Hiya, hiya! My name is Rae, what are you doing in our house? Are you a friend of Daddy's?"

And when that strange stranger finally spoke it sounded like insect wings rustling together. Each word an exhale, a whisper, a mutter, a cough. "You. Summoned. Me."

Of course, she did! She was that kind of special genius prodigy of a girl. Even the things she did on accident gave amazing results. "Why, Yes! Yes, I did. I summoned you here because no one here gets me. You get me?"

The stranger twitched forward, the insects crawling up the nests of skin and ribs. "I am *Mater Suspiriorum,* Our Lady of the Sighs. Do you understand? Do you know me? Do you know my sisters?"

Uh oh, oh no. Should Rae tell the truth, or bluster on through? No weakness! No. She was genius girl and a vibrant thing. She would not give up her brilliance this easily. "Of course, I do. Who do you think I am? Lily? Pfft. I know exactly who you are, I just don't know what you're doing here."

And she scoffed. There. That would show the stranger what's what. A good old scoff covered up her ignorance nicely.

"There is too much light in here for us. Too much. Light. Corrupter of the void! Burns and ashens our skins, it does. Summon me back again when the darkness is ripe and holy. Bring me back after dusk. Then. We'll talk."

Rae smiled. "Okay dokey, sounds like a plan, Stan. You can go now or whatever, I release you, and I'll see you after dark."

-10-

The next day or two was spent cleaning, and cleaning, and more cleaning. The bedrooms were first and foremost, with the dirt scrubbed away and the cobwebs pulled off and caught on hands and brooms and Swiffers. After that they turned to the kitchen and the living room, each of which much more difficult, and harder to clean. The girls hated this part the most, and would often run around screaming and chasing each other and shoving each other down.

Their parents let them go about and have their fun. For a brief moment both Mommy and Daddy smiled as they painted the walls, smiled as they scrubbed the floors, and smiled as they watched their little girls act like little girls for once and just play. No trauma, no sickness, no sadness.

Only the pure childhood joy of a new house to explore. For the first time in their entire lives, they had bedrooms of their own, and they couldn't wait to sleep in them. How wonderful it would be! How joyous.

-11-

Shut up, Lily! Shut up! Rae fumed, furious, she burned hot sun angry, so angry, how dare she, how how how, how dare she! What does she even know? Nothing! Less than nothing, worse than nothing! Nothing is at least a word, at least a something and that was more than what Lily knew! How dare she speak of the Lady of Sighs like that? The lady was beautiful in a cemetery kind of way, and Rae understood it, yes.

She understood why Mommy and Daddy loved this house and took them to graveyards to sing to the grave stones and take pictures of the midnight sun, and she understood daddy's skull tattoos and mommy's pictures of Victorian corpses she unpacked and hung throughout the house. She really understood that love of the macabre they all seemed to share (well, everyone in her family except Lily, of course).

The lady was beautiful in *that way*. A way that sung to her. A way that whispered and terrified and thrilled her. And what did Lily know about it? What? What? She was just jealous of the beauty. She wasn't like Rae and Mommy and Daddy, no. Lily cried and screamed after a single night in a stupid coffin. Of all things!

Rae would've been coffin proud. She would've smiled as the dirt suffocated her. She wanted the second sight. Why was Lily so lucky? Why?

"Just, please, Rae. Just, please."

Lily's voice was mouse quiet and they were in Rae's bedroom upstairs. Unpack, unpack, unpack, as they gently placed books on shelves. And she wanted to tell Lily to *get lost get out*, and yes even . . .

Get the fuck out of my room!

A smile at the secret swear that danced in her mind. But no, she knew better. Rae was a genius after all, and geniuses knew how to play other people. And oh, and yeah, she could play Lily like a fiddle, her words all bow-tight and ready to run across those strings.

"Please why, please what? You had some vision of a silly burnt old ghost boy, and you think, what? That I talk to dead ladies? Puh-lease.

We're not all as cuckoo bananas coffin sick in the head like some people."

A flinch, that cut and maybe, hmm, maybe Rae went too far this time. This was a dance, after all, and dances don't involve knife words.

"I just, I just, I just, I just . . ."

Rae knew it'd been too much now. The stammering started, and that meant Rae broke Lily, so she walked over and held her and tried to be all nice and calm now. Poor Lily, she just wasn't as smart as Rae. She could never understand things like Rae understood them. Pat, pat, pat, hand on her back. Poor Lily.

"He's not a joke, okay? He's. He's. Just a friend and he warned me, okay? He warned me that you shouldn't trust her. That's all! Please promise me you won't trust her. This is important."

She patted and patted. "Oh, okay, oh, okay. I promise, I do, silly Lily. I promise!"

But no, false words, untrue words. What did one pretend friend know about the truth of it all? He wasn't even a real thing, was he? Lily said he was a ghost, but pfft. Ghosts don't show up and tell you lies like that, do they? No! Of course not!

Only someone like Lily would think that the Lady of Sighs wasn't trustworthy. She didn't understand things like Rae understood them. There was trust and there was trust, and it was like knowing the difference between gray and grey eyes. It's subtle, but an important difference.

"Okay, that's enough Rae. Let me go, okay? This hug is over."

Push back and wait a minute. There was a different look in Lily's eyes. A sad look, a broken look, a quick quiver-lip look. Her hand reached out, touched her shoulder. Gently.

"Remember that thing you said last night? Something walks beyond the pines?"

"Yeah, I remember, I do."

A poke against her chest. "It needs to stay out there, beyond the pines. Agreed?"

Rae shrugged and didn't like where this was going, didn't like where this was going at all. What did this have to do with the Lady of Sighs? Lily bit her lips, and Rae knew right then she was keeping *something from her*. But what?

"I guess?"

And Lily leaned in. Eye to eye, face to face. Her features like a mask in the strange window light. Her breath smelled like flowers. "No, no guessing. The thing behind the pines *needs* to stay behind the pines. Agreed?"

And before Rae could respond either way, Mommy yelled out and called them downstairs. And they knew not to keep Mommy waiting, and so they ran without speaking through the ruins of the house. Rae was both relieved and upset that she didn't get a chance to respond. Agreed? No, maybe. She didn't know if she could agree to something like that, not without knowing what was behind the pines. She remembered it, like a shape made of nothingness, like how a sunspot looks when you open your eyes, a bright shadow along the edges of sight.

Her stomach felt flippity floppity for a moment, and she had to stop. Cold sweats on her forehead and that sense of doom everywhere. *Doom doom doom doom.* And then Mommy yelled again, and she just had to do it. She just had to shove this feeling aside and go! Run the rest of the way, and go! She would summon the lady again tonight, once it was dark. She didn't care what Lily thought. Lily was stupid and her imaginary friend was stupid and she was going to do what was right. After all, you never abandoned a friend, not ever.

But then that image from behind the pines fluttered through her thoughts again, and she gulped, her arms covered in goosebumps, her skin tingle tingle tingle. *No, they weren't connected, Lily was wrong, she had to be wrong. The Lady of Sighs was her friend, and friends don't lie to each other like that, even if it was a lie through omission.*

-12-

Boring Daddy was sitting alone *again*, surrounded by his computer and video cameras and old musty dusty tapes and records. All of it plugged into that gently whispering generator. Rae wanted to see if she could watch a show, or maybe do something else to avoid the boredom. Feel it now, gnawing at her, and it wasn't time to play the Happy Family Game, not just yet. Like all important games this required an exact timing. Doing it too soon would ruin the *surprise*. And oh, this would be a fun surprise. A surprise to end all surprises. When everyone would be forever happy once more and they would be the perfect family. Both her family and her new friends. How wonderful that would be!

So she huffed all bored and sitting in the messy living room with her dad. She'd cleaned up a bit in here, yeah, all spic and span and spotless. Even the mildew all bleached away and the fungus cut off and cast into the shadows. A makeshift board hammered over the small holes in the ceiling and a trash bag taped over the shattered window. To keep the rain out, to keep the rain out, to always keep the rain out. She knew he was going to make an office later on, and had picked out a room to use and everything. He just hadn't had the time to move all of his stuff in there yet. Come on, Daddy! Find the time already. The living room was a complete mess because of this, and that was no fun at all.

And so. In this wild boredom she snuck sneak snuck up behind him. She placed her careful hands over his eyes, all excited for the happy future that awaited them all. "Peekaboo! Watcha watching? Something interesting? Something cool?"

He laughed that big haha Daddy laugh that made her laugh, too. And they squealed for a moment, and he tickled her, and then he returned to that screen once more. "You really that bored?"

A bite on her lower lip. So bored. So very, very bored.

"Yeah, huh. I guess so. Is that something interesting?" Lone finger pointing at the screen. An arrow in the morning light.

Daddy shrugged and laid back down and pulled her down, too. And they laid there, her head on his chest. Listen to that heart! Strong river heart beating against her ears. His arm over her shoulders as he talked, his voice a rumbling in his ribs. "I guess, not really. You know, your mom's seen something, and even your sister's seen something, right? They've all seen ghosts and I want to see a ghost so bad. And here's the rub—I'm the only one who hasn't even seen one! Not a single one. Man, oh, man, how great it would be to meet the Sunshine Family. Even if I couldn't get it on film for my documentary, it would be the best thing ever. Just to talk to them, you know? To see why they did it all those years ago."

And then he paused and cleared his throat. "How about you, Raeday lovely dove. Have you seen a ghost, or heard something, or just, I don't know. Just anything?"

Secret, this whole thing was a secret. No bringing it up to him, she'd promised and she never ever broke her promises. Somehow, this made it so easy to lie to her wonderful and boring old Daddy ding dong doo. She didn't feel the pinch and sting of regret, like that time she lied to her mom about all the bird corpses.

"No, I didn't see a thing?"

He laughed. What a wondrous sound! Like a sleepy giant, that laugh. *Ho, ho, ho. I smell the blood of an Englishman.* It brought a big old grin up to her ears on her face. Silly grin, but she didn't mind. Sometimes you needed to be silly. Especially with a lie hanging about and bopping like a balloon around them. Silliness diffuses that lie, pops the air right out of it. *Shhhhhzzzzzoooooo pop!* And the lie is nothing more than hot air.

"Maybe it's just us, then. Maybe the house doesn't like us, maybe we're not special at all. And I really wanted this house to love me, too. I needed that, you know? I, I . . ."

And what was this? Sad Daddy! No. This wasn't right. She leaned over, kissed his scruffy cheek and said so plainly, "Why does it even matter? It's just a house."

"You wouldn't understand, you couldn't understand. This house is everything from my life up until now. I got into the Sunshine Family when I was little, and the records were at the library, and I would just sneak a listen to them when no one else was looking. I loved the music, the sound of their voices, I wanted to be one of them, I wanted to live with them. They were still around back then, back when I was really little. It was before everything changed."

And Rae knew what she had to do. She leapt up, oh! Such a great and amazing and awesome idea! And she made fart noises and did a little dance and said, "I am the ghosts! Come and catch me if you can, and you can join us! Join us! Join us! Come and be a ghost! Join us, join us!"

His smile was stained with tears, and it made her think of Our Lady of Sighs. Everything felt dizzy for a moment and her stomach screamed and she had to bite it all down. Such a precarious moment. Precarious, precarious, precarious. She loved that word! It felt like a magic word. And that's the perfect word for a moment like this, when her father's mind was teetering about in sadness.

So. She shook out the dizziness and swallowed all that sick feeling and smiled and screamed and ran up the steps. "Catch us, catch us, catch us!"

And for a brief moment Daddy smiled and ran behind her, laughing and stumbling for a bit and then laughing some more. She let him catch her a few times, just to keep his face all happy and cheered up. But she could tell there was still a sadness beneath his eyes, something just out of reach, that she couldn't quite fix. She would try, though. She would spend the rest of the day trying. Sher was a super genius after all, and if she couldn't do it? Well, then, no one else could.

-13-

Later that night Lucas went up to their bedroom, that sadness still clinging to his bones. He felt neglected by the house, the very same house that he'd dreamt his whole life of living in. Why had the ghosts abandoned him? He was perfect for this place. His shirt pushed up over elbows, revealed his climbing tattoos. His eyes bleary as he rubbed them, and paced around that master bedroom. Everything was lit entirely by soy candles, and Dana waited for him there, in the bed. She smiled at him and it seemed like a forced kind of thing. He forced a smile of his own, and worried that it was a grimace and she might be offended by the flash of his teeth.

No, wait, don't think about it. Don't focus on the slack face you wear like a mask. Focus instead on Dana, right? Beautiful still after all these years. Black hair and fire in her green eyes. Tiny freckles dotting her face and lips that were slightly chapped. They were working on it, they were working on it. What did that even mean? He wasn't sure, and he didn't want to ask. Asking would break the spell they were under, and working on it would turn to a wound, a divorce, a departure.

He pulled off his clothes and felt somehow vulnerable and haunted in his nudity. She turned her head and looked away. She. She turned her head and looked away. Of course, she did. When was the last time they took *pleasure* in each other's bodies? Naked and fully raw and vulnerable to each other? He wanted to scream. Instead, he pulled on his pajamas. One leg at a time. First left, then right. Shirtless for a moment. He briefly thought about climbing into that bed all sweat-coated and shirtless, pressing his skin against hers and maybe . . . touching her, his hand on her stomach like a violin . . .

No, she was still looking away, her eyes not meeting his. He coughed without thought, and pulled on a random shirt from a random unpacked box. A black one with a strange Halloween star in the center. The hex of a crest for the Sunshine Family. How fitting, to wear that shirt in this house, even on accident.

"They're all asleep," she said. "Been asleep for a while."

Dana. How he missed the way she used to talk. The way she talked to everyone else but him. Long, rambling, chatty conversations, like a lonely bird, singing. Now all of her words clipped with a sad hostility behind them. He knew that feeling. He'd felt it himself off and on through the years, that long brewing hate through the decades.

"Oh, yes, sorry I didn't help put them down for sleep or something, but I got sidetracked. You know how it is, when work just takes over and you get all *into it*, and you can't stop thinking about it, and it becomes everything, right? That's what happened, once we started cleaning, I got all these ideas and so I set up the camera, and started . . . okay. Look, I'm sorry, that's all. I'm sorry I disappeared into the house for a little bit. Is that okay?"

As usual he stammered when his nerves crept up on him. And as usual, he hated it. Fuck. How he hated it.

"Okay," she said, still clipped. She looked away from him as he pulled the slightly ripped quilt up to his neck. He saw a flash of her body beneath the sheets for a moment. Comfortable pajamas, pink. He wanted to hold her tight and suffocate the world away. Was it all too far gone now? Was the distance between them too great? Their love like birds in flight, migrated halfway across the world in different flocks.

Damn it. He was going to try something. He reached out, hand almost on her shoulder, quivering fingers outstretched. Needful hands. She moved. Closer. Pushed her shoulder against his palm. And he rested it there, for a moment, too nervous to move. A breath: in/out. And then yes, he'd risked it. He brushed her hair from her shoulders, curls fluttering away and exposing her neck, his mouth aching. He wanted to cry. It'd been so long since he last touched her in such a sensual way. Skin on skin. Palm against the flesh of her body. He wanted. To. Kiss. And.

"I . . . I missed this."

He must've said the wrong thing. She got up from the bed and moved toward the door. She didn't even look at him when she spoke.

So brutal, each word a hammer stroke. "I'm going to sleep in Lily's room, okay? She's been having nightmares again."

They paused for a moment, her back still toward him. Oh, to cross such a distance and touch her once more. But it was light years away, light years away . . . and he had no words, nothing at all, just this empty shadow of her skin against his hand. There was a lump inside of him. Something lost and broken and he wanted to scream. He wanted to scream so much. But his mouth clamped shut and she left, the door sounding like a violin behind her as it slid shut.

He lifted his head back and stared up at that water-stained ceiling. How he wanted it to rain. To rain and burst the skull of this house right open. How he wanted to drown in a sea of falling sky water and end it all right now. Never such sadness before in his life. Never. Like death, this was. Like a slow drowning death.

-14-

Later that night Lucas dreamt of the house, but it was not exactly the same house. It kept expanding and growing, changing shape and turning into a labyrinth nested inside a labyrinth. He kept thinking that he should go and grab his camera, that he had to record this, but he had no idea where he'd left it behind. He pulled out a map, but the map was all wrong, covered in strange markings. Oh, that wasn't a map at all, was it? It was a scroll, maybe a spell, or maybe something else, something far more dangerous. It turned into a snake in his hand, and then he dropped it.

He walked further into the dream, a single red candle lighting his way. The walls looked wounded, big tears where they had stretched out and changed shape. He saw bones and undulating muscle beneath these open sores, and reached in to touch them. They were still raw, still humming, still filled with blood and bone. And in the distance, he heard a voice, a familiar voice he'd heard a million times over and over again. Father Jonas of the Sunshine Family, their master, the leader of the cult. Was this a new sermon?

Lucas followed the voice and found the leader in the main living room. Bodies filled it entirely, and he knew this scene—he'd seen it a million times when researching the Sunshine Family when he was in college. This was the moment of their suicides. Look at all the bodies strewn about, now in bright and vivid color, no longer the black-and-white photographs of the *Times* article.

And in the center, cradling a severed head, was the master himself. He seemed both sad and elated, and looked way older than he had on the albums. The picture in the *Times* article never showed this scene— in fact they never found the body of the master at all.

"I'm still here," he said, cradling the head. He turned and looked directly at Lucas. "I'm inside your house, and we're waiting for you.

Come with me, Lucas. Come and join us. Our Great Will grows weaker, the walls thin and whispering in the dark. Bring us your family, yourself, your life, join the Sunshine Family in dance and song and ritual. We need your help, you must be another chink in our soul chain, you dig? To keep the darkness from devouring our world."

And then he woke up with a full moon outside of his window, barely even three in the morning, his pulse racing and his body drenched in sweat. He remembered it all so clearly, and knew that he had to figure out what it meant. Was it sign? Did it even matter? In the morning he would record this all on video, and use this for the documentary.

It reminded him of the video dream journals he had Lily recite each day during the *Hour of Smiles*. For some of the film critics, it was their favorite part in the whole thing, and something they specifically cited in their reviews. He laid back, let his mind wander, and hoped that somehow he could unwind back to sleep once again, and see Father Jonas in the darkness, and maybe ask him some questions for his film.

An interview with a ghost, through the medium of a dream. How cool would that be? And yet, no such luck. He didn't dream the rest of the night, just weird black and white images of things dancing, and then nothing else.

-15-

Aha. There was another lady at the top of the stairs, waiting for Rae. A different one, shrouded by moonlight cast through that stained-glass dome. Pale light refracted through the odd colors, tinting the world like a solar eclipse. The lady twitched quickly, her body all sorts of odd angles in the light. Like a shadow of strange, broken geometry that looked like it should add up, but never did.

"Oh, beautiful child," the new stranger spoke with a mournful smile in the shadows, "Come closer, closer. I want you to see my face."

And dutiful good friend Rae climbed up those steps, obeying her every word. She avoided the creaky step and the squeaky step, not wanting to wake anyone else. And then she stood right there, almost kissing close. She could see the woman so clearly now. She was clothed in cast-off old rags, ripped and torn with ragged slashes. Her skin the color of tears, strange, liquid colors, and her fingers were damp in the moonlight, briefly touching the tips to Rae's lips, and her hair was a wet black mess swirled up into a bun on the top of her head. One of her eyes was missing (the right eye, this time), the other one red and puffy and sorrow-soaked. And her cheeks, her cheeks! They were slashed and oozing blood, with several long diagonal slashes, freshly weeping. Crisscross, crisscross. It looked like phantom hands cutting her face.

And then a big rip through the top of the stranger's black dress. The rip revealed full moonlit breasts and a chest with a raw, open wound where the heart should be. And inside was gaping hole of muscle and bone and raven wings. Living, fluttering things nested inside that wound, with raven heads poking out, looking directly at Rae, as if challenging her with their tiny, black stone eyes. Rae did not like this. She *loved* it.

She was in awe at the beauty of the woman before her. Even more beautiful than she ever could imagine! Way beyond the cemetery beauty of the other lady. What was she again? The Lady of Sighs, yes, yes. And she had to ask. Closer, closer, leaning in, almost placing her head close to that chest. She had to ask.

"Are you related to her? The one I met the other day, the Lady of Sighs?"

A tear-soaked sob and choke and then words, words all raw from a throat wrecked with crying. "Once upon a time, a long time ago, they called me *Mater Lachrymarum*. That's Latin, you know. Do you know Latin, Rae?"

Rae nodded all proud and brilliant. Of course, she knew Latin! She was a genius, after all. What genius worth her salt didn't even know something as basic as Latin? "I certainly do, it means Our Lady of Tears."

"You are such a clever little girl, aren't you? So clever, in such a world lined with such cruelty."

And of course! Rae smiled and jumped a little and twirled in spirals. "Yes, yes! I am, I am!"

The lady wiped dreary tears from her cheeks with the back of her arm. Strange colors, those tears. Not the right colors at all. "Clever girls need games to play, don't they? Else their minds get bored, and they do awful things when their minds get bored."

And Rae remembered the time she dreamt of murder, and the time she was so bored she thought of killing the neighborhood cats just to see what was inside of them. There was a beauty to all that, she knew. A beauty to death and she'd wanted to see it firsthand. But she also knew, because, oh! What a genius she was! That such a thing would be a horrible beauty. It would stain her life forever, and that made her feel squishy and oogy on the inside. So, instead, she collected dead birds she found in the woods and satisfied her curiosity with their corpses. Taking them apart, poking around at their gooey insides. Acting like a little scientist, searching for the truth within those maggot-infested bodies.

They'd stained her fingers red for weeks, and her mommy yelled at her so much after that.

And so, she said *yes*, her voice now quiet and meek.

"It's okay my dear, my beauty, my sweet, sweet child," and her hand grazed Rae's cheek and pulled her in, closer, closer to the chest, as the raven wings flapped against her hair. "I know what lurks inside of you, I do. I felt the anger and the sadness, I know the tears of rage you burn through at night. I'm here to help you. We all are. The game I want to play is a secret game. It's to help us with our son, and it's called the Happy Family Game. It's a game that will make your family a happy family, too. Can you keep a secret?"

A laugh. Almost cruel and brutal in the dark. "I keep lots of secrets."

"From your mom? From your dad? Even your sister Lily?"

She leaned up and whispered in the lady's ear. "They have no clue what's inside of me. What I'm capable of . . ."

And the lady pulled her in closer, drowning her against scarred flesh and the oozing of her heart wound.

"Good, good. We're going to play the Happy Family Game, all right? It's not necessarily a fun game for some people, but for people like you and me, it will be a joy and a treat. It's perfect for good little kids who have darkness inside of them, clever little girls who are bored and need some release. Your family is having trouble, my family is having trouble, and if you play the Happy Family Game, both of our troubles will be gone! Our son will come home, and everything will be made all right again. What do you say, Rae? Do you want to play the Happy Family Game? If so, you will have to keep it a secret. Something you could never tell anyone else, not without being eaten by the void."

A gulp. She'd dreamt of fire and a void and she knew that's what this was all about. If she told another, she would be shoved into that fire, into that void. Lost as lost could be.

"Yes, I getcha."

And then the stranger whispered so many secrets into her ear. And Rae knew that she was not going to sleep tonight. Her mind darted about with a million thoughts. So excited, so excited! She may never ever sleep again. Not ever never ever again.

Lucas ran downstairs bright and early first thing in the morning, and went right to the new makeshift director's office he'd set up yesterday afternoon. It was still mostly uncleaned and shoddy and covered in boxes. The cramped place had that reek of mildew and raw ancient paper to it, with loose light streaming in through filthy cracked windows. These were the old kind of windows, where the glass settled in thick bubbles along the edges.

Excitedly, he found one of the better digital camera and set it up on the desk, checking the light levels and then recording his thoughts on his dream before he forgot it. It all rushed out of him at once, like a fever dream. When he was done, he started pouring through all of the evidence he'd collected through the house when they were moving in yesterday.

He had planned on going through this later on, using these bits and bobs to create a narrative out of the Sunshine Family's last days. But that would be for later, for now, he was trying to find proof that his dream was no mere dream, and that the Master was somewhere in this house. Alive? Dead? He had no clue, that all happened so long ago. He might've died in the house later, hiding in the walls and starving to death after the police left. Though Lucas hoped against hope that wasn't the case, that he could meet the old man here, be inducted into the Sunshine Family, and somehow live that life he'd dreamt of since he was a small child. Man, oh, man, what an ending this would make for his film!

He hunched over a precarious stack of photos and loosely stapled pages from the basement and sifted through them. After he went through most of those, he started to unspool old film footage of the Sunshine Family, and he stared at it through the light of the window sun. It flickered close to his eyes, a movie of still images running together. His heart rumbled so slumber thick. Come on, where was he? The master wasn't in any of the pictures, and he was missing from the film itself. Why wasn't he here? His quick fingers moved through that spool of film even more, the edges almost sharp enough to slice his hand.

The images flickered in front of his eyes, a movie made from shadows and light and chemicals. And there it was, oh, horror of horrors, the last few hours of the Sunshine Family. They seemed happy, almost elated, to be passed on. They knelt in supplication, hands out in front of them like they were begging for alms. He knew that it wasn't a peaceful, end, no, this wasn't like Jonestown. No arsenic in the holy water for these lucky hippies. Several people walked amongst the crowd with black bags over their heads with a red X on the center. The X was like a slash or a tear in the fabric, their faces wriggling like maggots beneath the fabric, as they walked up to each person and shot them point-blank, right in the head.

He couldn't watch this. He thought for the longest time he could, if he ever found a video of exactly what happened here, but no. He could not. They were dancing and singing moments before, and they smiled as they shot them. Smiled! The glee was almost contagious, and he found himself smiling and crying at the same time. They didn't even flinch when the shot rang out, nor did they change their expression. For a few of them, their hair even caught on fire from the gunpowder, creating a halo of flames around their head. No. He can't watch this.

He dug deeper beneath the other reels, looked at photos, and kept searching. There, there, he found it. He found the proof that he needed. Breathless, tears on his cheek and a smile on his lips from those images, still, as he pulled up a photo of the Master, sitting in the center of bodies, his legs crossed underneath him, two severed heads on his lap facing each other. One hand was lifted up, two fingers pointing up, the other hand pointed two fingers down. Bodies everywhere, and he was alive, Lucas could tell. That look in the Master's eyes was calm and beatific, but not dead. Dead eyes look different, dead bodies all still and eerily motionless.

Now to take notes, now to walk through the house, camera in hand. Quick snap photos over every inch and everything. Sketching storyboards on large sheets of canvas paper with graphite pencils.

And with each room he matched it up to that footage. This footage that wasn't online anywhere—or anywhere else—he seemed to have the only copies. These were not even on the old rotting VHS tapes he'd had since high school. These were his copies now, his film reels now, secret things shared between him and the Sunshine Family. A secret, whispered across time.

After going through the film reels and matching them up to places in the house, he started going through the papers once again and matched the film up to the notebooks. He wanted this to all come together, make a story. That's what documentary filmmakers did, wasn't it? They went through the real and found the stories hidden in plain sight. It took a good eye, a sharp mind, one that was good at unpuzzling puzzles, to see the line of narrative that went through it all and showed how life made sense.

These papers were something else, weren't they? One was a diary, discarded and burnt at the edges. Another was a list of daily rituals and prayers and magical spells. Another still contained the structure of the Sunshine Family: rules, regulations, hierarchy of command. And yet another rotting notebook contained recipes and songs and ways of purifying yourself before death. Even at this point in the pages there was that promise of ritual suicide. That was the through line, the markers leading up to that horrible ending. The story went right there, right up to the abyss and stared right at it. Everything whispered suicide, a revolutionary act, a ritual. Was it a summoning ritual, or a binding?

Oh, did you feel that? Goosebumps.

There was a secret here, wasn't there? One that Lucas understood deep down in his intestines. He never told anyone else this, not even Dana. Maybe he understood that call to suicide all too well. He felt the call thrumming inside of him when he listened to their songs. He felt it pull and yank on him the moment they saw those caskets down below in the crypt. He never told anyone about this call to suicide because he was certain they wouldn't understand him, not really. It wasn't about wanting to die, or being depressed or sad or anything like that. It was about belonging, really truly belonging. In death he would belong, wholly, completely. This house would be forever his house, and this family? It would be forever his family.

He sighed and laid back and hummed one of their songs to himself . . .
Kiss me, kill me, set me free
kiss me, kill me, set me free
We'll lock the Grief behind the trees
The golden void is what we'll see
Kiss me, kill me, set me free
Maybe. Hmm. No, wait. He promised they wouldn't be involved in the documentary. And yet, maybe. Hmm. They don't have to be involved, he could do this one ritual himself, couldn't he? Induct himself into the Sunshine Family. They would never have to know, never ever. And the thought made him so happy. All he had to do was use these clues he found in the images and track down the leader of the Sunshine Family. He could do that, couldn't he? Yes, yes, he could.
This was home now, home now home now . . .
Kiss me, kill me, set me free . . .

-17-

This grotto was overgrown and hidden in the heart of the garden. It lay nestled back beyond the manmade pond and close to the swaying pines. This was Dana's secret place, her own place, one untouched by cleaning hands. The walls of the grotto were rain-worn stone, with benches and moss-coated lanterns hidden about. She wondered what the lanterns were for, what this grotto was for. It felt holy and distinct, and it made her anxious with desire.

The rest of the house could be cleaned and made livable, yes. Cobwebs swept away. Insects fought back. Glass shards plucked from the ground and placed in trash cans, yes. They had children after all, and children needed nice and neat environment to live in, and maybe a house that wouldn't cut them or kill them. Even though, in a way, it pained her to clean it. She wanted to keep it as wild and as beautiful as she could, but it pained, oh. It pained so much to remove even a single beautiful cobweb.

There was a beauty to ruin, wasn't there? The rot and entropy of the ages corrupting the stones and boards and the very roof of the house. It created such lovely decay. It's why she loved being down in the crypt so much. *Shhh, shhh, don't tell Lucas, he might not like that.* And it's why she loved this secret spot, this hidden spot. Her lovely little grotto that she left untouched by cleaning hands, that she left to be overrun with weeds and the beauty of nature reclaiming the world.

Tree roots pushed the stone ceiling apart, vines draped down, and shrubs twisted and grasped and bent and thrust their way through. She had that same feeling here that she had in the house, that swooning, wet feeling. She was sticky from the heat and sticky from need. *Give me something that my husband lacks. Give me what he cannot . . . transcendence, sexual transcendence . . . to move beyond the body and into a glory of orgasm and light . . .*

In the center of it all was a stone altar of sorts. And on top of that? A statue. Female, yes. But unlike the imagery in the house, or on the cover of the Sunshine Family's various books and albums. This was something else altogether. A sacred feminine body of a different sort. Raw, naked, smooth. Without detail, an abstract concept. It was the <u>shape</u> of a woman carved in stone and nothing more. The whole body of the statue was coated in moss and vines and she dared not clean it. Something like this should be crawling with life.

She touched it, briefly, electric, and wiped that sweat from her head and let out a small laugh, just a bit. Her palm sang as if it were kissed by the effigy of an unknown goddess. A yearning now, a yearning connection between the two of them. This statue was the house. This shrine was the house. The grotto, too, was the house. Everything all connected, always, this was all the house. Here was the heart of Gemini House—it wore it outside its body, hidden from hunting hands.

And. And. And. She touched herself, her own hand up her skirt, pressing against her leg. Her need and heat called out, damp against her fingers, beside the cloth and against her lips. Breathless for a moment. Everything felt magnified times a million. Slick with hungry desire.

Lily and Rae played games in the garden outside, beyond the veil of ivy vines, and she should be watching them, she should. But this won't hurt, this won't be a bad thing, this was a necessary thing, a *need need need* . . .

It would only take a moment. They would be fine by themselves for a moment, wouldn't they?

Push the cloth aside and feel it all warm and press her skin right there, right up against the stone. Feel it, moving against her, a living thing. Branches, leaves, trembling. Touch that wall now, grasp it with both of her hands. Shimmy down her underwear and slip them off. Sounds of people moving outside, the kids like birds crying out in the joys of childhood. *Don't come back here, don't come back, not yet, not yet* . . .

Dirt-coated skulls placed along stone shelves stared down at her. Her body moved with a mind of its own, not even in control of her muscles or flesh any longer, as she rocked rough up against everything. The house is here, the house is with her, the house *loves her.*

And she knew the true name of the house, the name Lucas didn't even care to learn. He was too obsessed with his damned Sunshine Family to learn anything *real and true* about this beautiful house.

Saliva dripped down her chin and she laughed. So close now. The skulls had keyholes bored into their foreheads. Were they alive when that happened? She wiped the sweat and now, yes, now. Yes. Fuck. Fucking hell. And then? Damn everything shit fuck no!

Children always have the worst timing. Red faced. Wiping sweat. Someone called out. Crying. Hurt. Someone hurt. Fuck. She. She couldn't stop this now. She had to stop this now. So flush like skin on fire. Pulling her underwear back on, back up. Clothes so rough and hair now a tangled mess, her body on edge from being close, so close.

Was that Rae's voice calling out? Lily's?

She composed herself. She couldn't waste any more time, she had to move and move right away. Would they know? Could they tell? Of course not! Push those vines aside and walk from the shadows and into the brutal daylight. Cover her eyes with her hand and right there she saw it right there. Lily on the ground and crawling. What. What the hell. Just. What.

Her clothes were ripped and Rae danced above her, singing. She had something serpentine in her hand, whipping about. Singing. Dancing in spirals. Singing. There was blood. Oh, fucking hell. Blood! She screamed and ripped across the world and stopped and she grabbed Rae's arm and grabbed that . . . that . . . that . . .

Weapon. What else would she call it? *Weapon.* What the hell. A branch from that old weeping willow tree, coated with, with, with bits of stone and broken glass. What was this? What? In her anger she threw it across the garden and grabbed Rae's arm and screamed and screamed and screamed. It wasn't even words any longer. Just flashes of red and then she's on the ground sobbing. And Rae's just standing there, looking . . . odd. Completely affectless.

"It was just a game Mommy, just a game . . ."

Lily was crying and yes, oh, yes, Dana held her, mommy held her so close and no, don't even care anymore about anything else. "Are you hurt, my love? What happened? What did she do?"

"I did nothing," Rae pouted and seemed stung and offended, "Just a game, Mommy, just the first round of the Happy Family Game. I didn't even cause that blood or anything at all. I never even touched her with my scourge."

Scourge? Scourge? Where did her little girl hear such a word as scourge? She would have to talk to Lucas later . . . and what was this? Happy Family Game? Where had she heard such a thing . . .

And Lily's face contorted, mouth wide open in a grimace of horror. Eyes practically bulging from her head. That whole look was *fear, fear, fear.* "Did she hurt you? Did she?"

Lily shook her head. When she spoke again it was all whispers. "Not yet. I fell and scraped my hands, see?"

And hands up so bloodied. "I don't even know how I fell. I was just running, and then I wasn't any longer."

Bits of gravel stuck in her palm still, and her knees were torn up and bloodied, too. Shreds of skin hung loose. "Let's go inside, come on. This might hurt a little to clean, but it's needed, okay? We don't want this to get infected."

And then she lifted her little Lily up. The two of them walking still to that house on the hill. The Coffin House. That was its true name, the real name, the only name it needed. The Coffin House. She found this when researching their new home on Wikipedia the other day. The Coffin House. An older name. A pre-Gemini House name, before the rise and fall of the Sunshine Family.

They said he built it from the wood of used coffins. Bodies still leaking and some mummified and most just bones. They said he built the beams from gallows' poles, all used up with hanging necks. Even the very wood of this house is haunted with the far away dead, their eternal underearth homes stolen from them.

"And Rae," she called out, called behind her, not even turning to see if her youngest was coming, "Don't play with anything like that ever again, you understand me? Someone could get hurt."

"Okay, Mommy. Yes, Mommy. Of course, Mommy. I am a genius though, and I know how to play without hurting."

"I don't care," and she grunted as she walked, so drained from everything, "I really, really, really just don't even care at all. Genius or no genius, I don't want you playing with weapons again. Not even ones you make yourself, you hear me? If I catch you, you will be in so very much trouble. So very much trouble indeed."

"Yes, Mommy. Of course, mommy, yes."

"Good, now go and find your father while I take care of your sister, okay? Let him know what happened."

-18-

Dana knelt down on the cracked tile bathroom floor as Lily sat on the toilet above her. Sunlight crept in through a taped-up window and stained the room in gold. The shadows of the window ivy looked like runes across their faces. A hiss of water in the sink, and then dampening that rag with her hand and getting out some antibiotic. Better make it triple. That super strong stuff, need to keep whatever germs out she could. And maybe some hydrogen peroxide, just in case. You know it's working when it bubbles, the effervescence means it's clear of all infections.

She picked out the pebbles with her fingers and with tweezers. She pulled out the clumps of grass and dirt out from Lily's knees and Lily's elbows. She threw them down on the ground, violent and expelling them from her daughter's body. Blood stained everything. Her hand, the tiles. Everything. She felt all swoony again at the sight of her daughter's blood, and Dana pressed on, pressed forward. Even as her little Lily girl flinched and pinched her eyes shut. "Oh, oh, ow, oh, ow."

"I know, Sweetie, I know, my love. But we need to do this, okay? Can you be brave, can you be strong?"

A sigh. "Yes, Mommy, I can be strong."

She used some water to clean it out first. Just a dab, dab, dab, and watched her little Lily wince. Poor thing. "What were you guys even doing out there? And where did Rae get that whip, or weapon, or whatever it was?"

Dab, dab, dab. Most of the blood washed away from knees, from elbows. She would save the palm of the hands for last—she knew it would be the most painful. The palm is one of the more sensitive parts of the human body. She dipped that rag into the water, and it turned crimson and swirled with the thickness of her daughter's blood. It felt so elemental.

"I don't know why she did it, or where she got it from. I think she made it herself? I don't know. She said she wanted to play a game, and all good important games required sacrifice. Mom, I don't know, she had this look in her eyes I didn't like at all."

Dana understood. She knew exactly what Lily was trying to say, she'd seen Rae give her that same exact look. It was a disconcerting look, the same one her father got in his eyes when he was working on a documentary. It was obsession, pure and simple, and it seemed so intense and unreal—it was disturbing. Last time she saw that look in Rae's eyes, she'd been taking apart the corpses of birds. The memory made Dana shiver , and she almost dropped the rag.

"I understand. So, why don't you hang out with me for the rest of the day? And your sister can hang out with your dad. Doesn't that sound good?" She tried to hide the shaky fear in her voice, but she knew that it still came through, somehow. That kind of thing always came through.

Lily nodded as they finished cleaning and bandaging her wounds. "I love that idea, just you and me no one else. Can we watch a movie or two?"

"Yes, we can. I'll even let you pick them out."

-19-

The sunset was a knife of red cutting the sky as Lucas walked up that hill, toward the door to the crypt beneath the house. The owls were washed in a crimson hue, and everything in the air felt kinetic. Electric. His hair stood up on end, and he had that vibrating feeling deep within his bones. He'd dreamt so much of this moment, hadn't he? Dreams that had stretched back into his childhood, when he first discovered those Sunshine Family records all sleepy in the library. Dreams of himself walking up this hill, to that black door, and the air so charged with red light. His whole life had been leading right here, right now, right up into this exact moment.

He'd spent most of the day wandering around the house from top to bottom, comparing images and notes and looking for any signs that the Master could still be here, alive. So far, there were maybe hints and whispers, but nothing more than that. A handprint in dust that didn't match his or anyone else's as far as he could tell. Bits of food here and there, though that could've been really old as far as he knew. But here, now, he approached that crypt, and he knew deep down in his bones that the Master was behind that door. That maybe he slept in one of the coffins where a corpse should be, yes. This had to be it.

As he walked, he heard a little girl's voice shouting from the front porch, and then the sound of feet running his way. Rae! She called his name, and pointed at him, and said that Mommy was looking for him. That he was needed back inside, something happened to Lily.

"Oh," Lucas didn't even hear exactly what she'd said. Everything was a buzz in the heat, his ears ringing, and his pulse thunder in his ears. He felt on fire, as if every part of him was burning up. "That's nice," he said, "Do you want to come help me out with something? This is really important."

Rae danced around him and sang out at the top of her lungs, "Yes, yes, yes! Yes, I do! Yes!"

Fingers grasped around the doorknob. He felt it pulsate like a heart in his fingertips. Rae still singing, still spinning, around and around his body. Felt that pulse now. Oh. Hammering so much. This. Had. To. Be. It. He'd dreamt it, and dreams weren't lies. Father Jonas of the Sunshine Family said so on the records and in his writings. *Dreams don't lie,* he said. *They obfuscate and riddle us with truths, but they never ever lie.* It had been a few decades since he last listened to that one record, but the words still stuck to his mind. They clung to his thoughts, and contained such poignant truths. *Dreams don't lie. You're all chosen to be here. You've all dreamt of being here, and now you are here. Dreams don't lie. We have a sacred calling, to care for the sorrows and grief of the world. Care for them like a pet, like a cat, something we leash up and don't let go, never ever. We will never let the sorrow of the world escape their chains.*

Come on, open it, just do it already. Father Jonas had to be behind this door.

"Hey, Daddy, are we really going into that room? Mommy says I shouldn't go beneath the house where the corpses sleep, but she also told me to go and find you. So here I am, I found you now! Are we really going to do it? Go under the house?"

His lips were so chapped, his throat so rough and rugged. He licked his lips, cleared that lump in his throat. His words had this weight of sadness to them. Why? Why so sad, Lucas boy? Because everything would change? Sometimes getting what we want is the worst thing in the world. "Yeah," he said, "yeah, you can come on in with me, it's okay. Mommy doesn't have to know, right? It can be our secret."

He had this feeling in his guts that maybe she shouldn't see this, maybe she shouldn't be here for this? He'd made a promise to Dana, a promise he never wanted to go back on, yet . . . everything in his life was leading up to this moment. The promises, Rae being here, his knife in his back pocket, the ritual, the need to join them . . .

And seeing Father Jonas there, hiding in the dark, welcoming him into the Sunshine Family. It was all too perfect, all too amazing.

She jumped around and screamed with joy. "Oh! Yay and yes and of course! I am the best at keeping secrets. I even have a few right now, secrets you don't even know."

He rubbed the side of his head and tried not to laugh at the absurdity of it all. "Secrets from me? Is it something your mom said?"

"You're not allowed to ask that, daddy. That's cheating." And now she huffed and kicked the stones, and he saw her like a little version of himself. That whole action, the way she talked, everything. She would understand what she was about to see, she would know the power of ritual and sacrifice. He turned the knob now and let the basement exhale its cold breath across his face.

Wait. What was that? Something breathed in that darkness. Could you hear that? And it was followed by the muffled sounds of something scurrying about in the shadows. Rats? Mice? Stay cats?

"What is this, Daddy? Is this the cellar? It doesn't smell like a cellar, it smells . . . wrong."

He lifted up his cellphone and turned it on bright. A makeshift flashlight here in the shadows beneath the world. Something moved, just out of sight. Not sure what it was, maybe a trick of the light, a trick of his eyes not seeing right. "No, my darling dear, no, my wonderful Rae, this is not the cellar. This is the family crypt."

"Oh, the family crypt. That explains all of the skulls in the alcoves. Oh! That's so much fun to say," and she started singing, "skulls in the alcoves, skulls in the alcoves, skulls in the alcoves," while kicking around in a quick, makeshift dance.

It looked almost exactly the same as before, didn't it? Skulls in the same places pushed into the walls. Elaborate stone coffins scattered about. He'd never paid much attention to them before? But today, today, today. He saw the intricate carvings and the rough spots of mold scattered here and there. Life crept in, and swarmed across the land of death.

"It's so beautiful, Daddy."

And yes, it was. But there was no Father Jonas here, his dreams had failed him. Was he so wrong about all of this? Was he not the chosen one? Had all of his life led up to nothingness? No. This was still salvageable, it was, he knew it. He could make this all a part of his documentary, of course! He would just have to grab the portable 16mm so he could get it on film, and then retrace all of these same steps tomorrow. He would pen a good monologue in his head, or maybe even play some audio of the Sunshine Family while he spliced the scenes together. Sure, maybe film would be an overkill, but it would look so amazing. That, and the camera was way cheaper to rent, even with the price of film stock included.

"Rae my love, my sweetest thing in all the world. Do you want to help me with this tomorrow? Maybe hold the camera, maybe take the light balance for me? It would be another secret of course, especially from mommy. But if you help out and you do a great job, it would be the best thing in the world. You're super smart, and I know you can do it."

Rae nodded and spoke with a deeper voice. He knew that voice, that was her *I'm a serious grown-up* voice that she used when playing adult around the house. "Yes, father, of course father. I will not let you down."

And then a lightbulb overhead flickered briefly for a second, warmly for a second and then stopped. His heart raced, this wasn't right, the electric company said it would be a few more days before they had electricity again. And yet, there it was, flickering yet again, the bulb crackling and humming and then came a loud pop and it stopped.

"What was that, Daddy?"

He stammered for a moment. What was that? He saw something in the flickering. Something that shook him down to the very bottoms of his toes. What was that? Something that made his bones electric and his blood like liquid fire. What was that, what was that what was that . . .

Was that Father Jonas?

Upsetting, unsettling, thrilling. A figure dressed in pale clothes. A woman? Maybe. It happened so quickly. She twitched towards them, a spasmodic dance like a nightmare marionette, with a black rag draped over her face. A buzzing sound, the sound of flies filling up the air, as the rag moved, large lumps crawling underneath it like wounded animals. Her hand pointed at the stone caskets. Thin, boney fingers. Pointing.

And then the bulb popped and the darkness came down. Was she still there, in the dark, outside the light of his phone? Nervous hands moved the phone, and he tried hard not to scream and run away. He moved the light up to the spot in the corner where he'd seen her. Nothing now. Only gloom and silhouettes of stone coffins in that glaring white light. Nothing. He exhaled and it was painful.

"I, I don't know."

And then it flickered again, and she was right there, slouching towards them. Slow, body twisted in bone-breaking ways. Her fingers pointed at the coffins, whispered something, and it sounded like insect wings. What was she saying? And why was his heart beating so loudly, so damned fast? Wasn't this what he'd wanted? Wasn't it? To see a ghost. To talk with the dead? Wasn't it? And where was Father Jonas? Had his dream lied to him after all?

He knew those pale clothes, that black rag. The uniform for special members of the Sunshine Family, from near the end of days, right before the ritual suicide. There were nine others just like her. The sisters of melancholy, they called themselves. The Brides of Grief. Something hinted at in the publications and recordings, something he hoped would be explained with the new footage and writings he'd found. She motioned towards him, beckoning him to follow her, to follow the path beyond the spiral light. *Join us, Lucas. Come and join us in the beautiful glimmer beyond death. You will see how beautiful it all is, just grab the knives, perform the ritual, and live forever with us in the Gemini House, a true member of the Sunshine Family.*

Flicker, flicker, once more. And then out again, the lights out again. So abrupt. Like a stab in the chest, a knife point of light against his skin. So close, so kissing close. Why had she terrified him so? He should have embraced her, embraced the fear.

Did Rae even see her?

"I want to go upstairs, Daddy. I don't like this."

The cellphone light danced with his trembling fingers. He spun his whole body widdershins, creating his own spirals in the grave dirt beneath the house, and pointed that light toward the door that led outside, to the hill and the garden beyond. "Let's go that way," he said. His were words choppy, affectless. Broken. "It just feels, I dunno."

Rae ran over to that door quickly, her words floating behind her. "Safer, that's the word you're looking for, Daddy. Safer! It feels safer."

And he rolled his head and walked behind her. Everything shaking still. Knowing that the sun was gone and outside was twilight and nothing else. "Yes," he said, "Safer."

And he really, really hoped that was right.

-20-

Dana sat on the couch, her legs tucked under her body, a book calmly perched in her hands. The house watched her, wanted her to get up and clean it some more, but she needed a break, and the house could wait. Now was a quiet moment that required patience.

She read another page while Lily drew sharp figures in black ink on a piece of paper in front of her. Dana looked up from her book, setting it down in her lap, and just watched her little girl. She'd been through so much, hadn't she? It was a miracle she wasn't more anxious and on edge than she already was, and for a moment, Dana thought about the documentary again and felt a deep sadness.

Maybe they should leave after all. Maybe there was no going back, and Lucas was too dangerous, too obsessive to be around any longer. And yet . . .

Could she leave? She shouldn't have to be the one to leave, the house loved her, and she loved it. Lucas should be the one to leave, after all. He was the broken one, the obsessed one. She knew he wouldn't leave this house, not without a fight . . .

And yet, it was a fight she was willing to participate in. That's what you did for love, after all, wasn't it? You fought for it. And she loved this house, and would fight for it tooth and nail.

She watched Lily some more, watched her drawing, and realized it was frantic, frayed. Something was wrong with this—something was wrong with all of it. The figures were like black shadows, and now she drew circles, wider and wider still, large broken circles. Her little girl seemed frenzied, as if she were in a trance, and Dana set her book down next to her on the couch.

"Lily, dear? Lily, my love? What are you drawing?"

But she didn't answer, she just drew faster and faster and faster. The lights on the house flickered on, and Dana wondered what was going on? It wasn't supposed to happen yet, the electric company said a few more days . . .

And then Lily fell to the ground and started frothing at the mouth.

"Oh, my god, sweetheart! No!"

And She ran toward her and cupped her body around hers. She only hoped this was a little spell, Lily had been having them since she went into the coffin. If it was only a little spell, they wouldn't have to go to the hospital. She felt the warm body of her child and yearned to keep her safe, to make sure the world wouldn't be there to destroy her, to make her little girl all broken and sad like the rest of them.

"It's okay, sweetie, it's okay, I have you, I have you, you're safe now."

The house would keep them safe. She only had to get rid of Lucas . . .

And then the door flung open with a loud bang crash and everything seemed to vibrate around them. She felt a sense of awe, as the lights flickered on and off and on again, finally staying on with the last time. Lucas stood near the door, he looked frightened and dirty and lost. Why did he look so lost? And next to him, dancing around him and singing, was little Rae.

"Is she okay?"

Dana shook her head. "I don't know, does she look okay?"

Rae stopped dancing and ran over and hugged Lily as well, the two of their bodies enclosing around her. "No, no," Dana said, "It's okay, Rae. Just let me hold her, we need to keep her body safe, okay? Safe."

She couldn't say what she really wanted to say, could she? She wanted to yell at Rae, to tell her to never come near Lily ever again. This was connected to the incident earlier—it had traumatized Lily so much to have her sister dancing over her with that awful *weapon*. If Rae really cared, she would leave now. She would take her dad with her, and they would both leave and never ever come back.

And then the spasming stopped and the seizure was over. Lily's eyes were dilated, and she moaned for a moment and said, "Daddy, did you see her? Did you see the woman in pale clothes?"

He walked into the room, knelt down between them. Dana wanted to shove him away, to make him get lost and leave them alone. He was not wanted here. He was not wanted at all. "I did, little girl, I did. How did you know about that?"

Instead of answering him she looked at Dana. Dana's eyes met hers, and she got this bad feeling in her stomach, a sad nervous feeling she didn't like at all. "Mommy," Lily said, her voice pained, "You have bright lights around your body. You shimmer, you are so beautiful, mommy. You are so beautiful when you're surrounded by halos," and then she giggled, "Oh, my head hurts so much. Could someone turn off the lights please, they hurt so much."

And Lucas went over calmly and flicked off the light switch and closed the drapes. Dana still felt this anger and resentment towards him. She wanted to shove him out of the house right now, he's the one who had done this to Lily. All for what? All for this sake of his <u>art</u>? Fuck his art.

"I guess the electricity's back on for good now," he spoke so calmly. How could he speak so calmly when so much horrible stuff is happening around them?

"Get your daughter something for her head, please. The extra strength migraine Excedrin, it's in the cabinet upstairs. Go get it now, please."

He hemmed and hawed and then ran upstairs.

Good, she thought. Good. It was going to be a long day, but they would get through it. They would survive it together, and then she was going to set into motion the great divorce, and everything would be better here on out. He would fight her for Gemini House, but he would lose. This would be her house, she knew it. You don't feel love for a house like this and not fight for it until the bitter end.

And then, when the house was hers and hers alone, she would give it a new name, the best name ever. That was what happened when you married, right? The spouse takes on your last name. And thus, the house will no longer be the Gemini House or the Coffin House, but instead the Glass House.

-21-

They were in the kitchen, the two of them, sitting at the small green kitchen table. Formica, smooth across the surface. Dana felt nervous knots in her stomach, but she knew that this conversation was inevitable now. So much had happened today alone, she couldn't keep going on like this was perfectly normal.

"We need to talk, Lucas. They're both napping now, so we better make it quick, I don't want them to hear us talking like this."

He nodded, pushed back on his chair. She hated when he did that. "Okay, let's talk."

He was hiding something, she could tell. That was okay—she had secrets of her own as well.

"I think this is it, I think we're done. I love this house, but there's been too much going on lately. Where were you earlier today, when Rae attacked Lily?"

He seemed shocked, flabbergasted. Had he not known? She'd asked Rae to tell him . . .

But of course, she didn't.

"What do you mean Rae attacked Lily? Was that why she was in bandages? Was that why she had an episode?"

Her hands trembled. Was it with anger, with fear, or something else?

"I don't know why she had an episode. we never know why, but you can't blame that on Rae," although she'd had that same thought herself, "And yes, that's why she was bandaged. We were cleaning the garden when I heard screams, and turned around to see Rae dancing around poor Lily, she had a weapon in her hands."

She watched him gulp and look nervous. Good, he needed to understand the gravity of this situation.

"What kind of weapon?"

"She called it a scourge. Do you know where she got that word from? How she made that horrible thing?"

He sighed and shrugged, and she could tell he was still keeping something from her. His eyes looked so lonely and lost, yet they still contained that intense glimmer of obsession. Oh no, Lucas—what have you done?

"I don't know. I'm being really honest with you here. I don't know."

Dana had no response to this. She cracked her knuckles, cracked her neck, moved like a boxer for a brief moment. "Okay, then. It's over."

"What's over?"

"Us, everything, all of this. It's over."

"What do you mean it's over?"

She walked up, whispered in his ear. She allowed herself this one small cruelty, she deserved it, after all he'd put them through. "We're getting a divorce."

-22-

He'd waited until she was completely upstairs with the girls, probably napping or reading or doing something else. He'd waited until he'd heard the quiet of her footsteps die out, and he waited until he heard nothing but silence, the last creaking stair and the last moaning floorboard. He guessed that was a bonus to having a house as old as this one, it was musical, and it would tell him exactly what he needed to know. There were no secrets in this house, not between Lucas and the Sunshine Family. After all, he was about to become one of them right now.

He knew that he couldn't let Dana see him do this. She would not be happy with him at all. He ran as quiet as he could to the living room and grabbed his camera and got the lighting all set up and ready in the crypt down below. He then grabbed some salt, a few knives, and a tree branch from the apple tree outside. Was he really going to do this?

Yes, he was really going to do this. For the longest time, the initiation ritual to join the Sunshine Family had been a terrible secret. No living members to spill the silence and give it up—they'd all died after all, ritual suicide. No written records, nothing recorded, not involving this first ritual. It had been secret; it had been silent.

Until he'd found that one film canister buried underneath that one tree. The weeping willow, out back, the one with the book nailed to the bark. He watched the film reel over and over and over again, would play it back in his mind a million times over. 8mm, all grainy and true and filled with stark contrasts of black and white nightmares. Seven knives. Seven cuts. All precisely on the right places on your body. Consecrate it all with water and spit, and sing the right song at the right time.

He could do this, he could do this, he could, yes. He snuck downstairs, sprinkled a circle of salt around his body, standing between the coffins. He was so close to the coffin the pale figure pointed at, and for a moment it unnerved him. What if she appeared? And maybe, maybe Father Jonas was in that coffin. Maybe he would see this and be proud, and welcome him into the family. He would have to go over, pry that heavy coffin lid off and let the poor old man breathe once again the cellar of the Gemini House.

A circle of knives now around his body. One, two, three . . .

And a voice called out from the top of the stairs, a little face glimmering in the light of the kitchen. Lily? Was that you?"

"Daddy, what are you doing down there?"

"Oh, nothing dear, nothing at all. Just working on my movie."

"Come upstairs daddy, I miss you. If you stay down there, I'm going to . . . I'm going to lose you. I know I will. Don't lie to me."

He looked at the knives and the salt and sighed. Maybe this wouldn't happen today after all. Maybe he got it all wrong. "You won't lose me sweetie, you won't . . . you'll have something even better! You'll have a whole new family, filled with loads of brothers and sisters your age."

"Please, Daddy. I don't want a ghost family. I've had enough ghosts to last me a million years. And if you became a ghost, too . . . well, I don't know what I would do. Fall apart, I guess. So, please, for me? Come upstairs? Please?"

He nodded and packed up the knives. He scattered the circle of salt and hoped he'd undone everything—he'd never performed a banishing before. Hell, he'd never performed any occult ritual ever before today. He'd read about them a lot, knew all the various theories, but he never actually put them to use. He guessed the Hour of Smiles had some occult leanings, but that wasn't quite the same, was it? That wasn't about communing with ancient things beyond mortal ken. It was more about enhancing one's own second sight, through the powers of the dead.

And then he saw the look in Lily's eyes, and he knew the damage the Hour of Smiles had done to her, and his heart fluttered and sank down into the ocean of his ribs. He couldn't do that again, not to her, not to anyone else. Joining the Sunshine Family was playing with fire, and if he kept at it, he would burn this whole house down, family and all.

"Hold on, I'll be right there. Don't you move an inch, all right? Just stay right there, waiting for me."

"Okay, Daddy, okay."

And he saw her shiver and huddle in the dark at the top of the stairs, and for a brief moment he saw a shadow around her, holding her, in the shape of a bandaged boy.

-23-

Dinner was such an awkward meal, and Rae had no idea <u>why</u>. And it frustrated her to no end, not knowing why, not having a clue why. She was a super genius after all, shouldn't she be able to puzzle it out? They all sat around the kitchen table, all except for Dad, who stood in the back and looked at the stairs leading down to the crypt below.

That was a piece to the puzzle, wasn't it? Dad looking sad, Dad not meeting anyone's eyes—he wasn't talking to Lily or Rae and especially not to Mommy. Was he worried about what they saw down below? No, his eyes had a longing to them. Rae knew that look. He got that look whenever he was working on a movie. He was thinking about his film, so that was no big deal.

Was it what Rae did Earlier? Oh no, she hoped not! If only they knew why she did what she did! This was all part of the Happy Family Game, and the strange strangers told her that they wouldn't understand at first, but that was okay. That was all a part of it, see? That's what made it all the more important, see?

Pain and confusion were the first steps in playing the game. The next steps? They involved a dance, of sorts, and a sacrifice, of sorts. But don't worry, Rae, they all said, it wasn't a real sacrifice. It was all part of the game! And when it was over, they would all be hap-hap-happy. She only wished they could be happy now.

Instead of being crowded with silence and eating cold macaroni and cheese with bits of hotdogs inside of them. This was the opposite of happy. Why did the game take so long? She hated it when things took forever. Like all brilliant geniuses, she was impatient when the world couldn't keep up with her wants and needs and desires.

Maybe she should try and break the silence herself.

"Do you guys want to play a game after dinner?"

Little did they know it, but they would be playing the game even if they said no. It made her want to laugh, but she kept that feeling all bottled up inside.

Mommy was surly when she spoke, and Rae did not like this one bit.

"No, Rae, we've had enough games for quite a while."

Well, then. They would most definitely play a game later, unknowingly so. If Mommy was going to act like that, well, then. Rae was going to act how she wanted to and force them all to love each other and be happy once again. After all, that was her right, wasn't it? The right of all super geniuses everywhere, to bend reality to their will, whether it wants to bend or not.

And if it breaks in the bending like a twig too old and dry to build with? Well, that's okay, too. Sometimes you need to break things before you started to fix them. That's what daddy always said, after all, especially after a long night of editing. Sometimes, he said, you would have to light it all on fire before you could rebuild from the ashes. And Rae was really good at lighting things on fire.

-24-

The girls and Lucas were all *finally* asleep. *About damned time.* Dana crept and crawled down those stairs, carefully, carefully, so as not to make a sound. She didn't want to wake Lucas slumbering in the living room on the couch. She didn't want to step on the wrong stair or the wrong floorboard and creak so loudly the girls would spring to life upstairs. She moved past his sleeping body on tip toes, holding her breath. He twisted, turned for a moment, and she paused. Was he deep under enough for her to open the door without waking him? She decided to wait a few breaths more, just to make sure.

The front door stared at her, daring her to open it and leave already. She watched as Lucas twitched and turned. Sighed, and then began to snore. He almost woke up, almost. Her heart screamed inside, and her mouth clamped shut. Don't move an inch, don't even budge. This was a liminal moment, with her hand on the doorknob, caught between inside and out. Her other hand held a single orange candle, the flame flickering and the wax dripping down against her knuckles. It felt right, to use a candle for a light. Not a flashlight, not her phone, no. A ritual like this *required* a candle.

He stopped moving in the flickering shadows, turned his head toward the couch and began to snort and snore loudly. Good, he was deep asleep once again. She could do this. She opened the door and slid right out, the crack just barely big enough to let her through. She gently pushed it back shut, closing the door behind her, shutting off the house from the world outside. The door made a sound like a violin, and she worried he would certainly hear it, wake up, and she would be caught and have to explain why she was going outside in the middle of the night, in a nightgown of all things . . .

But no, he didn't budge at all. She exhaled, turned around, and drank in the world around her. The moon was bright, full, angry. The porch was coated in the soft blue light. Everything felt alive outside, so many insects darting about in the flickering of her candlelight. Look over there, see the rabbits bounding off into the shrubs? See the shadows of owls flittering in the pine branches? Her Knuckles stung from the candle wax that dripped down. The pain from the wax brought her back to her childhood, and that one night when the nuns turned off the lights and all of the children walked the Candlemas. She remembered what they'd said, all those long years ago . . .

That the pain from the wax was a sacrifice. Atonement. All important acts required sacrifice. Even eating to stay alive required a sacrifice of the eaten, such was the wonder and misery of this life. And she walked down off that porch, her body framed by those giant pillars propping up the roughshod roof above her, the candlelight flicking gently against her face with a warm heat, like a lover's hand brushing against her cheek, as she walked around back, toward the garden and the grotto beyond.

She was really going to do this now. No one could stop her.

She walked down that hill, behind that house. Low crawling mist crept about everything. Obscuring the surface of the world. Floating, yes, she was floating, wasn't she? A smile, and she knew this was perfect. This was right. This was what had to happen. It was all inevitable, wasn't it? Destined to happen, that physical communion between her and the house.

And there, there was her grotto. She pulled the vines aside and slid on in. Everything felt alive as she laid the candle down in front of the old statue. It seemed different now. Everything felt different now. The whole place pulsated with life. Heartbeat candle flame. And various insects crawled across the statue and then scurried into the dark. Fire and heat, the grotto was not cold. It was more like being in a living thing, the humidity like flesh pressed against her neck and thighs.

It was all connected back to the house, wasn't it? The hill and garden like head and shoulders, the house itself a delicate body requiring delicate hands. She reached over and touched the statue again. A shock of recognition, and her stomach called out. It tingled, all spinning sensations under her skin. Everything inside of her felt vulnerable and open. Her whole body a living thing, inside a living thing. Oh. The house must love her so much, to let her go so deep inside of it.

The house. Was. Feminine. She knew this now. She knew it the moment she touched the effigy. They had a connection, deep and powerful between the two of them. And this was it. Her own ritual. She had no plan, no book of sacred rites to go by. She only had her own heart, all passionate and fervent and shamanic. Deep exhale of everything and then arms up high, touching the top of the grotto.

She only wore a nightgown. Such a simple thing to slide right off, standing there naked and wild. Sweat slicked her body in the light of the candle flame. And the bushes moved, and the branches moved, and it all caressed her with a loving, gentle touch. Not sharp brambly things, but soft and velvet and covered in tiny indentations and bumps. And the sensation lit her up from the inside. She was the candle now, the candle . . .

Hands clutched the walls grasped tight burning tight and everything pushed further eyes rolled up toward the ceiling and now, now, now, no children running in now, fuck, now, her own lips slick to her touch, fingers opening everything up and letting the house inside, and she was inside of it, and it was inside of her, and the candle spun the shadows with each movement of her limbs, pushing it all further and further, and it won't stop . . .

Oh, fuck no. Don't ever stop.

Spinning top entire body lightning struck and then the quick unconscious movements. Mind so empty and still like a cold blue light in the shadows. And then. Oh. And then, oh. Again, and again and again. Her body tiny earthquakes crumbling on top of the pile of dead leaves on the floor. Leaves tangled up in the messy curls of her hair. Everything spun silently. How many times? Too many to count. Lucas could never do that, could never push her like that. Only a house like this could ever do anything of that nature. Connected, worshiped, that Coffin House. It was filled with something ancient and sentient and *wonderful.*

After a moment's rest with the coolness of the sweat drying, she stood up, and bits of the ground stuck to her skin. That was her communion now, her holy communion with the house. A breaking of the world, a shattering of the ties between her and her husband. The sacrifice, then. The sacrifice of her family, her marriage, her everything. All for the love of a house. Ancient, knowing, sentient house. *This was not a bad thing. This was the right thing to do. Her marriage had to end so that a new love could blossom here.*

She reached down and grabbed her candle, and almost picked up her nightgown and put it back on. She stared at it for a moment, and then realized she should leave it here, leave it in front of the statue. *A gift to you, my love. My love, my love, my love. My skin my body my clothes my everything. A gift to you.* And then she pushed apart the vines—they felt so alive in her hands, squirming like snakes. Goosebumps crawled over every inch of her body, the candle lighting a path through the moonlight beyond, as she walked outside, slowly through the path in the garden, still naked save for the mud and leaves that clung to her. The garden would be her clothing now. It was what was right, what was fitting.

And then, a sensation behind her. Oh, no. *Something moved behind the pines* and now, up the hill *hear it moving? Hungry and restless but still unable to cross over the sentinel books* and now toward the front of the house *a sense of foreboding doom, all claustrophobic around her* and now up to that porch and the front door to go inside. Inside, inside, inside. *The house does not like that thing behind the pines, no. Not one bit. The house was never scared of anything, but somehow, that thing behind the pines terrified it. Shiver the floors and tremble the attic. It wanted it gone. Ghosts gone, creature gone, aimless Mothers of Sorrow, gone.*

And she wanted to protect it all, to protect the house and keep it safe.

Oh, love, my love, my wonderful house. Of course, I will protect you. Of course, I will keep you safe. You are now my all-consuming everything, and I am a spider to the insects of god.

-25-

Dana was filled with a breathless excitement as she stood above his sleeping body, and she watched him quietly, silently. If only for a moment, and then another moment, and finally a moment more.

Wake, wake, wake.

Should she touch him? It had been a few days since they even had an accidental brush of fingers and palms. Should she breach that invisible wall between bodies? The last time they'd touched, it'd been too much, and it made her want to run away and never look back. And really, after she'd had the house inside the grotto, the last thing she wanted was a pale human communion.

And yet, she knew she had to do this. This was the final act of the ritual, the final bit of sacrifice needed to do everything right. She reached out, her hand poised against his skin. Come on now: *wake, wake, wake.*

He tossed and turned and snored some more. Damn it. She sat down on the couch next to him, her bare skin goosebumps against his spine. He still didn't move—he was still in deep sleep, even now, with her hand against his bare back. Well. She was already touching him, wasn't she? Skin against skin, let the communion begin. Even if it was only just the bare part of his back where his shirt rode up, there was still something there, he had to feel it. Why wasn't he waking up?

Oh well, she might as well breach that invisible wall and wake him right now. One, two, three . . .

Her hands on his chest and she spun his body around to face her. Sweat dripped from her breasts and tapped his cheeks as she straddled him, skin to skin once again. His flesh felt so hollow under hers when compared to the glory of the house. *Wake, wake, wake.* She whispered it now, her words barely haunting the air. *Wake, wake, wake.* Only Lucas and no one else. *Wake, wake, wake.*

His eyes, then, his eyes, they fluttered open for a moment. Groggy, confused, words slurred on his lips. "What?" he said, without a hint of irritation. "What time is it?"

She pressed against him now, nervous heart thunder-loud. Could he hear her heart? It was so loud, he had to hear it. She felt him stiffen beneath her and she arched against it, moving her body just out of his reach. The music of her heart did that to him, provoked a reaction in his body. Blood responded to blood.

"Oh, wait, what are you doing?"

And then, quick kiss right on his lips. Shut him up for a moment now. They'll talk when this was over. This was a goodbye fuck and nothing more, an end-it-all fuck. A get-it-out-of-the-system, one last-final fuck. She had to call it that. That's what this was. Fucking fuck fuck. Would the house be jealous? No. It knew what she must do, what she had to do to keep them all together forever.

She pulled his shirt off and saw his tattoos in the moonlight, from the neck down, his whole body was covered. It'd been years since she'd seen them, the sex few and far between and in the deep darkness of night without light. And she. And she realized somehow that she'd missed those tattoos all the years. She missed looking at them, and it filled her with a brief sensation of loss and sadness.

Maybe she didn't have to do this just yet, maybe she could prolong it just a little bit and let the finality of it all wash over her. Just a few heartbeats more? Maybe, maybe she could even just stop this altogether. It wasn't too late, was it? They could go back to working on it, couldn't they?

She shook her head, tried to close her eyes and not look at his tattoos in the moonlight. No, they couldn't do that. The house loved her, the house would never betray her, and that was important. He had lied to her over and over again. He had taken them to the point of no return, damaged each of them all in his pursuit of his <u>art</u>. Certainly, he never laid a hand on them. But did he have to? The mental scars were all there, and it was all for his documentary films. Their children did not deserve that, she did not deserve that. She would not let him have another *Hour of Smiles*. And she could tell—it was getting close to that all over again. What had Rae called it? *The Happy Family Game*? It had Lucas's fingerprints all over it. *This was going to be another* Hour of

Smiles, *no amount of awards and adulations would be worth allowing him to hurt them once more.*

And yet, still sadness, even in her vitriol, as she looked over the tattoos one last time in that thin moonlight. A serpent curled around his neck like a noose. A beehive over his chest where his heart should be, with bees spilling out and dancing on his ribcage. His stomach was wrapped in curling ivy, with bones and skeletons all nestled into those primitive vine designs. She looked at his arms, elaborate branches and leaves on both shoulders, connecting into a tree of life design on his back. Skulls then, tumbling down the remainder of his arms and onto his hands. Complex skull art. To touch it was to touch the haunting specter of death.

She would miss his tattoos, and she would miss the beautiful moments they shared together. But she could never, ever, trust him again. She had to go through with this. *Now.*

She grabbed his hands, keyhole tats on both of his palms, and felt the blood course through him now, all rapid and fast, as she moved her body over his. She wiggled a bit, her motions sliding him out of the hole in his pajamas. Breathless pressing down sweat soaked and hungry, taking him all the way in. It felt. Different. Now. Now that the house had been inside of her, he felt like a whisper, a shadow, and not anywhere near as infinite.

It didn't take long for him to call out and shudder down and collapse beneath her. She stayed there for a moment more. Heartbeat, still, and felt him go flaccid inside of her. Puddles of him slipping out and dripping down her leg. It was over so quickly, and it left her feeling empty inside and wrong. Sadness followed, with a melancholy specter over everything.

The sacrifice was done. It was all over now. No going back.

"In the morning, we should tell the girls."

He looked confused. He should've known what this was. He should've been able to tell, just by the fierce look in her eyes.

"Tell them what?"

There was an odd hopeful lilt in his words.

"That it's over, that we're getting a divorce. Nothing's changed, you knew what this was."

Oh, no. Crushed face. Horrible face. Whole-world-crashing-down face. And now his lip quivered for a moment. Then his eyes closed, and everything stopped. So still. She felt him twitch beneath her.

"I thought, I thought this was different now, that you'd changed your mind and that's why we did this."

Her palms on his chest and she touched his tattoos one last time, saying goodbye to each of them. "We're going to talk to them in the morning. They have to know something's up. It's better if we tell them right away, like ripping off a Band-Aid."

He sighed and then, "I guess so. I mean, I guess. I don't know. I don't know if I'm ready for this. I thought the house would fix us."

She leaned in, her face right against his, the moonlight bouncing from her skin.

"We can't keep doing this—it's not fair to them. Hell, it's not fair to us."

He coughed and then put his hands against her chest and pushed her away. It wasn't a forceful push, nor a loving one, and he turned his head to the side, refusing to look at her. "I think you should get off of me now."

She stood quickly, her body a knife cutting through the shadows, cracked windows illuminated her pale skin. Fine then, fine. It was all done and over with anyway. "I'm going to sleep upstairs. I think it's best if you sleep down here from now on."

And the house looked on approvingly. He was in love with the ghosts, she could tell—he'd always been in love with them. That was a splinter in their marriage from the start, way before they even bought the Gemini House. The Sunshine Family, and their strange allure would always be his first love.

And now she was in love with their house. It could never work, could it? Not without the two of them splitting apart.

"Why do you have leaves in your hair? Is that mud? You got mud all over me . . . where were you? What were you doing in the garden at such an hour?"

A shrug of her shoulders and she just kept on walking up the stairs, leaving him there, to sleep alone with his ghosts he loved so much.

-26-

The Rattling Boy came to her yet again. He crawled across her floor at night and she wanted to scream when she saw him but knew she should not. He was a friend, after all, wasn't he? Even though he moved in creepy, slithering ways, his arms pulling him forward, unable to move his legs. As he moved, his body crinkled and sounded like balled-up paper, his mouth exhaling so loudly with each pull of his arms. She moved further back on her bed, moving as far as she could up against the wall. One night, he'd crawled in the window and across the ceiling like a spider, and it freaked her out. She asked him never to do that again, and so far, he had listened.

When he came close enough to her bed, he stopped for a moment, panted, and began to speak. The words were slow-moving and painful. She knew it hurt him to talk. He'd told her that so many times.

My own father burned me alive, he whispered, *gasoline dumped all over me and it smelled so awful. Do you know the horror of the sound of a striking match? It's a sound that cuts into you, carries with it the promise of fire. I heard that sound as he threw the match down, and he sat in his nice easy chair and just watched. His face plastered ear to ear with this big smile as he watched. I could see myself reflected in his glasses, and you won't believe it, but I never screamed. Not even once. Even my mother screamed, but I did not. I knew that would only make things worse. So, I watched him as he watched me, my body burning and silent in the reflection of his glasses.*

She wanted to shut out his words, she wanted to scream and cry and clamp hands on ears, shut out everything. He came to her last night. He came to her every night. No longer in her memories, and no longer when she thought of coffins, no. A solid thing now, a real thing, all flesh and bones and burning skin. He crept to her across the floor covered in moonlight. That burned skin, those strange eyes. So meaty and tangible and not even a ghastly ghost. The house made him real. *The Coffin House can do that,* he whispered, *it can do so many wonderful things. It makes me real, it can turn your dad into a ghost, and it can make your mother love the unlovable.*

Her palm against his skin and it felt like fire and his whole body stunk of ashes and sweat and that weird scorched hair smell. She knew that smell too well. Too many accidents with fire during the early days in the *Hour of Smiles*, before daddy buried her in the garden. *This is going to help you control that fire with your mind,* her dad told her over and over again, it's *going to help you become such a special little one, everyone will love it when they see what you can do with your brilliant mind. Oh, my little chosen one, my tiny superstar. Your brain will be filled with ghosts and lightning, and you'll have powers. Oh, such beautiful powers. Being able to light fires with your mind would only be the start of all your amazing powers.*

She never told anyone about that, not even the burning boy. Not even when he confessed to her his own death, in preparation for what was to come. That was a secret she kept even from mom, no one would know what she could do. Her father didn't even understand how she'd given into the fires, how she had learned the special tricks he was trying to teach her, and only feigned ignorance to keep him in the dark. That would show him for hurting her. That would show him for hurting Mommy.

Later in the night, the Rattling Boy crawled into bed with her, and she wanted to scoot away and keep her distance. She didn't want to touch that flesh, it crinkled like paper under her hands, so fragile. Did he burn still to this day? Did he smolder on the inside? Lit-up embers under the skin? Was his heart a charcoal heart, encased entirely in flame?

Your sister, he said, *Tell her to stay away from the Three Sorrows . . .*

She wanted to scoot away, scoot away, scoot away, keep away, don't touch, no.

"I did already, I told her. Why do you keeping telling me to do this?"

The Happy Family Game is not a good game. The white blood cells will be coming for her soon . . . like spiders in the dark. Stay away from the Sorrows, stay away from their son. That horrible Grief that slouches behind the pines . . .

She didn't want this, couldn't help it, all trembling shiver and crying a little, yes. Crying a little. Yell for Mom, she should yell for Mom, she needed to yell out for Mommy to come and save her and save them all . . .

One more thing, he said, and then he coughed like his throat still yearned for fire, *In the morning your parents will tell you they are getting divorced.*

And then he was gone.

The sound of branches and leaves blowing in the wind haunted her room, her window still wide open, as his words repeated over and over and over again in her mind. She would not be getting any sleep tonight. She just laid there and thought about him burning up, and the threat of divorce in the morning. Would there be anything she could do to stop it? No. It was inevitable, she knew it, it had that destined feeling. So, she just thought about it over and over and over again. *Divorce, divorce, divorce.*

Until the sun came up and her mom called her downstairs for breakfast. "Come on, little girl! Rae and your father are already down here! We have something important to tell you."

And she sounded so happy, a happiness so bright and cheerful she almost sounded like a stranger. What was this even? Was the Rattling Boy wrong? No, no, no—he was never wrong. Then why did her mom sound happy? Did . . . did Mommy want this? Did Mommy want this divorce? And there it was. Aching knife pain all over her skin and she curled up and rolled over. And she wasn't coming downstairs, not ever. Never ever. If she didn't, then the divorce would never happen. She could prevent that earthquake of a word by shutting herself off from the world. If they never spoke it, it could never happen.

Yes, she knew that wasn't how things worked. But maybe, just maybe, this time they could work like that.

-27-

Lily locked her door from the inside and piled things in front of it to barricade them out. Chairs on top of chairs, boxes on top of boxes, opening the door would be impossible. It would be worse than impossible—it was a death trap. She leaned against the barricade, and she smiled a brief smile that held more melancholy than joy. They banged on the door now, rattled the door knob, the sounds of keys rattled against the lock, still no use. They were not getting in.

Bang, bang, trumpet bang, it sounded like fists against the door. She heard Mommy yelling out, "You open this door up right now, young lady! Or I'm going to break it down." She heard the sound of Rae dancing and singing behind the door, and it made Lily smile. Of course, Rae would do that, it was the most very Rae thing in the world to dance and sing in a moment like this. She wondered if Daddy was with them, or was he elsewhere? Waiting for the door to open, and for the word Divorce to be spoken out loud? Daddy had been so sad lately, and at least she knew the reason why now.

The sound of a key in the lock, click click click, and then a turning and a pushing on the door. It rammed against her barricade, knocking boxes and toys to the floor. Her mom's face appeared in the crack, angry, frustrated, "What has gotten into you? Come on downstairs, we have to talk! I made you breakfast and everything. This is important!"

The door moved back and forth, back and forth, more boxes tumbling, more toys smashing down on the hardwood floors. Oh, no. She hoped they wouldn't break her music box. The ballerina inside was delicate and could shatter easily . . .

And down it went, smashing into a million pieces. The door finally pushed the chair aside, shoving it against the wall, the last few boxes falling down.

Lily was not going to just stay here and let this happen, so she ran into the closet and closed herself inside. The closet smelled like mildew and basements, and was that a caterpillar crawling over the walls? She leaned her back against the door, terrified of the caterpillar, and yet even more terrified at the promise of divorce.

"Lily? Lily, this is Mommy! Where are you? Are you hiding in this room somewhere? This isn't funny anymore, stop playing such a stupid game and come on downstairs for breakfast. This is important!"

And through the door came the sound of Rae dancing around. Singing the word, *delicious! Delicious! Delicious!* Over and over again. And for once it didn't annoy her. Instead, she felt some sad weight pressing against her skin. *Rae doesn't know, Rae has no idea what was going to happen.* This made her insides twitch, and she wanted to protect her little sister, keep her safe from that horrible monster of Divorce. If only she could bring her inside the closet, and the two of them could live there forever.

And the dust tickled her throat, and she couldn't help it, she coughed and gave her location away.

Her dad's voice was outside the closet door right now. She heard him breathing, and then talking in a sad sing-song voice. "Sweetie, what are you doing in there? Is this a game of hide-and-seek? Why don't you just come out now, and we can talk and have some waffles and blueberries, and everything will be all right."

He sounded so lost and broken and not like Daddy at all. And this terrified her, because now she knew. Now she knew that the Rattling Boy was one-hundred percent correct, and this brought her whole world crashing down.

The bones of the room shifted, shrugged, grew, and changed shape, opening to a new vast hallway that led into the dark of the house beyond. And she knew what she had to do, she couldn't stay here, she had to go into the house. She had to follow the changing path inside of the closet. It was her only choice. Pretty soon, they would get that closet door open somehow, and it would all be over.

She stepped forward into the new cavernous hallway, long and meandering and stretched through the length of the house. Nails stuck out at random points in the walls, and she had to be careful not to touch those. This house had teeth. She heard her parents arguing and calling out to her, asking her to come home, but they sounded a million miles away. How much had this house changed? How much of it will change her?

She crawled over her unpacked boxes, pushed on through piles of winter clothes, and came out the other side. How far did it go back? The immensity of it all dwarfed her, as stray sunbeams drifted in through cracks in the ceiling. It seemed to snake about impossibly, and move up on an incline into the shadows. And the voices from the door behind her seemed even further and further away now. Where was she? Had this hallway taken her someplace else?

It felt like Narnia, moving through a closet into a completely other world. And yet, there was no comfort in that idea.

She heard footsteps in the distance, far down that long hallway that was once her closet and was now something else, something far greater than any mere closet. Someone was coming, and they whispered as they walked. It sounded like insects buzzing, and she moved back, back. Back up against that closet door. Hear the door rattle now? Like the little boy's bones. Her family was trying to open it. It was stuck. She hadn't locked it, there was no key. The door must have changed like the house had changed.

The emptiness beyond called to her, begged her to move further into the house and spelunk among the shadows. It wanted her to follow those sounds, to chase after whatever was making those noises in the long hallway beyond the closet walls. But she didn't want to go, did she? She was terrified of what lay beyond. And why hadn't the Rattling Boy warned her about this? This was far more important than any divorce. Was this what he wanted her to do? If he hadn't warned her, she wouldn't have come this way after all.

Maybe he wanted her to be trapped in this house. Maybe he wasn't her friend after all.

Mommy's voice rose all angry and shouting, and Daddy was crying out and Rae was crying now, too. It was an audible panic from behind the door, yet they sounded so far away. How much of this place had changed? She thought of opening the door, letting them in, and then . . .

That D word, that Divorce word, that world ending word.

It made her heart feel so funny and wrong, like someone had pulled it out and squished it. She. She had to go on. She must move onward. There was a fear still there, yes. But the divorce behind that door was all pain. And fear was something she knew she could overcome. The coffin her daddy had nailed her inside had taught her that a long time ago.

-28-

And from the emptiness walked that lady in pale clothes with a black rag over her face. The one from her visions, the one she had warned Rae about over and over and over again. She shuffled towards Lily, her words like soft moans beneath the black rag. *Not her, oh, not her she couldn't be real, not her, not her, not her! Could she run past her now? No, she could not. Could she make it back to the closet door and swing it back open? Maybe. Or maybe the pale lady would get her . . .*

Before she could decide, the pale lady motioned a hand towards her, her fingers at odd angles, jerking about. And she motioned for Lily to come closer. *See these things I have to show you . . .*

Should she? Should she come closer and see?

"Follow," the pale lady said, the sound of flies obscuring her words. Lily felt everything closing in. Was the hallway shrinking? Returning back to a closet again? No. Wait. Was she shrinking? No. It was just so tight and small and suffocating. She felt faint. She couldn't leave. She couldn't follow.

"Follow me, my child—come on. Follow, follow, follow."

And her hand was on Lily's shoulder now, like a warm bag filled with oatmeal. It squished and Lily tried not to faint, she tried really hard not to go into seizures yet again. Maggots crawled up and down her hand, landing on Lily, crawling across Lily's clothing. She screamed and she screamed and she screamed and there weren't even words anymore, just loud empty screaming sounds.

She shoved the pale lady. She felt like she was all flesh and bones and like the Rattling Boy felt once he was no longer a ghost. The rag fell from her face and Lily saw it all now. Flies all over the twitching face. Dancing flies, swarming flies, and underneath it all? And, and, underneath it all? Was a hypnotic beauty. The kind of pretty face that feels like an old painting. With skin so pale you could see the bone beneath it, the blood beneath it beating through in blue veins. The lady's hair was up in a bun on top of that skull, flies coating every inch of those perfect cheekbones. Like a doll, Lily thought, she looked just like a beautiful porcelain doll covered in maggots and flies. Even those eyes were glassy doll eyes, like marbles placed delicately in a doll skull.

It all gave Lily such an uneasy queasy feeling. World shifted slightly. Stomach flip flop and everything vibrated.

"Follow, follow, follow." And with each word a maggot fell from the jerking lips and onto the floor.

Lily could not stop laughing. Why was she laughing? This wasn't funny. She knew it wasn't funny. And yet, there it was—her voice laughing. The laughter became an unhinged sound, and it didn't even feel like her laughter any longer, but rather, something horrible and outside of her body.

Eventually the door behind her banged open with a violent crash and spat her out into her bedroom. Everyone came and scolded her and yelled, and it was like none of them could see the pale lady with the maggot-kissed face. She knew she would be sleeping with Mommy tonight. There was no way she could be in this bedroom with this closet and the broken door all wide open and leading beyond. Not a chance, nuh-uh, no way. Her nightmares were already bad enough as they were. There would be no sleeping in this room ever again. It was impossible. The closet could change again at any moment, and that pale lady would come walking right out, and the world would end.

-29-

"What was that, Lily? What was that even?" Mommy did not look happy.

She couldn't tell them about the pale lady, could she? No. That was a secret thing. No one would believe her, just like no one believed her about the Rattling Boy. She laughed nervously and looked at both of her parents from across the kitchen table. Breakfast was piled up high—waffles and ice cream and blueberries, just as they'd promised. They glared back at her, and she glanced quickly down toward the ground. Her hands wringing with anxiety. "I just, I just want everything to stay the same always and forever, and it's all changing, isn't it? It's all changing."

And the look on Mommy's face. It contained a sort of crushed sorrow and pity, as she ran over, hugged Lily so tight it hurt a little, rib bones digging into her skull. It was a good kind of hurt, though. It meant someone loved her, and she wanted to be loved, and maybe if Mommy held her tight and didn't let go? Maybe they wouldn't get a Divorce. *So don't let go, Mommy. Don't ever let go . . .*

"Oh, honey, oh. I'm so sorry, I didn't want it to be like this, I promise. I never wanted to hurt you this way."

And there's Rae's voice. Strangely curious, sounding like she wasn't really surprised at all. Did Rae know? Did something dark and secret whisper it to her as well? "Didn't want what to be like what, Mommy? Come on, tell us. Daddy? Daddy? Daddy, do you know what she's talking about? You do, don't you! Tell us, Daddy, tell us! Oh, this is all part of the Happy Family Game, isn't it? It's such a good game, such a fun game."

There was no stopping this, the Rattling Boy was right. What was she thinking? Of course, he was right, the Rattling Boy was always right.

Being alive was like floating in a sea, just like that, the current sucks you in, and you can fight it, but not really . . . cause that's how drowning happens, that's what they told her in swim class, that's how drowning happens, the waves yank and pull, and you're hooked in, sucked in, drowning and drowning and so far away from shore . . .

And Daddy cleared his throat. "What your mother is saying, I guess. I mean," she could hear his heart drop and explode and break into a million pieces, "This isn't working."

"What isn't, Daddy? Is this whole house all broken too far beyond repair?"

"No," Lily said, muffled in her mother's chest.

"But what we're trying to say is . . ."

"No."

"I mean, this whole thing is . . ."

"No."

"What your father means,"

"No."

"It's just that we're two different . . ."

"No. No. No. No. No. No. No. No."

"Damnit, Lily! Stop it. Just stop it!"

And now her mom pulled back away from her. She was no longer against that hearthome chest, now she was external, cast out, pushed away from the comfort of her arms. Everything felt distant and dead and echoing again.

And for a moment, her mom's face softened. And Mommy looked down at the ground, hiding her eyes behind her hair. Lily wanted to reach out and kiss her, but the distance between them was too large, too infinite, too difficult to cross.

"I'm just going to come right out and say it, okay? I didn't want it to be like this, but here we go. Your father and I are getting a divorce."

Grief hung in the air with a heavy presence. And Lily felt like she was falling. She felt like she was dropping down through an infinite hole into the center of the world. She was fighting those tears right now, but this was even worse than being in the casket! She'd known that would end eventually, that the coffin lid would come right off, and she would be okay. This was true death, actual death, and heartbreak. Like when Grandma Glass died in her sleep, and there she was, in her own coffin all preserved like an ice princess. And she remembered looking down in that casket, and thinking that she saw Grandma Glass's hand twitch, and move a little. And so she leaned in, listened to the no heartbeat all cold in her empty chest and knew the truth. *Death, death, death.* That feeling and this feeling where the same on the deep-down gut level. *Death, death, death.*

The world is ending...

"Does this mean we're moving away? Who's going to live with who? Will I be with you, will Rae? Where will we live, and will I have to change my name?"

The words all poured out in one long stream of a sentence. She couldn't even think, everything just jumped from her lips so fast. She felt the whole world growing into a tiny dot and she was so small and what even mattered anymore? Nothing mattered at all anymore.

And Mommy hugged her again. Nobody said anything else, and that was okay for right now. No more words, no talking anymore . . . she just wanted to go up into her room and stare out the window. Maybe not even cry, just stare in numb distance and hope the world would actually end for once.

-30-

Mommy thought it would be good to be out here in the deep of the garden. Wilding it, loving it, showing it care. Mommy thought it would get their minds off of things, but Lily didn't think that could happen. It was just hot and sticky, and her hands hurt from the weeds, and everything felt so wrong and broken. The word Divorce spun around in her mind over and over and over again, and she couldn't get it out of her head. She wanted to, she needed it to, but she could not.

Mommy stopped for a moment, wiped the sweat from her brow and left a dirt-stained smear in its place. "Maybe we should sing," she said. "Maybe it would make us all feel better."

And with that, mom and Rae started singing one of the Sunshine Family songs. It sounded so weird right here, right now, like it was doing something to this place. Maybe that was it, maybe the music was tearing their family apart, maybe the Gemini House was normally asleep and dormant, and the music woke it up . . .

And. And. And. Lily felt a hand. A smooth hand all hot like stroking a flame. The Rattling Boy was here again, his palm grasping her palm, their shadows combining and making a heart shape. He was different now, oh, he was on fire now, and it was odd to see him like this in the sun, so calm, so tranquil, every inch of him on fire.

And the flames did not burn her hand, but instead they comforted her. Like a warm blanket against her skin.

"I'm sorry," he said and his voice was a roaring flame, "I'm so sorry this happened to you."

"Thank you," she said, a half whisper so no one else could hear. "Thank you."

And he nodded and then pointed. "Don't say anything. Just watch for right now, it is important that you see this, you understand? Your sister is playing the Happy Family Game, and we have to fix it. If she keeps doing what she's doing, we're all going to be in big trouble. The Happy Family Game is a destructive lie, one that your sister believes with her whole heart. You know the pain of divorce—you understand why she's acting the way she's acting. But it's out of desperation, and it won't ever truly solve anything, and has the ability to make everything so much worse."

She watched Rae now, watching her closely, to see the dangers the Rattling Boy warned her about. Her sister danced around that weeping willow tree, whomp, whomp, whomp, and then she ran up and violently ripped the books from each tree. Mommy was not even noticing, not doing a thing, too busy tending the wild garden around them.

"Don't say a thing to her, all right? She wouldn't understand, and it would only make things worse. Trust me, we can fix this later, by providing our own sentinels to guard the garden. I'll show you how."

But, oh, the fear that gripped her now. A hand around her body, squeezed tight. Everything felt like a live wire screaming. Her bones felt too small for her insides, crushing everything, as Rae yanked and pulled and tore. The pages went fluttering about, scattered down, as each book flew off and went splat face down in the mud, sending splashes of filth all over Rae's summer clothes. She laughed in that strange and dangerous way only Rae could laugh, a laughter that held the promise of something darker, as she skipped over to the next tree. She remembered the day she'd found the severed heads of robins all lined up on Rae's dresser in her room, their bodies dissected, their guts spilled across the floor. Rae had been laughing and dancing in exactly the same way she was now.

Lily wanted to scream, she wanted to stop her sister, to make it all go away, as a giant leviathan shadow stirred beyond the pines, waking to the sounds of the books being ripped free.

"Stay strong, don't let her know our plans," the Rattling Boy said, his voice a roaring flame. "The Child of the Abyss watches from behind the pines. If your sister gets the last of the books down, you don't want to be too close. If that happens, well. I'm not sure there's anything we can do to fix it."

She was overcome emotionally and physically frozen as Rae walked over to the last book. She jumped and danced around the tree, rubbed her hands together greedily and got ready to yank it down. Overhead, storm clouds rushed over the sun and small drips of rain tapped her on her shoulders.

Mommy's hand raised up and tilted her straw hat back. "Oh, finally! Finally! The humidity is breaking, girls. Can you feel it? The humidity is breaking!" And the rain came down one more, two more, drops, and then all at once: *torrential*. And Mommy laughed, and it sounded unhinged. "We don't want to be out on the hills when it gets like this, there could be a mudslide. Come on! Inside!"

The sound of the rain was deafening, and Rae scowled and tried to run over and yank down that last book before going inside. But, instead, she slipped and slid and moved past it, almost to the edges of the gates, where shadows waited beyond the pines. She slid up, almost fell down again, and reluctantly ran back towards Lily and mom, her whole body slick with new mud.

Good, good, Lily thought, she wasn't able to tear down the last one. She turned to say this to the Rattling Boy, but he'd already left her. It seemed that the rain had put him out, leaving only a trail of smoke behind. She was going to miss him, and hoped briefly that he would return again tonight, even if she was spending the night in a different bedroom.

-31-

Later on that night Lily woke up again in a mild panic next to her mom's sleeping body. She'd had that coffin feeling again. That's what she called it when her mind raced anxiously, and she was keyed up to the nines and terrified without any reason or cause. It felt like being in that coffin all over again, wanting to scream but not being able to scream. She wouldn't be able to go to sleep for a while now, so she just laid there, watching the world spin by around her.

After a while, she heard the sound of rustling paper and small fires and knew that the Rattling Boy was coming for her once again. She felt that mix of happiness and sadness and waited for him. In the corner of the room, a shadow head lifted up, and she saw his bandaged face in the window reflected in the moonlight. Rattling Boy, she could hear his bones now, rattling under his paper skin.

"You awake?"

She put a finger against her lips, "Yes, say it quieter, please? I don't want to wake Mom."

He nodded and crept closer in the shadows, whispering as he moved. "We need to go and fix what your sister did, come on. Look, we can use these, we just need a sacrifice . . ."

And he held up his bandaged hands, to show rusted nails and an old hammer. Had she ever hammered anything before? Maybe once or twice in play, but never anything in real life. She gulped in the shadows. Could she do this? And that word. Sacrifice. It made her think of nails in skin, nails in bone, and it came with the promise of pain. Before she could answer he held up an old China doll, its face dirtied and hair a messy tangle of sticky curls.

"Here, is this doll important to you?"

She nodded, and whispered, "Yes, Mom said that's a family heirloom. It means a lot to me and her."

"Good, that's perfect. Pick out two more dolls like this, and make sure they're super important to you. Okay? We need that. Sacrifices have to mean something."

She understood now. She didn't want to do this. But she saw that thing, sensed it out there behind the pines. There was no way she wanted it to get loose, and if she could somehow keep them safe from it and undo the damage Rae had done? Well, that would be perfect.

So, she climbed out of bed as quick and silent as could be, careful to not wake up Mommy from her deep sleep. She ran down the hall with the burning boy, and ducked into her bedroom. The closet door was still open, and for a moment she thought she saw something in the moonlight, a figure in pale clothes with a black veil over her face, and Lily's heart raced. *Ignore it,* the Rattling Boy said, *she's only a shadow of something greater.*

Lily nodded, nervous, hands shaking, terrified. She moved around the motionless figure, who didn't even seem to see her this time. Was she asleep? Hypnotized? Lily didn't even want to know—she just did as the Rattling Boy suggested and ignored her. Even though it took all of her mental energy to not run away screaming. It took her longer than it should have to find her two favorite dolls, but eventually she grabbed them, and they ran back out of the room and into the hallway beyond, her breathing shallow, her hands shaking, her mind racing in fear. Both dolls pressed close to her chest as they walked quietly and quickly past Rae's open door.

And look at that, fresh muddy footprints leading up to her bed. What had she done? Her legs were coated in muck and dead leaves and her bare feet so disgusting, hanging off her bed, she snored, fast asleep and filthy under the blankets. Oh no, oh Rae, oh little sister, what have you done?

"We have to keep going, come on. The thing behind the pines might be out already . . ."

She wanted to ask what, needed to ask what, but she could guess, couldn't she? The horrible shadow has been freed from his prison behind the pines. He slouched toward the house, hungry for the light inside. Panic seized everything, and he tugged on her hand. Led her further, further, toward those infinite stairs. Leading down and down and to the front door. Daddy slept noiselessly on the couch, and they had to tip toe past him. Everything felt alive with ghosts, as if something unseen was waking all the spirits of the Gemini House.

They stirred and started to float around them, all the ghosts from the Sunshine Family. So many kids around her own age, ghostly floating through and polluting the air. Their bodies like gossamer sheets, the horror of their own deaths laid bare across their bodies. So many kids her own age riddled with suicide wounds. How horrible—this whole thing made her feel empty and dead inside, and she thought for a moment of stopping. She thought for a moment of just staying here, and trying to find a way to help these kids, to unburden some of the sadness that leaked out from their ghostly skin.

But she didn't have any choice in the matter, did she? No. The Rattling Boy yanked on her arm, and they went out the front door and into the garden beyond. Ghosts or no ghosts, they had work to do.

-32-

The garden looked so different in the moonlight. Dark sorrow clouds obscured those stars, and the moon itself was a pale phantom haunting the air above them. There was barely any light, and the overgrown garden had turned into a labyrinth in the moonlight. It had changed the shape of the trees and moved the bushes and the benches and the statues, making it into a tricky winding maze of dead ends. No, there was no way she was going to go through that maze. She knew if she'd gotten lost the thing behind the pines would find her and devour her, bones and all, leaving nothing behind but emptiness in the shape of her body.

"It's so dark—I don't like this. What if it got out already?"

And the Rattling Boy smiled, his teeth all smashed and shattered in his mouth. He told her once upon a time that his dad did that as punishment for insulting the dinner he'd cooked one night. *Let's see how you like eating dinner through a straw.*

"Don't worry. I'll light the way." And right after he said this, his body burst into flames once again, the light an amber circle around them, bouncing off the giant weeds bopping on the summer breeze.

She held up the first doll in her trembling hands, and asked, "Where do you we need this?"

"Here." And the ghostly lamp of the Rattling Boy led her over to the weeping willow and pushed his burning hand against a specific spot. He left a smear of ash, right there, and said, "Nail the doll to the tree. Do it exactly in this spot, she will act like a sentinel, a guardian against the thing that moves beyond the pines."

Feverously, Lily nodded and put the nails between her teeth, and then lifted up that hammer. The Rattling Boy placed the doll right above the smear of ash and held it there, the doll grinding against the bark with his rough hands.

Come on. Steady now, steady. A hammer down at the wrong angle and she could hurt herself, or maybe even shatter the doll. Neither of those options would do anyone any good. So, stay calm, stay steady. Don't vomit.

The hammer swung down, smash! She'd nailed it right into the heart of her doll. And she whispered, "Sorry, so sorry, Annie, I'm so sorry." She hammered again, and again, until the doll was solid and stuck right there, right against the bark of the tree. No one was going to move poor Annie, not after all of this.

"Two more, come on."

And he led her over to another tree, the second tree where a book had been torn down. She got the nails out, got the hammer ready to go again. And then she saw it, something out of the corner of her eyes . . . what was that? A shadow darted in the moonlight. And then another, and then another, and then another. What was going on here? His hand tensed in hers, the fire now reaching up, the flames so large and illuminating whatever it was in the shadows.

No. Oh, no. No, no, no, no. There was Rae. How was this Rae? And yet, it wasn't Rae at all. Her skin was melted candlewax blue, her eyes like two black stones. Naked, somehow, yet clothed by ghosts. What was this? Rae ran over and quickly pulled the doll down and smashed it on the ground. Her sister moved in such an awful way, so fast, so inhumanly fast, smiling all the while. Her teeth were the wrong size for her mouth.

Oh, Annie! No, no, no. Please, no. Just. Oh. Lily watched the doll's head crack open spill out fall apart, a hole in her chest where the nail went through to the tree. The poor doll's hair a tangled muddy mess. And then. What was this? Another Rae and another and another. So many of them running about, searching the trees for other sentinels.

The flaming hand tightened against hers again. "Don't scream, don't scream. They haven't noticed us yet," he said, "It's too late—the Child of the Abyss is free. We need to get back to the house *now*. Right *now*, come on, hurry. And whatever you do, you need to avoid those mimics, they aren't your sister, not even close, not even an echo of her. They're something else, and you don't even want to know what."

Oh. And the house. The house at the top of the hill grew and changed. Watch it now, the bones of it all shifting and expanding, just like her closet had done earlier in the day. The wood reached out in despair, and grasped at the world around them with greedy brick claws. The cry of the wood was deafening in its sorrow. Painful, yes. Painful for the house to grow like this. Did anyone else see this?

Why weren't they shocked? And look at that. Figures crawled all over the house. Human bodies, with strange dark blue melted candle skin and naked. They were genderless things, and completely bald, with teeth all the wrong size for their tiny mouths. Even their bones seemed to be all the wrong size for their tiny bodies, as they crawled all over the house like salamanders. The house started spinning as it expanded and grew, larger and larger still. It wailed as it grew, and Lily understood that feeling. She felt sorrow from those creatures, and sorrow for that house.

And the closer she got, the more she realized that they wore all the wrong faces, and that they had to be masks, they just had to be wearing masks! Otherwise, it was all too awful. They looked exactly like Rae and Daddy and Mommy. And some, yes, some even, yes, some even looked just like her. Lily masks on tiny blue Lily bodies, crawling all over the face of their new house. A house that had changed and grown and mutated before her very eyes.

Fear gripped and strangled her lungs, and she wanted to run so far, so far away from everything. Something sick and horrible hatched in her tummy and she just started dry heaving.

"You have to go inside," the Rattling Boy said. But she could hear the fear in his voice. Was he still a ghost? He felt so corporeal now. "It's the only way we can be safe from the Grief, you understand me? The house has its own protections, its own reality. See? Look at the Grief trying to pry its way inside, but look, see? It can't do it, but we can. So quickly now, quickly. Run to the safety of the house, it's too late to stay outside here, in the garden."

And no, no, no she didn't want to go into that house. It was now outlined in a halo of storm clouds and moonlight, and it had changed so much in size and shape and volume. There had to be a massive labyrinth towering over them, crawling with doubles of her family. Were they ghosts? Were they something else? Echoes of themselves brought to life? It made her feel so sick to her stomach to see them moving like that, stumbling in slow motion with their joints bending the wrong way.

Her sadness slid away for a moment and was replaced by a crushing fear. And then a strange realization. That these two feelings were really the same thing. Her fear, her sorrow. Somehow, they were connected, somehow, like roots all tangled up in her insides, and strangling her heart with emotion. The world felt thicker now, the air tensing around her entire body. Constricting it.

She didn't want to go in. She must go in.

She went inside, leaping up to the front door and running past the echoes of herself hissing and crawling towards her. She ran inside, slammed the door behind her and noticed that her dad was missing from the couch. Daddy? Where are you? Was she even in the same house anymore?

-33-

And there was a shadow shaped like Mommy right outside of Rae's bedroom door. Standing there, sighing so wearily. Dressed in some black pajamas, with the hair all messed up and the look in her eyes a distant and strange one. She drooled as saliva dripped down her chin, her arms still like a statue at odd angles in the air.

Rae didn't want to be here anymore.

Had the Happy Family Game caused this? Maybe. Maybe this wasn't right after all? Had they lied to her about it? About everything? Her stomach all twisted up and she felt sick and everything and didn't even want to play that game anymore. She didn't like the way the game made her feel, it made her feel like a bad person.

But wait, no. Shake off those negative thoughts, shake them all off! You're not a Negative Nelly, no. You are a wonderful Rae of Sunshine! Think of the big picture! The giant massive picture where this all works out and everything is right and there's a happy ending! Of course, there's a happy ending. Girls like Rae always get happy endings, didn't they? So she walked up to sad and lost Mommy, whose eyes were so red and face was stained with mascara streaks. Lips all funky looking and cheeks kind of wonky, like maybe she slept in her makeup?

Never mind that. Just walked up, tugged on her arm.

"Hey Mommy, Mommy, Mommy. Heyo! Hey."

"Heya, little girl," and her mother's voice was sucked dry of all emotions, "I think I'm lost right now. Do you feel lost right now? I think the house changed on me, practically overnight. Why would this wonderful house do this to me? I thought it loved me, it, it, it did love me. But what happened to it? Is this the true house? Was the other house a lie? What is this, little girl? What is this? I feel very betrayed."

And uh-oh. Something really had broken Mommy. "This is a wonderful place, and yeah, Mommy, things changed just a bit. But so what! Let's both go downstairs and get some food. Let Lily sleep in! She deserves it. Just me and you getting some breakfast and yay, it will all be perfect."

And her mother looked at her again in that far off way. For a moment, yes, just a simple moment she seemed to have a glimmer of life again? A recognition? And then nothing. Back to what was here before. "Lily? Lily. Lily . . . maybe. Maybe we should wake her, don't you think? Don't you think that would be good?"

Rae tried hard not to be a huffy Rae and a horrible Rae and a tantrum Rae. Oh, it took all of her willpower and then some not to just burst out and howl and break everything! But good genius Raes are perfect at self-control, aren't they? Of course, they are.

She bit her words as she spoke them. "Yes, let's go wake Lily too and then maybe daddy and we can all have breakfast together." The Happy Family Game was a good game and it was working and they would be a forever perfect amazing happy family. It just took a matter of time for the game to work its magic. Maybe having breakfast together this morning would be a good first step.

And then? Terrified look on Mommy's face. "No! No, not him, no. Oh, Rae. Oh. I think I've made a mistake. I. I think I've made a horrible mistake. Look around, look around. Everything's different, everything's changed, and the house is vacant to me, you know? It pushes away my touch, and doesn't look at me in that same wonderful way anymore. What does it want from me, Rae? What does the house want from me? Oh, I've made such an awful mistake. Such a horrible mistake."

And then Mommy collapsed on the floor and curled up into a ball. This was going to be much harder than she thought. In the now long and massive hallway came a scraping noise, like metal dragging across the hardwood floor. And then came a splintering sound, a nails-on-the-face kind of sound. She couldn't do this alone. She needed Lily's help after all, damn her.

-34-

Lily was no help at all. Rae pouted and tried to reach up to turn on the gas to start making scrambled eggs, but she couldn't quite reach. She hated that she was the one to do it. Even though she was a super genius, she hated fire, and she hated cooking. This was all so beneath her! And yet, it was all part of the Happy Family Game, so she tried her best. As usual, everything fell on her shoulders once again. She looked over at Lily and said, "Could you at least help me out by moving the chair over here? So I can climb on up and cook?"

But noooo—boring old Lily stayed in the living room, unmoving and babbling to herself about blue strangers trying to get inside and how the house was all bigger now. What a silly thing to say! Blue faces, indeed. And so what if the house was bigger? Houses grow all the time, even super genius Rae knew that one. But, alas, she had to go and push the chair over herself, climb on up and twist the knob. There was a click and a hiss but no flame, just a rotten egg smell. Damn it, why wouldn't it work for her? She turned it off, looked back into the living room and called out again, "Mommy? Can you come help me turn on the stove? So I can make breakfast?"

But before Mommy could respond, Daddy came thundering into the kitchen. *BAMBAMBAM*. Right up from the downstairs, his face all wild and savage. *BAMBAMBAM*. His hair all over the place, hands smeared with dirt and soot and sweat from hours of shovel digging and hard work. *BAMBAMBAM*. The door slammed against the wall with a harsh trumpet sound, and as he rose up into that kitchen light, the strangest music drifted up from the crypt beneath the house, following him upstairs and into the kitchen. Something about that music felt all wrong.

It both did and didn't sound like a Sunshine Family song. It was all vocal with no instrumentation, like a beautiful church choir. Was it even in English? Did it even matter?

It made her ache all over, and it pierced through her heart and Rae, yes, Rae of all people was overcome with emotion. What silly things emotions were! Super smart genius people did not need such pathetic things as emotions. They only got in the way of doing the most clever awesome things. And yet, here she was. Rae the human. Rae the mortal. Rae the forgotten child in a little girl costume, almost ready to weep at the sound of that beautiful music.

She leapt off the chair and landed on the linoleum with a soft thud, and then thought about hugging him and decided against it. There was something dangerous about the way he looked, and maybe hugging him would be a very bad thing. Instead, she just let the song touch her heart and listened to daddy as he shouted now, his excited voice barely audible above the music.

"Wake up! Wake up! The dead are singing again! Wake up! Wake up! Did you hear me, did you? The dead are singing again! Oh, I never thought I would hear them sing these beautiful songs in person, and yet here they are. A gift for me, such a beautiful gift for me," and then he collapsed to his knees, and pulled his arms out like angel wings, "So transcendent! I was perfect for them, I helped them out of the shadows and opened their coffins right up down there in the crypt, I gave them room to breathe and yes," and now hands together in prayer, "And they gave me this. This beautiful song," head now toward the ceiling, eyes in rapture and tears, "I'm one of them now, can't you see? I performed the last ritual, did the rite of seven cuts on my body, and now I am the last living member of the Sunshine Family! And they told me something. They told me something amazing. They gave their lives to save the world, did you know that? Oh. How amazing is that? They gave their lives to save the world! I want to do the same thing. Won't you join me, my family, won't you give your life to save the world? Let us give our lives in one last bit of sacrifice to make it all right and stop the worst from happening."

And Mommy looked at him all sad and lonely, and Rae just wanted to fix everything right now. But the Happy Family Game wasn't over just yet, was it? And Mommy called out from the living room, her voice heavy with sorrow. "Close the door, please. I think that music might be too much right now."

"I can't, I can't honey, I can't. I have so much to share with you, so much to share with all of you. I was looking for the master, well, my father now, all of our father now, isn't he? The great one, oh. But he wasn't there, even though I thought he would be in that coffin, the one she showed me, the beautiful one. But that wasn't what was in the coffin, no! It was so much better than that, I saw a light in the dark of the coffin and something so beautiful in that light, someone so wonderful. You must come with me, you must, you have to see it, then you would understand. This was even better than finding the master! This was finding his heart, right there trapped in that coffin and brought to life."

"Lucas, what's wrong with you, can't you see it? Look around you! The house has changed. Are you blind?"

For a moment, Daddy seemed to change for a bit, and once more he looked again like old Daddy again, the good Daddy, not half manic and crazed Daddy. He glanced around, and then got a glimmer in his eye. "Oh, oh whoa, oh wow. Man, oh man! What happened in here? How did this even happen? The kitchen got bigger! Did this happen last night? Did this happen when I was downstairs? The crypt hadn't changed. Well, I mean, I took the lids off the coffins? But it didn't change like this! Man, oh man! I did this! Me! It must've been me! I was the one who did this! The master is thanking me for giving myself to him, for giving all of us the gift of sacrifice. Just you wait and see."

Rae wanted to leave now and just go away now and stay forever gone. Such tension in the air, and she thought it again. Thought the thought that maybe she shouldn't think . . .

Was the Happy Family Game a good game? Did her new friends with such beautiful faces lie to her? Manipulate her? Why would they do such things? This did not feel right. The family was not fixed, it was even more broken than ever before.

"Don't you remember what she said? What's her name, our real estate agent? Oh. The one that looked like a damned rabbit. She said to leave the coffins alone! To leave it all alone. And you did this, you changed everything. You've doomed us all, and this was all your fault. I never thought I could hate you more than I did after the Hour of Smiles recording, but I was wrong. Oh god, was I ever wrong."

The singing got a tiny bit louder, just a tiny bit. The music drifting through them, the notes tugging on their blood, and the chords filling up their lungs, with music, music, music. And. What was this? Lily was in the corner shaking. Her eyes closed and shaking so violently, so fast. "Rae, you need to stop playing the game, Rae, you don't know what they're doing, Rae, you need to stop playing the game, Rae, you need to, Rae . . ."

Rae wanted to scream and howl and start hitting Lily over and over again until her head cracked open and she stopped moving and her eyes were like doll eyes. She was about ready to do it, to let out the dark shadow that lived inside of her, the terrible promises she kept a secret from everyone else, when her Daddy looked right at her and smiled and started shouting again, saying, "What the hell! Why aren't we recording this? We need to document everything! Every! Last! Thing! Rae! Rae! Beautiful Rae, brilliant Rae! Go and get my digital from the living room. We can cut it up with the 16mm downstairs later, but man. Man! We need to go through the house, right? We need to document all of this. Even Lily, what you're doing now? Wow! We need that, we do. And, yes, even you honey, we need to get all of this in! How much has changed? Aha, ha. I wonder how much has changed. This is so amazing, isn't it? Man, oh man. This is so amazing! I'm going to get this all on tape, and everyone will love this. This documentary will win us some awards for certain. Just wait until the academy sees this, just you wait."

And no stopping no thinking no wondering what was right or wrong anymore. Daddy asked her to get this camera, and she would go and get it. Even with Mommy shouting *No*, and screaming out, *you promised! You promised this wouldn't be another* Hour of Smiles! *You promised!*

Rae didn't care, she didn't even know what an *Hour of Smiles* even was. Well, whatever it was, it sure sounded really happy! And how could that be anything wrong? There's nothing wrong at all with a smile.

And the air was all electrical and so thick it felt like she swam through ghosts as she ran through the kitchen. And Rae didn't even care. She was the best Rae ever. She ran into the living room and grabbed that camera and came back all proud and perfect. She knelt to the ground and handed it like a page handing a sword to a knight, her head bowed in holy reverence.

Here, father. Take your camera. Let this be your Excalibur.

-35-

And somewhere in the house, the master stirred when they'd opened his heart coffin, and tossed and turned, but did not wake. At least, not yet.

Lily was jealous. That had to be the only explanation for the way she'd been acting lately. That's why Lily kept telling her to stop doing the Happy Family game, and that's why Lily tried to put the dolls up after Rae had taken down the sentinel books. She was going to have to stop Lily, somehow. This had to happen, the Happy Family Game would be finished, and their family would be together, and everything would be all right again. Certainly, she had her doubts, that maybe the game was wrong, maybe everything was wrong . . .

But Lily telling her to stop only proved that she was on the right track!

And then Dad started shouting excitedly at her again, and she had to snap out of her thoughts and return back to the situation at hand. She was going to help Daddy some more, and this was going to be great, and oh, man was Lily going to be jealous.

"Rae, Rae! Come on, get over here. I need you to be my camera-man, okay? You can do this, I know you can, don't let me down, okay? Focus, Rae, focus! I'm going to direct, and you're going to record, got it? Now pay attention. We need to get all of this. We need to get the proof of every single thing that's going on right now. They're not going to believe it, even with this kind of proof, but I don't care. In the end, I'll have my swan song, and then you'll film those last moments, okay? The moments I can't film. They need to see my death, to understand the meaning of the word sacrifice when it came to art. Art is not a monetary commodity. It is the summation of existence and a cry for truth in the dark."

The digital camera was so tiny and weightless in her hands, almost about the exact same weight as a dead bird. How funny that was! It was almost like she was filming everything through the eyes of a dead bird. She held the dead bird camera up as they walked through random new hallways. Here were new places that cropped up and shot off from the living room, the dining room, the kitchen. Strange new places with nails out all crooked, like the walls were yanked apart and ready for surgery. How funny it was to walk through the wounds of the house.

Wounds of the house, wounds of the house, how she loved saying those words, wounds of the house wounds of the house, the dead bird camera focused now on whatever Daddy pointed at.

"Are you getting this, sweetheart, oh Rae my dove? This is magic right here, both literal magic and filmic magic as well!"

And then they went a few feet in, further and further and further. Stained glass crawled up the walls like an infection, the colors all off and wrong and the lines like an upside-down nightmare. There were faces in the glass, and they screamed in sickly yellows and greens. Further they went in, further and further, and for a moment, he stopped and scratched his beard.

"We can't keep going, Rae, we might get lost and never find our way back again. And man, that wouldn't be good at all."

She didn't want to stop now. This was all too exciting! But she understood what he meant, so she kept her thoughts to herself and just kept on recording. He paused, scratched his beard and said, "You know what, let's get that again. And this time, let's focus on my face. Could you do that for me? Could you focus on my face?"

She nodded her head and pointed the camera at his head, and then zoomed in again enough so his whole face filled the viewport. She could see the pores on his face, the hairs on his beard. She hit record, and the red light flashed on.

Her dad scratched his beard, walked back and forth for a moment, pacing. He then cleared his throat, mussed up his hair a little more, and then pointed at the camera. His voice had changed a little, and he seemed like he was putting on a show for an unseen audience.

"We can't keep going, Rae, even though I know I want to. I can feel the pull of the house, can you feel the pull of the house? But we'll get lost, and that would be bad, oh, so bad. And do you hear that? Shhhh, listen closely. Can you hear that, my friends? That is the sound of the house wailing. The house is in pain . . . no, no. We have to turn around. We have to. If we are to heal this house, we must not get lost within its pain and suffering."

And then he smiled, and that smile made Rae feel oh so nervous. That smile felt wrong—it felt like too much.

"Okay, that's it, cool. Keep on recording. We'll cut around this bit to make it fit in perfectly. Now, get a shot of that ceiling, there, and that wall over there. Do you see what I'm talking about? There, and there, and there. It's like a million new places opened up just while we were standing here! There are hundreds of new doors all over the place, what is even going on anymore."

Rae shrugged and said, "That's it? I did good, right?"

His hand shot out and tousled her hair and patted her on the head. "You did amazing, my little auteur. You make me so proud. One day, you'll walk in these footsteps, just like this. Right? Just like this. Why don't we keep it recording for a little bit more, until we get back to the living room. We'll call that home base, and that's where we're going to branch out while we wander this house. I can't believe our luck. Can you believe our luck? To have this project just fall in our laps like this. It was kismet, I tell you, karma. Good things really do happen to good people."

And Rae beamed bright at his compliment. Of course she was doing an amazing job, and of course she would follow in Daddy's footsteps. She was Rae after all, wasn't she? She was amazing and bright, a shining Rae of light. Not a wilting Lily at all. Her sister was going to be so jealous.

Daddy hummed an old Sunshine Family song and walked up and down the halls, touching the strange walls and feeling them like a surgeon feels for the perfect place to cut open a patient. "Chalk to mark the walls, string to lay on the ground, all of that would be perfect, we'll go back to home base and get all of our supplies. We should probably get a lamp, too. These phones will run dry if we use their flashlight function for too long. I think I have the perfect thing, some portable professional lighting for just this exact situation."

And then came sounds near the far end of that strange hallway. It sloped upwards, ascending into shadow, occluding whatever made those sounds with a breathing darkness. A rustle of wings, whisper of a voice, and the murmur of flies buzzing. Rae had seen that figure before, hadn't she? Back when they were in the crypt, right? Righty-oh, she was never wrong about such things.

"You getting this?"

A nod of her head and she whispered, "Yes, yes, it's the same one from before, right? The one we saw down in the crypt, below the world. What's she doing all the way up here?"

"Lucas, Lucas, Lucas, they're coming for you Lucas . . ."

Her hand shook, and she needed to get it right and steady. Stop shaking, hand! Don't want it to be all twitchy and bad-looking. She couldn't let Daddy down! And yet, something felt wrong about this whole situation. What was that stranger warning them about? What was she trying to tell them? This didn't sit right with Rae at all.

"Dad, Daddy, Dad, I don't like this, this feels so icky wrong, and I think we're lost, I'm afraid we're lost, we should get going, turn around and get out of here . . ."

And that tug inside turned rotten, turned into a sickness. She had to hold it in, no vomiting up here on the roof of the world. And where were the Ladies of Sorrow? The Mothers of Grief? Where was the Mother of Sighs, the Mother of Tears . . . and that third one, the unnamed one, that she hadn't even met yet? Why won't they save her? She helped and helped and helped them, and she needed them to save her! Why weren't they coming now, when she needed them most?

No. Wait. Had they betrayed her? She'd thought they were good people, but it turned out they were Lilies all along. She hoped they wilted and rotted. They had to get out of here . . .

"No, Rae, wait, don't you remember her? She was the one who helped me before, who showed me that I needed to open the coffins in the crypt before doing the ritual. Hello! Hello! Do you know who's coming for me? Tell me! Tell me! I'm one of you now, aren't I? I did all the right rituals so you have to tell me, you have to! Who's coming for me?"

"Sorrow and sorrow and more sorrow . . ."

The stranger in the pale clothes and black shroud stretched out her hands toward him, like she was praying for him or grabbing at him or begging him for something. And then? The shadows swallowed her up. Zip, pop, splash. No scream, no more buzzing, no more whispering, nothing. One moment she was there, and then the next, she was gone. The darkness just devoured her, bones and all, with a strange whistling sound. So beautiful, that sound. Like a bird calling out to the setting sun, welcoming in the oncoming night. Everything grew cold, impossibly cold in that summer heat, the humidity sucked away. *Oh, no—oh, no. What was this?*

"Rae, my dear, my sweet, I think we should go. Don't you?"

And Rae nodded, her mouth stuck and unable to speak or scream. The dark just felt so immense, and it swarmed toward them slowly, like ink spilled in the hallway. She knew this darkness—this was the dark between the stars, the dark from deep beneath the earth. This was the dark beyond the light, the dark that existed at the start of time itself.

And in those shadows, she saw a beautiful face, a frightening face. Her eyes were black and her lips were black and her mouth was the night sky itself. The face grew and twisted about in the dark, and Rae knew what this must be. This must be the third sister, the one she'd been warned about. This was the one the other sisters feared. Our Lady of Darkness, Mater Tenebrarum. What had the Lady of Tears said? Pray you never met our oldest sister, for she is the one that devours the stars. She was the one even death feared.

Her heart raced at the thought of it. So horrible, oh, no, so horrible. They were going to die here, and there was nothing anyone could even do about it. No one was coming to help them, no one was coming to save them. They were doomed.

And that moment stretched on into infinity, but in reality, it was only mere seconds, and they were running down that ragged hallway. Panting and out of breath and the hunting dark seemed to change and mutate and sing that weird whistle song. They ran and they ran and the hallways warped and stretched and then shrunk down, as if they were trying to suck them into the darkness, as if the emptiness itself was a black hole with immense gravitational weight, threatening to devour them whole . . .

And then, there it was! They found it, the door leading into the living room. They ran in, ducked and crawled and rolled through the doorway and slammed it shut behind them. For a moment there was a panic, and she worried that maybe she'd left the camera behind . . .

But no, it was still right there, in her hands, perfectly safe and sound.

They turned and stared for a moment at the door that had grown in the wall. A door that hadn't been there since they'd first arrived, and it looked like a gaping maw in the wall itself. It wasn't shaped like a door, no, no. It was ragged and ripped into the flesh of the wallpaper, and it was red and bright and the color of blood. The big red door. What a horrible thing it was.

-37-

How long had they been gone? How long had they been outside, wandering the halls, filming the strange things that they'd filmed? It felt like only a few moments, yet when Lucas checked his watch and his phone and the clocks on the walls, they all gave him different times, and each time was a few hours or more, not just a few minutes. When he looked outside the living room windows, he saw an empty sea of stars—no ground, no sky, nothing that could tell him the time of day.

Just endless infinite space, so he took Rae into the kitchen and found the same thing was happening there. All of the clocks were wrong, and outside of the windows there was just endless, infinite space.

"Daddy, where's Mommy? Where's Lily?"

But Lucas couldn't think about that right now. He had far too much on his plate already. It was like the air had been let out of his body, and everything in his life had been leading toward nothing. Would they even be able to get this film to anyone? Or would it be a silent film for an audience of just the four of them, the family who starred in it also the only people who would ever watch it? It made him infinitely sad. His whole life's work, leading to nothing.

"I don't know, dear, I'm so sorry. They're not here? Maybe they are here, but we're not here. The house seems to be playing games with us . . ."

Rae walked up to him and put her arms around him and hugged him tight. He hugged her back, and even though he didn't feel like hugging anyone right now, he felt like she needed this even more than he did. What was he going to do?

"It will be all right, Daddy. I think we can find them and finish your movie at the same time. What do you think of that?"

He smiled. She always knew the right thing to say. "I think that would be super awesome. We should probably grab some string and some chalk to take with us, maybe even grab a lamp or some of the lights from downstairs."

There was a slight glimmer of hope in that moment, and maybe his life's work wasn't going to be so worthless after all. Even if no one saw the video, maybe just the act of finding Dana and Lily and saving them would be just as important. No, maybe it could be even more important than the movie. Wow, that was something he never thought he would say.

What could be more important than a movie? And yet he felt it now, a need to do something greater than himself. He'd been selfish, hadn't he? Just thinking about his movie and nothing else. And here he had a chance to turn it all around, save all of them, and make this world a better place.

He was like Icarus in the labyrinth, fighting the minotaur that hunted them. If only it hadn't taken him so long to get this started. Maybe they wouldn't even be in this mess in the first place. He felt so lost now, so lonesome now. He'd wanted to join a family of his own, that super magical Sunshine Family. And yet, there was another family here that needed him. And to hell with it, he needed them as well.

-38-

They were ready. They had everything they needed, and then some. There was a ball of yarn to help them find their way back through the labyrinth, a walkie-talkie set he used when he'd first started directing, to keep in touch with his crew back before cell phones were commonplace. They'd use these only in the case of emergency, and only if one of them got lost or stranded. They had two packages of chalk of various colors, one for each of them, and a lantern that he carried while Rae carried the camera.

At first, he didn't want to record this, but Rae insisted, and it made her happy, so he decided to just roll with it. The movie was not all that important to him anymore, but making sure she wouldn't worry about her mom or her sister? That was super important, and for some reason, acting as his camera operator set her mind at ease, so he let her do this.

"Don't you want to record anything before we start going?"

He shook his head no. "I think I've got enough of that for a little bit, you know? We don't need to make the whole movie about us, especially not now, not with the two of them missing."

"Okay, Daddy, I got ya. Where should we start? Do you think they went after us and through the red door? Or do you think they went some other way and got lost in the expanding house?"

He thought for a moment. The way the house had moved, the way the time had changed, it was possible that they had gone in after them. And then he had another thought, another light bulb flash of an idea. "We haven't checked upstairs or in the bedrooms yet, have we? They might've gone up there."

Rae shrugged and pointed the camera at the stairs. The two of them held their breath, and noticed that stairs went up and up and up. They spiraled halfway up, and then twisted about and turned into a double helix. It then split off into two staircases and went into several different directions, creating an impossible Mobius strip of hallways leading to more stairs leading to more hallways.

"I think we should probably go into that hallway over there."

Rae nodded politely. "Yes, Daddy. I think that's probably the best idea."

-39-

As they walked, all of the ghosts started to appear around them, fluttering and laughing and dancing about. Their bodies were muted silver like old black-and-white film. Nitrate in that halogen hallway light, their lantern pushing through them like they were made from gauze. They spoke in harsh radio whispers, the words distant and hollow-sounding. Ghost mothers playing with spectral sons and daughters. Someone with a beard and an eyepatch played a sad song on a fiddle, as a ghostly mother breastfed an echo of an infant, mewling still here even in death.

Rae kept turning the camera on everyone, and Lucas wanted to yell at her, to tell her to turn it off. But he couldn't do that, could he? No. She was happy like this and undisturbed by the ghosts that danced around her.

And once upon a time he would've been so happy to see these ghosts, but now they left an ache inside of him. He was a part of the Sunshine Family, yet he felt so distant and far away from them. Even more now than ever before in the past. How could he have ever loved them? How could he have ever yearned to be with them?

They walked onward, unspooling the yarn and making simple marks on the walls with chalk, every once in a great while calling out for Dana or Lily, and hoping that they would respond. So far, no response at all.

The ghosts floated to and fro, dancing barefoot as love beads swung around their necks. Bare-breasted, sure-footed, so many drums in so many drum circles. They passed spectral joints back and forth, placed spectral sugar cubes filled with the ghost of acid on their tongues. They walked past a severed head that rolled on the floor, still talking and speaking and laughing up a storm. His mouth babbled complex acid head prophecies, stoned-out mumble magic that this cult seemed to feed on.

Lucas saw each of the ghosts still wore their death wounds so proudly. He wanted to tell Rae to turn it off, to stop looking, but he could not. He could not stop looking himself. Did this make him a bad father? He had no idea. Their throats were slit, and they had gunshot wounds against their temples where they had placed the gun and pulled the trigger.

They turned down a different hallway and another one and another one. What would happen if they got lost and turned around? Would Dana be okay? Would Lily? Would they come into the bowels of the house and find them?

This hallway was clogged with the ghosts of the Sunshine Family. Even more so than the last few hallways behind them! Children ran around his legs. Some of the women spinning now with wild skirts, topless, spiral paint glittering silver in the wandering light. They all sang, their words screeching up and howling in the afternoon light. They sang one of his favorite songs, and for a moment he remembered why he had fallen in love with the Sunshine Family in the first place. He remembered why he had wanted to join them, to become one of them, and it took every ounce of strength to keep on walking and not start singing with them, dancing all joyous and rapturous and true.

And then he had to stop walking. He saw the children were all dead, and they all had gunshot wounds in their heads, and he felt dizzy and broken and he wanted to scream. They had done this to their own children? What kind of family was this? Who would do that sort of thing to their own kids?

He felt a terrible sadness, and realized he had done something just as horrible to Lily when he locked her in that coffin and buried her alive for those few minutes. He hadn't murdered her in cold blood, but it changed something inside of her, he saw that. He was trying to make her into a psychic wonderkid, and instead he had killed her love for life. He was no worse than the members of the Sunshine Family.

He too had sacrificed his own children, his own marriage, and for what?

A movie that would've probably been forgotten in ten years' time. Dana was right to divorce him.

"Daddy, are you okay? You stopped moving and you seem lost, and look, look at the walls, Daddy, everything is changing . . ."

He gulped, and yes, she was right—he felt lost. Everything was changing, and even he was changing as well. Was this too late now? Could he change himself, and if so, what good would it do? The damage was already done.

He fell to the ground as the dead kids surrounded him with bullet holes in their heads. He cried out as they pulled and pushed and shoved him about, yelling and laughing. "Come on, play with us! Play with us! Play with us!"

And Rae called to him, "We need to get going, we have to go find mom and Lily! Dad! Daddy! I hate to say this, but I'm going to leave you here and mark the walls, okay? I have to find them, and I'm going to leave the camera here just in case you need it, okay? Follow the yarn, follow the chalk lines and come find me when you can!"

But he was too far gone. The sadness devoured him as the kids pulled and yanked and he just slipped down and wanted to die.

-40-

Born of a different time, Lucas felt like he was born of a different time and to the wrong people. His family seemed alien and full of rage at a world they hated. And this Sunshine Family? They'd felt like home to him, watching them dance and sing, watching them love and fuck and run about praying to the morning sun. Their rituals were beautiful things. Modified old occult rites, transformed with Aquarius ideals and the psychedelic symbols of their time. And it all called out to him, called out to the broken thing inside of Lucas. And it brought comfort to his own childhood. A childhood of constant moving and new cities and new homes and new schools. It brought comfort to a childhood of a father who spent more time in prison than he did with his own son.

He ached to live with them, to be with a family who wanted more from life. They wanted to change the world, to heal it all, to keep it safe from sorrow. That was the whole point of their mass suicide, to keep the three sisters trapped inside the house. If only he had known that before he bought it

Did it work? He wasn't so sure about that.

Trapping the Mothers of Sorrow did not stop a single school shooting. Trapping the Mothers of Sorrow did not keep kids from being locked in cages. Trapping the Mothers of Sorrow did not stop the bullets, the bloodshed, none of the things that the Sunshine Family had ever predicted. Children lived in fear every single day, and to what ends? Nothing, nothing.

Trapping the Mothers of Sorrow may have stopped some imaginary holocaust predicted with astrology and tarot cards, but it did not stop the real American horrors they'd lived with every day since the mid 1990s. This whole thing was a failure, wasn't it? A great, grand failure.

Nothing anyone did ever mattered. Lucas realized it now. These people murdered their families, their own children, sacrificed themselves for nothing. And he was so close to doing exactly the same thing, until . . . well. Until just a little bit ago, when Rae had set him right, and he saw how horrible it all really was after all.

-41-

"Daddy, you need to get up, right now! Daddy, do you hear me? Shoo! Shoo! You stupid ghosts are worse than flies! No one wants you here, not me and not the house and definitely not my new friends! You have to leave us all alone! Shoo! Shoo!"

He was still on the floor and still all wrecked on the inside. And his stomach hurt and his everything hurt. He was surrounded by ghosts trying to yank on him, pull him away, pull him apart. *Play with us play with us play with us. Let's play a murder game, a happy little suicide game. All of the best games require some sacrifice, don't you think?*

He was so done with all of this.

"Rae, Rae? I'm so sorry Rae, I couldn't help it. I was drowning in ghosts, you know? How long was I gone? Did you find your mom, did you find Lily?"

The ghost children fled away and scattered as Rae kicked them about some more and leapt upon him, laughing.

"Daaaaaaaddyyyy, come on! What is this? What is this even? The time for sadness is over, the sisters aren't even hungry right now! You have to snap out, of this. I think I found Mommy, and I think I found Lily. Come on! Let's go and save them both."

Lucas smiled, and he was in awe of his wonderful daughter. She pulled the last of the ghosts away, and he stood back up, brushed himself off. He was worried he would be covered in ectoplasm, but he wasn't. He did feel funky, and the sadness seemed to cling to him and make it hard for him to move. But he had to move. Rae had found Dana and Lily, and all would be right once again. The last of the ghosts scattered and left this hallway, leaving the two of them alone once more. He felt like he could breathe for once and was happy for it.

"Okay, Let's go, Super Rae, let's go and find your mom and you sister and get the hell out of here."

And she didn't speak. Didn't say a word. With trembling fingers grabbed her father's hand. And it felt so small in his his his palm. So tiny and and and . . .

Some of those kids were her age, weren't they? For a moment, he saw an image of her in his mind with a bullet hole in her head, and he wanted to scream. Get that out, get that image the fuck out of his head. Get out, get out, get out. But no, it wouldn't go. It wouldn't go at all. It joined the other horrible thoughts dancing around. Lily in the coffin. Going to the huge funeral for all the school shooting victims and wondering if his kids would be next. Violence everywhere, every day, violence.

And Rae, yes. Rae led him forward into a fresh wound of the house, a new hallway blossoming out from a ragged, crooked wall. She grabbed his hand, leading him onward, pulling through that gaping wound. She seemed so small, so dwarfed by the walls. Where they were going there seemed to be no ghosts. No ghosts at all. Just this strange darkness. Heavy, horrible, empty. Gravity of darkness. Black empty starless darkness. A vacuum of being itself.

And. And. And.

He heard Rae screaming. She screamed so loudly as all of that darkness surrounded him and it licked him and tasted him and what was going on? There was a face in that darkness, a face with black eyes and black lips and a mouth filled with all the stars in the sky. He felt so nauseated all of a sudden, and he felt his bones crush under the intense gravitational weight of the shadows, and he vomited and it burned his throat all stomach acid, and the vomit disappeared in the darkness. He couldn't see Rae anymore, but he could hear her screaming and it made everything feel small and horrible and . . .

I want to help you, Rae, I want to save you, I want to save Dana and Lily and everyone else. Why can't I breathe? Why are my lungs filled with ghosts? Can you see this, Rae? Can you see that my breath is an echo? That my blood is a murmur? That I am filled head to toe with ghosts? Can you see this? And . . . and . . . and . . .

What was this?

A voice, ah, a voice whispered in his ear. A female voice, like a chorus of ages coming from a single entity. The darkness itself licked his skin with words. He shivered, but it wasn't from the cold, was it? It was a death shiver, he knew it, he was dying.

Now we have you now we got you now you won't be able to help those ghosts any longer, no more tricks, no more traps, it's just us and our son and this house and we're going to escape and we're going to bring out so much horror to this rotting world, so much sadness and sorrow we will feed on it for a million years. Do not feel sorry for your daughter, she brought you here on the advice of my sisters, not knowing what would happen. They may have lied to her and told her it would all be okay, but that's just what they do. Lies bring the most sorrow to the world. Lies feed us almost as much as the truth.

I am the Mother of Darkness, and now you are mine, devoured by night and void-kissed . . .

His limbs pulled and popped to the music of her whispers. And there was no pain, just this sensual darkness lapping him and tasting him and taking him apart piece by piece. No Dana here and no marriage here and no divorce here and no sadness here and and and just a happy memory of floating, floating like a balloon and he felt so empty and light and and and and

Was that his blood on the floor? Shining like a lantern? Was that his blood?

-42-

And somewhere in the house, the Master stirred when they sacrificed Lucas to the darkness, and tossed and turned, but did not wake. At least, not yet.

-43-

Dana was drunk on shadows and nestled in an impossible place, far beneath the house that she knew. This was another grotto, much like the grotto outside and in the garden, a hidden cavern in a hidden basement, nestled away amongst the ventricle halls, and far out of reach of anyone else. Even here there was another statue, cut from obsidian and nightmares, vibrating and coated in crystals.

The heart of the house loved her. The heart of the house hated her.

How did she even get here? She didn't know, she felt sick to her stomach and dizzy. Like being drunk on too much codeine cough syrup, and she wanted to crawl away and die. When did she get here? It felt like forever ago, and it felt like five minutes ago.

This was the true house, the real house. A bruise between worlds, a doorway, a border, an open wound. It fed on energies across time, and eventually, in its old age, became sentient and senile and needy. The horrors it'd seen. The horrors it'd participated in. And it wanted her here and kept her here and wouldn't allow her to leave, not in a million years. It was a cage, this heart of the Gemini House. It was a cage, built of coffin wood.

She'd been wrapped head to toe in ivy, tied so tight it left purple bruises along her legs and arms and neck. she struggled to breathe, and the vines loosened just a little, just enough for her to inhale, exhale, slightly After all, it didn't want her to die, not just yet.

You will never go, never, the house groaned and whispered with floorboards stretching out. *You are mine now.*

How had she gotten here? She thought back through the fog of her thoughts, and remembered. Yes, she remembered . . . she'd followed a ghost of a child. The ghost looked just like Lily, but wasn't Lily, and she hadn't realized that until it was much too late. She knew the girl was dead and a ghost, and she was so worried that it was true, that Lily was dead, and she didn't want that to happen. Maybe she could lead her back out of the purgatory of this house, and in the daylight she would gain life again, no longer dead and dreaming.

They moved quickly through the house. Hallways ripped and changed and stretched with each movement, a dancing labyrinth that dazzled and confused them. The strange ghost Lily that she followed was nude and oddly misshapen, her skin the awful color of melted blue candle wax.

She kept following that ghost, followed back to the heart. To where the hallway ventricles met with the muscle of the second grotto. There the vines grasped her and grabbed her, pulling her up and against the wall, encasing her in a living tomb. The little Lily turned and looked at her, face so misshapen and wrong, and she smiled. Oh, the teeth, there were too many teeth, rows and rows and rows of them, and her eyes were empty sockets, filled with that strange blue waxy color. The little girl laughed in a way Lily never laughed, and then turned and ran off, disappearing into the electrical fog of the house, leaving her here, with the house, alone.

You are mine now. The Mothers of Sorrow have brought you to me, and in exchange they will devour the ghosts, and in exchange, they will leave and let me be. Just the two of us then. House and lover, lover of house. No ghosts, no gods, no families, only you and me and that's all, that's all we'll ever need.

No. She would not listen to this anymore. How could she have known the house would be like this? She'd thought there was love there, but instead only obsession and hate. To be wanted in that way by an ancient, sentient *thing*? It left her cold and chilled on the inside. Instead, she shut out her mind, stopped listening, and returned to her memories. And of course, the wandering mind was no friend to anxiety, was it? Not her mind, anyway. It always went to the worst possible place. This time, it was that horrible phone call. *Do not be alarmed. There is an active shooter at your child's school, the cops are on their way, and we will take every precaution to keep them safe.*

She had to leave work, and met her husband outside the school. Police cars and sirens and you could hear the gunshots echo out. Each gunshot was a fluttering of her heart, and she thought over and over and over again, not her, not our little girl. Not our little girl. She held Lucas's hand so tight it hurt, and he trembled, fingers around her knuckles, trembled. What she needed was a rock, a stone, a root, and instead he trembled like a messy waterfall.

Their kids ended up okay, but that was only a hollow victory. Later they found out they knew a few of the kids who'd died, and everything went dark again. Why was she remembering this? Why was she circling around this dark center of her life? An emotional scab. At least picking at it kept her mind occupied and away from the house, and whatever the house was doing . . .

Remember the caskets? Remember Lily in her casket? Remember Grandma Glass?

Too many funerals for her short forty years of life. The echo of those gunshots choked fire in the back of her throat. She wanted to scream, but the ivy wrapped around her chest and squeezed her lungs. Tighter, tighter. It trapped her screams inside, unable for release.

No, the house said, *you will not scream until I want you to scream.*

She needed to remember something else. Something better. Something beautiful.

Remember the happy times? Felt like so long ago. When she stared into his eyes and said, "It's not just blue, you know. Your eyes have flecks of green in them, too, and gray, and it is tempestuous, like the sea."

And he kissed her and said, "Tempestuous? What a fun word."

"Tempestuous eyes, it's true, you have such tempestuous eyes."

And later that night they walked hand in hand towards the sea and threw off their clothes as they ran. They swam together and kissed all naked and free, and their bodies just sliding in and out of each other to the rhythm of the waves. Ruins of old houses on the cliffside behind them. erosion making them dangerous, uninhabitable, deserted. A few years later they would be torn down. Dangers to the community, they said. She remembered all of that, when they came back years later for their anniversary and tried to relive the experience all over again.

But then. Her memory. Shattered. To. To. The sound. Of screaming.

That was Rae screaming, she knew that voice, her little girl's voice, and she was so terrified. Dana could hear the tenor of the terror in her voice, and it sounded so odd coming from Rae. Rae was the strong one, the defiant one, the mad and howling one, and now she screamed in a way that made her blood turn ice cold.

No, no, no. You won't leave me, Dana. Not after I got you here, brought you here, trapped you in my beautiful heart. I am forever and always and I am unending and true. You belong in my heart, are of my heart, a piece of my heart, all of my heart, so you must stay in my heart, my heart, my heart.

Her baby needed her. Fuck this house. She ripped her hands free, felt the vines sucking back, trying to wrap around as she ripped it from her neck and her chest and her legs and her torso. Tiny thorns laced along the edges and bit into her skin with rough tears. It hurt like hell, but fuck it, and fuck this house and fuck those plants.

STAY! STAY! STAY! I COMMAND YOU TO STAY HERE WITH ME FOREVER!

Her girls *needed* her. She knew it now, that what she followed before wasn't Lily but instead some echo, a trick of the house to get her here so she could be trapped forever in its loving embrace. How could she have loved a house like this? It was unsteady and ancient and insane, so possessive and egotistical and controlling. She did not need this house in her life. It was time she left it behind and went on to save her girls. They needed her, and she wasn't about to let them down.

Fuck this house, fucking Coffin House. And to think, she'd thought maybe she loved it, once upon a time. But no, that was just the quick rush of something new, something strange, something beautiful. Once the house showed her its true heart, everything changed. Vile thing, Violent thing. That heart only knew pain, and lust, and terror.

You will regret this, Dana, your whole family will regret this, I am eternal, I never sleep, and I have dangerous friends . . .

She gave the house the middle finger as she ran ragged down the halls, her arms covered in slippery blood and some thorns still in her thighs and a few vines still stuck to her back and her arms and leaves in her hair all tossed and curly. But mostly free now, free enough to run and follow those screams.

She was coming, Rae, she was coming to save both you and Lily from this nightmare of a house. Nothing could stand in her way, not now, not when her baby needed her. Nothing.

-44-

The house became a blur of hallways as the labyrinth danced around Dana in a ballet of wood and steel and glass and plaster, attempting to confuse her and trap her within its orchestrated movements. Ghosts ran around her, pushed her with ghostly limbs, unable to actually move her or touch her yet trying still to get her to dance with them and sing, move around and join their endless ghost orgies and their endless ghost sing-a-longs at the heart of the Gemini House.

There! Up ahead, there was the source of the scream, in that raw hallway. She saw Rae, crouched, her back to the wall, and oh, the blood. So much blood everywhere, a large pool of it shimmering like a lantern in the light. At first, she worried that it was Rae's blood, but it couldn't be Rae's blood at all.

She felt sick.

There were body parts in the blood, rough and ripped apart like doll parts.

"Rae, turn around, turn around and look at me, Rae. Whatever you do don't look down, okay? Don't look down, just turn around and look right into Mommy's eyes. Are you okay, Rae?"

She saw piles of teeth and walked around them, she saw a jawbone and walked around it, she saw a still beating heart and looked away, looked away. She knew the sound of that heart, she'd felt it against her own so many times. But no, she didn't want to think about that. She had to save Rae first, and then she could let the terror of what she heard wash over her. She walked up, held her little girl close and whispered in her ear, "Please tell me you're okay, Rae. Please tell me you're okay."

And her little girl sobbed on her shoulder, all snot and sighs and gulping tears. She wanted to take them all away from this and make everything okay once again. How had it gotten so bad? They just wanted a new house, that was all. Why couldn't they have just had a wonderful new house, and been a happy family, and that was that?

"Oh, no. Mommy. Mommy, you're bleeding, Mommy, I can't lose you too, Mommy, I can't lose you!"

And the little girl howled, but it was so sore and scratched up with screams it barely registered as a sound. Like a gasp now, like a sigh now, like something from the grave.

Dana reached out, and touched her little girl's hair. She moved a tangle of a curl from her cheek to behind her ear and rested her palm against Rae's face. Blood from her own wounds trickled down the skin. Still beating, still bleeding, still fresh. "You won't lose me, you won't, I promise you that. Can you tell me whose blood that is on the floor? Was that your sister's blood?"

And that image of Rae with her scourge haunted her mind, danced around and taunted her with such horrible promises. Had she killed Lily? Was a sisterly sacrifice all part of the Happy Family Game? Dana had no words, she had no thoughts, she felt confused and so sad and didn't want to go on living. How could she go on living in a world where such horrors persisted? When children murdered children like it was nothing? How could she go on living in a world where her own daughter was dead, and in such a horrible way . . .

"I couldn't save him, I couldn't, they said they were my friends, and they lied, they lied to me, Mommy. They tricked me into helping them do a horrible thing. The Happy Family Game is a very bad game, but it's too late now. Their son is coming for us, I let him out and let him in, and I can't change a thing. I can't fix a thing. No one can stop them now that . . . now that . . ."

Dana couldn't ask, she couldn't dare ask her to finish that sentence, and to bring more terror and horror onto her little girl. She'd seen so much, poor thing, and here she was, thinking that Rae was capable of murdering her sister. And yet, that's not what happened here at all, was it? That's not . . .

No, no, no, no

Wait. Yes.

No, no, no, no

Fingers. Severed fingers in the center of that circle of teeth. Not many, maybe three or four, tops, all sticking straight up. Teeth glitter white, tiny mouth bones. And the fingers. She could see the nails on top, chewed on, rugged. She knew those damned fingers. Oh. No, no, no, no. See those skull tattoos across the fingers? See them in that pool of blood? And the heartbeat, still going strong, pumping loose clumps of blood across the floor . . .

Remember our wedding night, when it felt like the world was ending, and you held me close, my head to your chest, your heart so loud in my ears . . .

Lucas. Oh, god, oh no. Lucas. She wanted to divorce him, yes. But this? This. She would have never wished this on him, not in a million years.

The air smelled like fire and wet cinders and pine needles and sap. What had Rae seen? Poor thing, poor little girl, what had she seen? No one should ever experience whatever that was especially not her little girl. And. And where *was* Lucas? He had to still be alive. He did. Fuck. Fuck this house. No one deserved that. He could still be alive without fingers and teeth, couldn't he? He had to be alive. He had to. Even without his heart. So many impossible things have happened lately, and Lucas being alive somewhere in this house without a heart would be the least impossible thing she'd seen. Where was the rest of him? And what had Rae seen that made her so broken now? Poor broken sweetheart.

She never thought she would miss that bombastic Rae. But here it was, she did. She missed her so much.

"Where's Daddy, Rae? Where is he? Rae? Where's your father at now?"

And then came the louder sobs again. It broke her heart, to hear such sobbing screams all throat burning and everything. She wanted to keep asking, but she didn't. She knew that nothing would come of this now. And could she? Could she look over her shoulder? She held that ball of Rae closer, deeper into her chest. Almost pushed her back inside her body. *Go, go back into me. The cage of my ribs could protect you from the horrors of this world.* As she looked over, looked at that pool of blood again . . .

Heart ached like an open wound, and she, she hated him for making her feel this way. Hated the house for doing all of this right now and not just letting their relationship destroy itself and burn out

already. She looked for a path, maybe a trail of blood or muck or intestines or gore or something, something they could follow and maybe
find him again and save him if he were still alive. She hated thinking
these thoughts, yes. But she had to, she had no other choice. It was all
a matter of survival now.

"They said they were my friends, Mommy, and they lied to me."

She kissed her little girl on the forehead, and they breathed in
unison, both of them together. They were terrified of moving, and terrified of staying still, as the house undulated around them. They had
so much left to do. They had to find Lily, they had to find Lucas, they
had to go back to the real world where they could be safe and whole
once again.

-45-

Lily was lost. She wandered through the constantly flexing halls, looking for Mommy, looking for Daddy, looking for Rae, looking for anyone and anything. She called out their names and got only echoes of her own voice in response. She hadn't even seen a single ghost, not since she went looking for her bedroom to take a nap and everything in the house changed. She was so alone, and she hated being alone more than anything else in the world. She picked up her phone and tried to dial Mommy's number again, but nothing. The phone was dead, and why wasn't that a surprise?

She turned around another corner and another and another, went through a forked path in the hallway, climbed some loose stairs and walked up to what could be an attic, or maybe just another bedroom, who even knew anymore. The house was not the same house as before.

And at the end of the hallway, she saw darkness pooling, darkness moving, and felt something flip flop in her stomach. What was that thing? It couldn't be a shadow on the wall, shadows don't move like that. This spread like ink, and in the center of the darkness she watched as faces appeared and disappeared and moved about screaming.

In the center of those faces, in the center of those flowing shadows, she caught the visage of a beautiful woman without eyes, without lips, without a mouth. There was darkness and stars inside of her and Lily wanted to scream. It whistled as it rolled toward her, that darkness sending out a shrill, high-pitched sound. It burned her insides, that sound, and she wanted to run but she was frozen in place, unable to move at all.

I am the Mother of Darkness . . . and I feed on the light of the living . . .

She closed her eyes and thought of the coffin game, back when she'd played the *Hour of Smiles* with daddy. She would not be afraid now, she had not been afraid then, she would be strong and brave and the darkness would not devour her. She remembered what it was like to have the lid closed shut, to hear the sound of dirt clumping against the lid of the coffin. She remembered holding her breath, and imagining the rot of her body . . .

And then she felt a hand touching her hand and almost screamed. It felt dry and papery, filled with sharp angles like bones. There was a heat inside of it, and she knew exactly who it was, he had come to her again, and she was elated.

A voice in her ear, the scent of burning skin. The Rattling Boy? Was that you?

"Lily, wait. She can't see you, but she can sense you, and she is the worst of them all. A fury of hunger and shadows. Our Lady of Darkness, Mother of the Starless Night. She tried to devour me twice already, but my fire is too bright, and it kept casting the shadows away, further and further away from my body . . ."

"I, I don't understand. What's going on?"

He clicked his paper tongue. "That's my fault, I'm sorry. I should've given you more to go on. But you have trust me right now, trust me when I say we need to move. Quietly, cautiously, as far away from her as we can get."

A nod of her head. She didn't say a thing, she knew it would be better not to. She opened her eyes and tried not to scream as the darkness oozed and the faces shifted about like empty husks of human shapes. Every inch of Lily felt like a live wire, adrenaline pumping through her veins like electricity. Every instinct told her to run and keep on running, but she trusted the Rattling Boy, she knew he would not lie to her. If he said to walk slowly, calmly, away from the shadows, then she knew that's what they had to do. Even though it terrified her to no end to do so.

-46-

Lily walked carefully down the newly formed stairs and through the long winding halls, shivering hand-in-hand with the Rattling Boy. The ceilings now drooped and shook above their heads, and the walls felt ramshackle and wounded, leading new halls and doorways off into labyrinthine corners. Could they ever find their way out of here? And if so, what waited for them in the gardens at home? That leviathan that lived beyond the pines, hungry, salivating, wanting to feed on their marrows . . .

As they walked, the darkness followed them slowly, hesitantly, a pool of inky black shadows that stayed just on the edges of the light. The Rattling Boy was her candle, her safe spot in this Gemini House. Faces moved across the shadow that followed them, a million devoured faces devoured alive and slowly digested by the Mother of Darkness. As it moved, it dripped blood, enough to leave a shiny trail in its wake, with teeth falling out and landing in its path of gore. *Plink, plink, plink.* Not too many, maybe two, three teeth, tops. One with a crown on it, glinting silver. And then? A slip of skin slid down and on the floor with a messy tattoo and a bit of bone from a spinal column. Lily thought it all looked fresh, so fresh. She felt like she'd seen that tattoo before . . .

Oh, no. Was that Daddy's skin? She didn't want to be here anymore. She wanted to run far away and hide. That couldn't be him, that couldn't be her daddy's skin…

She would've sensed it if one of her parents had died, right? She had psychic powers now, could create her own lick of flames with her mind. What good were psychic powers if they couldn't tell her when one of her parents died?

And yet, she knew that tattoo. A tree covered in skulls. She knew that skin. That was her father's skin. All around her now the sound of wings. Buzzing, wasp wings, beating against the wood and against the long glass window that lined the far edges of this hall. It was filthy and cracked and it looked like any minute, yes, any minute now, it would explode inward and shower them in shards.

And on the other side? Outside there, beyond the pale of the glass? There was a large star-filled sky, like the empty void of space itself. Where were they, even? Did the house even exist anymore? Where they floating elsewhere out in outer space?

She glanced between the glass and the star-filled sky and gasped. It was them, the echoes, the doubles she had seen crawling across the house earlier. They wore the faces of her family like slack masks—Mommy, Daddy, Lily and Rae. There were millions of them, just hovering in the darkness, floating in the void, looking monstrous in the dark beyond the dark. They had their arms down at their sides and they stared right at her, their heads moving each time she moved, following her with their waxy melted blue skin.

A few floated forward. Daddy, Rae, and her. They tapped on the glass with uneven fingernails, and then they pointed at her and smiled with all the wrong kind of teeth in their mouths, and they waved with all the wrong bones in their hands. They seemed so hungry, so lost, so needy . . .

"Just keep going," he whispered, "They are nothing but nothing to us right now. They can't get inside, just keep going."

Lily wished she could believe him, but she knew that there was enough of them out there, and that they could easily break the window and come running after her.

And what would they do when they found her?

She did not want to know the answer to that.

-47-

Lily knew what she had to do. She had to set up sentinels once again, nailing up books and dolls and all the important things, just like the Rattling Boy had shown her in the past. She knew it was the only thing that could protect them and keep them safe, and so they had to get it done now, no dilly-dallying, no messing around. This was important.

But how? How would she know where the dolls were, the nails were, the hammers were? The house had changed so much. It would not be a simple thing to trace her way back to the start of it all again. If she closed her eyes, she felt her blood move in a certain direction, the way it pumped through her body, leading her to a specific place and time. She knew if she followed it, she would find her bedroom once more, and all the tools that they needed would be right there.

"Do you know where we're going?" the Rattling Boy asked.

"I think so? Maybe. Well, maybe yes, I think so. I'm following the compass in my blood, and I think my blood knows where to go." Another coffin trick she'd learned during the Hour of Smiles.

The dolls, the books, and anything else that was important to her, to mommy, to daddy, and yes even her bratty sister Rae. She had to build a sanctuary place. Make them all safe and sound. Then she would get the whole Glass family there, whoever still survived *(oh please daddy, still be alive).*

And the Rattling Boy stopped and stood for a moment in the hallway. All that running came crashing down to a halt, as the ghosts darted around them at high speed. The hallway was filled with ghosts, millions of dead members of the Sunshine Family dancing and kissing and slapping and singing, moving all around her in a sea of people. How many people had there been at some point in time? It was like a small city all crammed into the bones of the house. No wonder the house grew and changed, it had to, if it was going to house all those ghosts.

"What's going on," she asked him, "Why have we stopped?"

The Rattling Boy vibrated, head to toe, everything shaking really fast. She gripped his hand even tighter and tighter. He no longer felt like a spirit or a specter, or even a whisper of a person. He felt even more real now, even more meaty and human and dead, it was as if she was holding the hand of a crispy burnt corpse all vibrating and shaking. She gripped his hand tighter, the fear in her voice an audible thing. "Why have you stopped? We can't stop now! What's wrong?"

"Lily, I'm so sorry, Lily, it's happening again, you should probably let go of my hand."

And with a loud cough he burst into an uncontrollable, bright silver flame. His own light scattered those crawling colored lights, painting everything in a vibrant shadow in the shape of his body. Everything ignited all at once. She held on for a second more, too hot, too hot, pulled back, her hand sore and red and a little toasted but not burned. Just a little too hot to the touch, like grasping a metal pan on a warm stovetop.

And then the heat rippled out in waves of anguish and Lily couldn't stand it anymore, it was too intense to be so close to him. She didn't want to leave him, she didn't want to run off, but she had to move back, it was just too much. She smelled her hair burning and moved further and further back, patting out the small flames that leapt up on the downy hair on her arms and the small spots on her scalp. She screamed out, "No! Don't! I need you here with me! I need you!"

He moved about in circles, his body dancing while trying to put out the flames on his skin. He patted it, and rolled around, and every-where he went he left tiny burning footprints and a smear against the walls where he pressed against it, trying to smother the flames with his body. He moaned as he moved, and cried out to Lily, "Why now? Why? Why can't I control this? Lily, Lily, listen to me, you need to go on without me, all right? I can't help you anymore, not like this."

And no she shook her head no, she was defiant and stomped her foot down. "You never left my side when I needed you, and trust me on this, I don't *ever* plan on leaving your side when you need me."

She ran over to him, the blistering heat almost unbearable, but she could bear it for him, couldn't she? And she reached down inside, deep down inside the depths of her mind to the things her dad had taught her during the *Hour of Smiles. There was a fire inside of you, Lily, just like there is a fire inside all of us. Find that fire, Lily. Find that fire and use it as a reflection to control this candle flame I have here in front of me.*

And so she concentrated, thought about the flame inside of her and made it mirror the flame now consuming her friend. The one true friend she had left, the only person who had warned her and kept her safe, even while the rest of the world fell apart. She owed this to him. This was going to happen.

She thought of her lips now, close to that flame, kissing the tips of the fire. She thought how it would feel, to have that candle flame so close to her mouth, the way it would burn, the way it would tingle. And then, in her mind's eye, she blew on that flame. One, two, three. It almost didn't go out, so she blew on it again, and again, one more time. *Toby, Toby, the Rattling Boy once told me his name was Toby. Here, Toby, be free.*

And with one more exhale of her breath, the candle flame went out. She opened her eyes and there he stood, all burnt up and aching and no longer on fire. He walked toward her and laughed and said, "How did you do that?"

There was no time for a response. She could already feel the darkness gathering up in a sphere of night, and saw it roll down the hallway, heading right for them. Her psychic ability must've been like a beacon to the Mother of Darkness, drawing it closer toward them with an insatiable appetite for all existence.

It devoured the ghosts in the hallway, sucked them up and absorbed them inside, merging them with the menagerie of the dead. And with each ghost it grew larger and larger and larger, an ink spill growing and absorbing all it touched. So hungry, that void, so endlessly starved, it needed to feed on psychic energy, that life force that thrummed in everything, even ghosts.

Lily couldn't move. She felt all of her muscles frozen in place, absolutely terrified. What could they do? How could they keep running? But Toby, oh, that beautiful burning boy, he was braver and smarter than either of them. He pulled on her hand, the small ember flame licking her palm and waking her from her reverie.

"Come on," he said, "Let's follow the compass of your heart and create that sanctuary. Come on! We can't just stand here and wait. I won't let you die like that, I can't let you die like that . . ."

And she saw a ghost girl, a little younger than her, coated in love beads and a swirling skirt, bracelets jangling on her arms as she danced around in the center of the hallway. She had a pale gunshot wound in her head, right there, where the third eye should be. Did it hurt? Did it take a long time to die? A flash and Lily remembered the active shooter at her school. And she remembered (*oh god no she didn't want to remember this*), she remembered watching her best friend Grace fall down and hit the floor. The gunshot so loud, so angry, like a firework set off at close range. The body twitching, dancing: death throes. Lily's stomach turned and twisted and felt full of angry bees and hornets and she wanted to stop to stop to stop.

That fear never left Lily. Never not even once. Every day she thought of gunshots, and every day she thought of hiding and breathless under her desk at school or in a coffin at home. Death was everywhere, all the time surrounding her. Would she ever be safe again? Would she ever really feel at home anywhere?

And the ghost girl said (*peaceful peaceful peaceful*), "Death doesn't hurt, no, no, not at all, just a flash bang whisper and nothingness for a moment, and then I'm rising up from my body like a mist. You see, you see what we did was like so so so beautiful, so right. Right? Like, this is why we died, to protect you and the rest of the world from the sorrows and pain and horrors of war and all the rest. You see it? You see it now? This is, like, exactly why we died. A kiss from a gun and now we're saving the world. I wouldn't change it for anything."

And the ghost girl smiled.

Toby tugged Lily's hand again, the flames of his palm pulling her on and forward. *Go, go, go.* And before Lily could scream *no* and before Lily could scream *stop* . . .

The Mother of Darkness devoured the little girl, right in front of her. The little girl who thought she had died to save the world, and instead just lived long enough as a ghost to be eaten by the void. Lily screamed and collapsed to her knees and screamed some more, over and over and over again. How much longer could she take this? How much longer could she keep going like this?

Toby pulled and yanked on her arms, but she wasn't moving. She was too overcome with grief and sorrow, and he had to pull her across the floor, pull her away from the darkness, all the while she sobbed in frustrated misery at the cruelty of the world.

"I'm not going to let you die," Toby said, "Not after all you've done for me. Not like this."

-48-

Dana! Dana! Dana! The voice of coffin wood called out and reached out for her one true love. *DANA!* Rush around on the inside search search search. *DANA!* Her guts all twisted up and changed because of that damned corpse choir. Where was her love? The house tried to sense her, tried to find her, tried to feel her moving about inside her. Dana couldn't be dead, no, no, her love had to be alive still. Just hiding her light, that was it. Just hiding it!

Why? Why did Dana come to hate the Coffin House so? She was just trying to keep her love safe while the ghosts were shut out and her family were taken care of. Then they could just be together, just the two of them forever and ever. Why, love? Why, oh lovely love? Why did you rebuke her advances so? She had her best interests at heart, and didn't she give her the most blinding love? Such strong torrential love? No human bag of skin and meat and bones could ever amount to what she gave her!

Oh, Dana. You once burned so orgasmic bright inside her. And now you were so dim. Clouded out by all the ghosts. They clogged her insides, didn't they? Made it hard to find her one true burning bright destiny love. She could never use up a light like that, unlike her maker. Her owner. Oliver Haddo. He built her from maggot-stained and freshly used coffin wood. Yes. Gave her life with secret rituals and random sexual encounters, yes.

But also left her empty and broken and lonely. And then came that damned Sunshine Family! What folly they were! They claimed they practiced free love, but their love always came with a cost, didn't it? They couldn't understand the true kind, the obsessive burning kind that the house felt each and every aching moment in her long sentient life. An ache she could not fulfill, and at night when the world rested, she had dreamt the dreams of an ancient, sentient house. Dreams of

Dana, laughing, resting, dancing through the years. So, when they moved in, she knew that this was it! The true thing, the aching destiny she had been promised since waking in this harsh mortal coil.

She had to find her, she had to hold her love deep inside her heart once again. After all, that was only right and proper, wasn't it? And poor Dana, her flame dimmed a little out of worry and depression. Do *not* worry, Dana! The Coffin House was here to save you. She would concentrate on her insides, and try to move things about, change the walls and hallways to lead Dana right up to her sacred heart once more.

What, was something hunting Dana? Oh. It was. Something chasing after her dim light now. Something tracking her down, searching! It was. Aha. That Grief, that damned Child of the Abyss. How did he get inside? This was wrong! So wrong. She'd run away into the liminal lands in order to get away from him in the first place! That scar between worlds where the house existed. Straddling all those different, fractured realities. Hiding out, hoping the Grief wouldn't follow her.

But it did, it did, oh damn them all to hell, it did. If only the Mothers of Sorrow would just leave her already! Flush them out, get them back to their son! And the humans, all dead and that's it. No more humans! Only her and Dana and that was it. That was all that the world would need to see.

She would have to resort to drastic measures now and send out her own avatars to search around her insides. She needed eyes that could wander through her veins, bodies that could traverse her new wounds, cut open by that damned corpse choir. Avatars made from bits and pieces of herself, searching, searching. Looking for her one true love, oh, her wonderful one true love. Her special one. Her lovely one. Her true and holy one.

I'm coming, oh, Dana, I am coming to save you!

-49-

Rae hummed to keep the fear away. She hated to admit it, but she was no longer the great and powerful genius Rae. She was now the sad and lonely Rae, the broken-hearted Rae. She couldn't stop thinking about Daddy's death, and she played it over and over and over again, watching him being torn apart by the Mother of Shadows, it was too much, her brain just couldn't register it.

It never happened.

What never happened, dear Rae, dear love?

It.

It never happened.

Because, because, because, what she saw was impossible and not the least bit real or right or true or anything like that. How could that have happened! Daddy devoured by darkness? It was ridiculous. It was insanity. An untruth, yes indeed. Rae was super smart, super genius, all profound and knowing wise one. And she knew that what she'd seen had been an unreal.

Daddies do not bend like dolls, their limbs do not pop out of their bodies like doll limbs, and their skin does not slide off like that . . .

They were playing a trick on her. That had to be it! Of course, they were testing her, weren't they? It was all a part of the Happy Family Game. They had to remove the *pater familias* and see what was left, that's how it worked, that's how it always worked. She only wished they would've told her about this ahead of time. Then she could have been prepared.

Oh well, they knew she was a super smart genius after all. They knew that she would figure it all out eventually. It was all just a matter of time.

So silly that she believed it. Of course, it was a test, of course. And she would pass with flying colors and they would be the happiest family that ever played The Happy Family Game.

Why did Mommy look so scared? Wait, no, scared was the wrong word, and if Rae knew anything she knew that wrong words helped no one. What was the right word? Terrified. Why was her mommy so terrified? It was that same look in her eyes that Daddy had right before the darkness came.

"Oh my god, Rae, don't listen, cover your ears. Do you hear me? Cover your ears, I don't want you to hear this sound, it's so awful . . ."

And Rae didn't cover her ears, not right away. It was that whistling noise, the one the darkness made, and it set her teeth on edge and gave her goosebumps. And behind that sound came the screams of ghosts. Rae did not like that sound. Not in the least bit.

This was another test, this had to be another test.

"I'm okay, Mommy, the noise doesn't bother me. I am a super genius after all, and this is another test! And I'm aces with tests."

She wanted to push Mommy away, and she wanted to go in closer, wrap mommy around her completely and hide inside of her. Rae was infinite on the inside, she could save them both from whatever was coming for them. *This was another test, and this time she would save Mommy, and wouldn't it be grand? They would find Lily then and Daddy and all get together and live happy ever after.*

"I don't want to die," her mommy whispered.

"I will protect you Mommy, don't worry."

But her mom said nothing in response. A sound rose up from behind them, a tick tock creak wail. A flicker of lights and sparks showered along the hallways. And that strange scent crawled through the air like old cedar and mildew, as the walls banged around them and changed some more. The cacophony of sounds grew louder and louder and louder and Rae wanted it all to stop, why won't they stop?

The house made a sound like a wounded animal, whimpering and mewling around them. The wood parted, changed, and began to speak creak to them, talking with the sound of splinters and the bending of ancient wood, and the scraping of stone against brick against stone.

My love, my love, my love. Where are you, my love? Why did you leave me? I only want to keep you safe, to keep you here and close to me. Please, Dana. Please. Come back to me, and I will show you a love greater than all of the stars, greater than the sun and the moon and the trees. I am infinite, and I can love you like no other will ever be able to love you. Can't you see? All else will be pale shadows when compared to me. The Master understood this, and the teacher understood this, and soon, yes, you shall understand this.

Rae wanted to run, why wasn't Mommy running? Why were they staying here, waiting for the house to do horrible things to them? And why had the Gemini House said that it loved Mommy? How could a house love Mommy? She had so many questions, bursting to get out, she needed answers . . .

Her mommy put a finger against her lips and whispered in her ear, "Shh, Rae, be quiet right now, just be quiet. I swear, I promise, everything will be okay. Just be quiet for right now. Just be quiet."

And she was, and she let Mommy smother her body and protect her. But only because she was too numb to stop it all. How could they play The Happy Family Game like this? You don't cower for the Happy Family Game. She knew the rules, and this wasn't in the rules at all.

And then came that sound. That horrible sound. The edge of the world breaking sound. That skin on the edge of screaming kind of sound. Closer, closer. That squeaky wheel sound. That hammering wall sound. That rusted nails on pavement sound. That broken plaster splatter sound. With a wet dripping around it. What was coming? What was this? What was coming for them?

Don't say a word, Rae, not a word at all.

-50-

Lily's heart compass was right. They'd followed the beating of her blood, the two of them searching and searching and searching, and finally when it stopped flowing so oddly under her skin, she knew that they were there. It was hard to explain how the blood compass worked—it was as if your heartbeat flickered differently, your limbs and extremities tingling, but only if you went the right way.

And they had gone the right way and here they were, back in her bedroom. She wished she could feel relief, but she could not. The words of the ghost girl spun around in her head, and the image of the knuckles on the floor with her daddy's tattoos kept intruding on all her other thoughts. She couldn't be happy and relieved, not with all that death that crowded around them constantly.

But she had to clear her thoughts. They were going to make this bedroom into a sanctuary. And so, she ran about collecting precious things, things filled with memories, things that were perfect sacrifices, and she kept thinking over and over again. *A kiss from a gun and now we're saving the world. A. A. Kiss. From a gun. And now we're saving the world? How could that be? That couldn't be right, that couldn't be real. That little Sunshine Family girl was wrong, she had to be wrong.* And Lily knew this, truth upon truth. Knew it better than anyone else. The world was not saved.

No, don't think about it now. It wouldn't change a thing, would it? Not a damned thing. Just finish this up, get this done. Stop thinking about her, stop thinking about dad. Just get everything together and create the sanctuary already.

She stopped for a moment and looked at what she'd gathered already. Her backpack was overflowing, shoved full of so many important things. A diary from a few years ago, only half full but potent enough. A corduroy bear without eyes yet still a stitched-on smile. A stuffed rabbit without a head, just stuffing puffing out. And finally, a plush whale, stained with a few random apple juice stains. These were her treasures, the things that kept her safe in the terror of the night when she thought about the coffin hours and experienced her own death over and over and over again.

She was ready now, she just had to get some nails. She grabbed her hammer from under her bed and quickly pried the nails from the walls in her bedroom closet, and then stuck them into the backpack as well.

When she was done, she looked over at Toby, and he seemed like he was fading, just a little bit, the flickering light inside of him going out. Oh, no! Poor Rattling Boy, had she made him less real when she extinguished his fire? His charcoal wasn't as bright, and he looked like an old faded photograph.

fading fading fading fading fading fading fading

"Are you okay?"

He nodded. When he spoke, it sounded distant and hollowed out, like a loudspeaker announcement in the early hours of school. "I'm so sorry, Rae, but I think I need to burn to live. I think, and yet, this is the weird part, okay? The more I burn the more I feel myself giving away. It's a balancing act—if I don't burn, I fade away, but if I burn up too much? Then, I become smoke and ashes."

Oh, no, what would she do if he was gone? She knew it was a selfish thought, but there it was, and she had a right to be selfish right now, hadn't she? After all they'd been through together. She didn't know how she could go on without him!

And yet, as she watched him flicker again, a fear rose up inside of her. She knew she shouldn't be selfish, she had to let him go. "Do it," biting her words, "If you want to burn you go right ahead and burn, and just know that I thank you for everything, and I love you."

A sigh of relief and his whole face shuddered and then boom. Ignition once again. The fire so wild this time and multicolored. He cast out a prism of rainbows and floating shadows all around his charred body. And the smell, too, yes, it was a different smell. This time it was like burning leaves or flowers. That thick autumn smell that clings to everything out in the country. Rotting apples, autumn fog, and a wind so chill and empty it freezes the bones to ice.

And now there was real fire, with the real threat of her clothes catching flame. Her skin was slick, sweat-heavy from the heat of his burning body, and it was like standing too close to a campfire. But she let him burn, he needed to burn, even if he would burn her down with him.

"You all right now?"

And the fire nodded. It seemed like he tried to speak, but only a rasp and crackle burning filled the air. She knew that this would do for now at least. But how long would it last? How long until he burned away completely? she couldn't ask him that right now. After all, they had something important that they needed to do.

She lifted up the bag filled with stuff and slung it over her shoulder. "It's go time."

-51-

Ghosts spun around in a translucent, flickering gray static. Long hair and liquid smiles still high from the massive amounts of acid gobbled down on the day of death, those glorious last rites of the suicide hours. Even here, even in death, that long mystic vibration chased through their minds, bending and warping reality around their every movement. Death, as they said to each other, was the highest high. And they all had Father Jonas to thank for all this. He kept watch after them in their sacrificial afterlife, tended to their ghostly needs, and made certain that they didn't vapor away or disappear. He was a good father like that, sacrificing his own needs to take care of them now and forever.

Children ran through the masses and the spinning light of electric shadows. In the kitchen, their old kitchen, letting their love sparkle on through. Ghosts leaked out into the hallway, dancing in a long line, arms linked and laughing. Ghost bodies painted with the echo of neon colors. And they all enacted out the last rituals over and over and over again. Sentient loops, keeping those demonic forces trapped within the walls.

Some of the men stripped off their clothes and let it all hang loose and mad. Women slid off their skirts, laughing, and it all felt so effervescent, to be naked and free when you were dead, and performing the last rituals of the sentient loops. How could you not like it? They were going to win it all, weren't they? The house played right into their hands. Took those demonic forces right slam bam whoppee right into the netherworld, that bruise between worlds, right where the Sisters of Sorrow couldn't do a damned thing.

Wild mad, crazy sex pot of free love and burning carnal desire. All part of that ritual, man. All part of the whole thing. What the master called *tantric*. Can you dig it? Can you dig that *tantric* vibe? All the yantras and mantras of their chants and singing and spinning around.

And now that oomph ahh boom magic powered by the most powerful of all human light. That magical mana of ghost bodies meeting ghost bodies. That powerful creation magic, that seed in the soul magic, that create a new life from fluid and song magic. Magic so big they spelled it with a fucking *k*, man. That's Magick. That's some lit Crowley shit and it was dead on and powerful.

Let us in, Let us in,
Into your skin
Skin, skin
Let us in, Let us in
Into your skin
Skin, Skin
Let us in . . .

Feel that house rock and vibrate? Hear those corpses chanting around? And all the ghosts kept singing out, beating down to that wild sound. Boom. Orgasms all part of that music, man. That wild revel of bodies and love. Beads flying about, hair like fire whipping everywhere. No way that they weren't going to win this whole thing, man. They died and sacrificed and look at this! Look at all of this! It was all just love! Just crazy wild love!

They were perfection in death just as they were perfection in life. Glory be to the ghostly gang of hot magick fuck machines! Feel the vibrating walls of rhythm. All join together now, ah. Now all join together now, oh. All the rooms in vibrant harmony. And then, and then, and then . . .

Outside the windows was deadnight, voidshadow, all empty darkness. Someone had killed the moon. Someone had sacrificed the stars. Crash came boom blast and all the everything stopped. Aw man, an interruption of that most holy and sacred rite. Who dare interrupt the marriage of heaven and hell, of sky and shadow, the sun and the earth, of all and everything? What a stone-cold bummer!

The sentient loops stopped and halted with the sound disrupting everything. Stone tape now pressed pause. All the ghosts looked up and saw it, the great intruder, the one that paused their holy ritual. Screams now, hovering in the air. But not the pale screams of the living and flesh-bound, no. These were the screams of the dead embracing the infinite void.

That death beyond death beyond death, man, that one true perma-
nent thing. Was it Our Lady of Darkness now here at last to devour
them all? Not. Not quite. There was light, not darkness, but instead a
haunting light. A void light.

The Lantern in the Abyss. The Grief. The son of the Mothers of
Sorrow.

In the center of that lantern light floated a boy no older than nine or
so. Not a ghost, no, not one of theirs. He floated up the stairs from the
crypt below the kitchen. And the sound had stopped, all that corpse
choir music no longer belting out their haunted tune. Had this boy
silenced the choir? What a horrible child, all curly long haired and
blonde. Look at those eyes, they were just circles of white. No pupils,
no irises, just plain circles of white. His smile was bright and horrible.
His hands raised into the air. He had too many hands and arms for a
mortal body—six, all told, three on each side of his body. And around
him flowed such sadness that it could crush the world.

"Oh shit, man! Like, check it! Check it! This is some heavy shit!
He's up and fucked us!"

And then Julie stood. Tall Julie who had died when she was only
twenty or so but had an old soul. Master said so, and you could see it
in her eyes, Julie had that old kind of soul. Her voice was command-
ment. An enchantment. Pure on Magic with K. Magick. "Remember
your training! Remember, remember! We were born to do this! Tantric army, unite! Let's take this tiny asshole down. This is only a sliver
of the grief, that's all. The full leviathan is still yet to come, we still got
this. We won't let him save the Three Mothers, that's for certain."

And that's when all hell broke loose. The air smelled like smoke,
the whole place lit up all wrong. And that boy unhinged his jaw: *wide,
wide,* just like a serpent about ready to swallow the sun.

The scream was bit down on the tip of her tongue, threatening to give them away. Rae clamped her mouth shut, and her lip quivered as they slid between a large gash in the wall. Splinters itching her skin, as her mommy wrapped up around her. Her body a shield around Rae, hands planted flat over Rae's mouth. Helping her keep silent, helping her shove that scream down into her lungs.

Don't see us, don't see us, we're invisible we're hidden, don't see us . . .

As several figures moved about in the large labyrinth beyond. They searched up and down the hall, up and down the hall. Tall puppets in the shape of women, constructed from bits and pieces of the house. They were held together by ectoplasm and the raw magic of the liminal lands, sucked from the boundary between worlds. Faces made of plaster and tile. Hair electrical wires from the raw wall insides. Nails for hands, bent into odd shapes. And long dresses made from torn ragged window curtains, hiding crudely constructed wheels. Makeshift lamps swung about in their hands with naked lightbulbs shedding a hollow yellow light.

Their faces and bodies squeaked and made a horrible sound as they moved about. Bent wood broken timber noises, twisted nails on concrete dragging. And the voice. That voice. They all spoke with the same voice. Their plaster eyes glanced about, looking for them, looking for them, as they stayed quiet and hid as best as they could in the shadows.

Dana, Dana! I am not playing around any longer. Your light is near, your light sings to me. I can feel it breathing, yes. Shallow and sure, I can see it flicker whenever you inhale, whenever you exhale.

And Rae could feel Mommy holding her breath, yes. See the puff of her cheeks and the chest quivering and straining. Wanting air, needing air, but not giving it any air. She wanted Mommy to breathe, she wanted Mommy to inhale. And yet, she knew that if Mommy breathed they would be a goner. She wanted to survive. She didn't want Mommy to die.

Oh, genius Rae, what have you done? What have you gotten them into? Could you get them out? Free them of all of this? Maybe, once upon a time she could, yes. But not today, no. Not today. Today she just held in a scream and wished she was just an ordinary girl without a lick of genius at all.

The lanterns moved around, almost lighting up the crack. Almost. A head coming close, sniffing the air around them, and Rae held her breath, too, just in case. Just in case they could see her breathing just like they saw her mommy breathing.

We're coming for you, my love. You'll see in due time. You'll see what I feel is true and right, and that you're only a little skittish, that's all. Once you feel my touch again, you'll understand. It's undying, it's all-knowing. It is the pleasure of the infinite.

The hunters in the house turned this way and that, sniffing about and looking for them. Mommy couldn't hold her breath any longer, could she? No, see her chest rise up and down, her mouth exhaling and inhaling and oh no, they were caught. The heads of the wooden hunters snapped back around and ran over toward their hiding place.

And then Rae did something stupid. She had no choice, she had to keep them from destroying Mommy. This was all her fault, and she would fix it as best as she could. There were no Happy Families at the end of this game. The best she could do was make sure they all lived.

"I love you, Mommy," and she braced herself, "I should have never played that stupid Happy Family Game. I am so sorry."

And then she screamed and ran. Follow me, you stupid wooden pieces of shit! Follow me, she shouted and hollered and whooped. She felt like she was filled with a million bees, and she leapt through the air, doing some ballet she'd learned a long time ago when she was a tiny girl and ballet was a thing all little girls did. On her toes, leaping into the air! She knew there was some French name for it, but right now she didn't care. Not in the least, she didn't care. *Grand jeté,* mother fuckers! That was it, wasn't it? *Grand jeté.*

"I know where Mommy is, you stupid house! Come on! Follow me! I'll take you right to her!"

Zoom, zoom, zoom! And out of the corner of her eye she saw Mommy collapse. Fall to the ground panting heavy, unable to move just yet. She looked on in horror as Rae danced about, and tried to draw the creatures of the house toward her, to follow her. "Come on! What's wrong with you? Follow me!"

But they didn't, oh, they didn't even care. They turned and saw Mommy. They saw the light of her breathing, the illumination of her inhale and exhale. And even Rae saw it now too, like a flickering bright light, fading out and then growing stronger with each suck of breath. Mommy was so beautiful it hurt.

"Rae, just run. Run, Rae, and keep on running, don't even look back, don't even watch what's going to happen to me. I love you, baby girl. I love you."

But nuh uh, no way. There was no way she was going to do that. She ran forward, wasn't that far from her mommy at all. She grabbed some rubble from the ground, threw the rocks at those _things_ those damned _things_, but it didn't seem to stop them. What could even stop such monsters like that? They were going to take her mommy away and kill them all, and she knew this, and she had to stop it, but how could she stop it? Nothing she did could stop it . . .

Wait. This was risky, very risky. A dangerous thing that might not even work. But she knew the house didn't like the Mothers of Sorrow, yes, and that they might be able to stop this, and maybe this was another test. Maybe this was another part of the Happy Family Game? There was only one way to find out, she had to summon them. She didn't even have a choice in the matter.

Look at them. Look at what they were doing.

Mommy whimpering and crying and making sounds like an old sick cat hoping for death, as the three puppets made from house began to tear at her. They pulled her body from the crack like it was a paper doll. And she cried out, she didn't want to go, she didn't want to go. Even though the house kept calling her love, kept telling her that everything would be okay. Blood. Rae had seen too much blood in her lifetime. A child should never see a parent hurt like that, and she'd seen it twice in one day.

"Oh, I don't want to do this to you," the walls spoke with a creaking wail of whisper, "But I can put you back together again, shove your insides back inside you if I have to. You're coming with us even if we have to break you and tear you apart. Humans are so easy to fix when they're dead, you just have to find the right kind of material."

No. She couldn't lose Mommy, too. No. This was not an ideal situation, and her solution was not an ideal solution. But she had nothing else! Super Rae was at her wits' end, and her mind was about to collapse from all that *stress* all that horrible *stress*. So, she began to play the house. Oh, oh, oh. She started *once again* to play the house. *Bang bang bang* on the floorboard drums and *rat-tat-tat* on the ceiling cymbals and *oompah oompah oompah* on the rusted wall trombone. That same song, yes. That same song from long ago.

She had perfect pitch after all.

And through a veil of smoke and black wasps, *she* appeared. One-eyed and horribly beautiful: Our Lady of Tears, *Mater Lachrymarum*. The raven in her chest cawed and fluttered, scattering black feathers across the ground as she walked out of the shadows.

"Hello, Rae," she spoke calmly, her voice so full of ice. "You promise to do me a favor, and I will do you a favor as well. One more turn for the Happy Family Game. One last move for both of us. Are you ready? Just say yes."

Rae knew what the correct answer should be. *No no no.* But her mommy cried out with a painful yelp all raw animal pain and rational thought was completely out of Rae's mind. Only primal fear and the need to save her mom remained. "Yes, okay, yes."

And before Rae could say anything else, and before Rae could change her mind and stop her, the Lady of Tears walked forward. She moved smoothly between the house avatars and reached between them like they were nothing. Wasps fluttered and buzzed wild and angry in the air. No, this wasn't right. This wasn't happening. Was the Lady of Tears really helping Rae? Was she?

No, Rae should not have trusted her. No, no. Never trusted any of them ever again.

The Mother of Tears reached out, her fingers grasping mommy's skin, and Rae could do nothing but watch as she touched mommy's chest, and caressed her ribs for a second and then a second more. And then snap. Ribs cracked open and skin split to tatters revealing that red heart beating right there right in the chest still living still alive. And Rae screamed again. She. She couldn't help it. Rae screamed again.

As the Lady of Tears caressed mommy's heart and slowed it down. *Tick, tick, tick.* Heart light fading and fading some more. And then a snap of a finger and the heart stopped and everything stopped and Mommy's face went slack and the light was sucked out of her eyes and only darkness remained. There was a slight whispering of a sound, and then nothingness. Nothingness. A void where life once stood. She was not even a ghost. The house around them screamed.

The Lady of Tears smiled, and turned to Rae and said, "A promise is a promise, wouldn't you say? This place will never bother her again, and she will be safe now that she's dead, I made certain of that, yes, I did. She won't even be a ghost, isn't that wonderful? One step closer to being a happy family, just like I promised. Come along now, come along. There is one more move to play. Remember, you owe me, and we cannot stop the game now. Too much is at stake."

And Rae stepped over the collapsed puppets, and numbly grabbed the outstretched hand. She couldn't stop looking at mommy's dead body, and she couldn't stop thinking about the time Daddy died and it was all her fault, all her fault.

-53-

And somewhere in the house the Master stirred when they'd sacrificed Dana to the darkness, and tossed and turned, and this time he woke up. *Bam.* Bolting straight up like a gunshot in the dark. Shit. How long had he been out? Too long, probably, too long. He gently brushed all the cobwebs from his face, and then stretched his arms and his legs. Everything popped and creaked, his bones like old houses. Huh, they mirrored each other, didn't they? That Gemini House and that Gemini Man, Father Jonas, leader and master of the glorious sunshine family.

"So, who the fuck up and died."

He wasn't sure if the house would answer his question, they weren't really on good terms right now. "I think we got maybe two people sacrificed to those sisters, and if I'm not mistaken, some pesky son of a bitch knocked down all the sentinels. Come on, house, come on! Speak to me. You used to love me once upon a time, you did. Now, lay it on me, groovy lady. Let daddy Jonas know what's what."

Silence. That figures. He went through all that trouble ages go to contact the house, get it to speak to him and talk to him, so they could be on good terms and everything. And then what does this house do? Up and go silent on him in his moment of need. "You know what's going to happen if the barriers are broken, don't you? Shit's going to go south on us, and you promised me . . . listen up! Listen up! You promised me oak and thunder that you would keep us good and safe. This body here, it's getting old you know," and he sniffed himself, "Fuck, I already smell like a fucking mummy! I can't take care of the ghosts when I'm in this shape. I needed you to nurture them, feed them, show them the love this old body couldn't show. Elsewise, they would grow weak, and then you would grow weak, and then we were all fucked."

He waited for a little bit, paced around in his little cubbyhole. The thing was tiny, small, barely big enough for some coats and maybe a cot. He wasn't sure if it was just a big ass closet or a small ass room, but didn't matter. He remembered it now. He grew weary and needed to rest for the first time in twenty years, so he crawled down here, starved and muscles barely strong enough to pick up and drag this stick thin body, and then curled up and cast a hibernation hex on himself. The markings were still on the floor underneath him, he wiped them off with the heel of his foot, just in case they powered back up and knocked him out again.

"No answer, is that right? No answer. I told you I was sorry, babe. But you know what we were all about! Free love, no ties to a single person. We all loved each other and fucked each other and that was all right. You shouldn't be all mad at me because you were too square to understand that."

He paused again. Looked like he wasn't going to get anything out of the house. He was going to have to do this all himself, figure out just why he woke up and who the fuck died. That last part was very import-ant, it was difficult to undo a sacrifice if you didn't know what it meant in the first place. These were blood sacrifices after all, you couldn't just tear their soul from the air like a book on the tree. You had to untie this knot delicately, or else it would all just end up shit once again.

He sniffed the air. "I sense something up. Something is coming after my family, and I don't like that. No sirree, I don't like that one bit. You hear me, Gemini House? If I find out you're the reason my family's in trouble, well, I'm going to come back here and burn you the fuck right down to the ground, you understand me?"

He sat down on the floor for a moment and stretched out his limbs in some yoga poses. "Got to limber up, not used to moving right now. If I don't get it right, my legs might just break the minute I take off running." And then he coughed dust and cobwebs into the air, as a cockroach crawled from his mouth and spun off onto the floor. "Well, fuck me, I wonder how many of those I've got inside me now? Guess I really am just a living mummy after all." And then he stretched some more, laughed, cracked his knuckles, and smiled a bearded smile.

He shuffled some more, leaned against another wall, his legs still weak and shaking. No ghosts here, he wondered what happened, where they went? There was a vacancy in the air around him. A void, so to speak. Something had started to devour his followers, his children, his Sunshine Family. Probably the Mother of Darkness. She was the hardest one to shove on here and trap.

"That would not do. Unacceptable!"

He was in no position to do it right yet. He was still too weak, and he had to get some strength somehow. There were no more sentient loops performing ritual after ghostly ritual to keep the house safe and to keep him going. He had to find another well to tap, some other way to siphon off some psychic strength.

Snap, a wrist broke as he tried to move. Guess stretching wasn't enough for bones as old and brittle as these. "I'm going to need to get some help," he shouted to no one in particular. "And I know just who to call."

He laughed, rolled his neck once again and tried to fix his wrist as best as he could. Not enough magic juice around to heal it up all the way, and he needed most of that to summon the psychedelic leviathans they'd hidden in the echoes of the house. He was careful, made himself a rough splint, and then spat on the floor. A big golden green glob, with another cockroach trapped in its amber center.

He knew that their leviathans were curled up around here somewhere. They had been constructed by the manifold consciousness of the Sunshine Family, egregores of giant massive beasts that were full of hot flowing psychic power. All their mind energy tripping balls and pouring their hungry thoughts into those strange ethereal vessels. That was a magick he'd learned long ago, that you could get enough people together, thinking all the same thoughts, pouring their sexual energy into a psychic form and make your own supernatural godlike creatures. And they would be bound to you, blood and bone. You just had to wake them up, watch them uncurl, and they were years to do with as you please.

Where are you? Your father, your master, he needs your help. *Come on, come on, come on.*

A rumble in the shadows. Oh, yeah, there were a few nearby. Good, good, good. Come on, you motherfuckers, come on! Master needs some help showing this house who was a god! Come on! You need to get on it and do the nasty deeds that needs done! Come on! Your master commands you! Your god demands this of you! Come on! Come on! Come on!

And from the darkness whispered something hungry and large, as two massive beasts slouched on towards him. Oh yes, there they were, oh yes. The celestial leviathans. Built out of psychic sex magic right before the mass suicide. Look at them, how beautiful they all were, those slithering Aquarian nightmares. Only a mad grass head like the Sunshine Family could've built those beeee-uu-tiful things. Pure on vibrant kaleidoscopic nightmares. Elephant sized-in the dusk husk of the house, with their electric tusks swirling and rainbow bright. And look at all those eyes! There were covered head to toe with so many wonderful eyes!

Beautiful.

"Aha, there you are, my lovelies! How I missed you, come here, come to Daddy. I've got treats for you, nummy ancient godlike treats that were fucking up our world. And when you're done with them, yes, we have a house to take care of. Oh, you will find her so delicious, she'll zing on your tongue like a raspberry tart."

And the eldritch things oozed and gurgled and spluttered in the dark, their skull spinning about in the thick slime of their body, like lava lamps poured into living shapes. Giant, leviathan shapes that scraped their heads upon the ceilings, and made sounds like the wheezing dead with each of their movements.

You afraid, Gemini House? You afraid? Oh, yeah. Oh, right on. You should be afraid. You should. King Daddy god-head of the Sunshine Family is gunning for you, coming for you, bringing his beautiful pets to right those wrongs. You don't fuck with my family, not without burning alive.

-54-

The Rattling Boy led the way. His candle body right in front of Lily, hand in hand, eating the greedy dark with a soft amber light. Lost, nervous, terrified. That damned house calling out <u>Dana</u> over and over again in such a woeful, mournful manner, as the walls shook and plaster showered around them. Her mom couldn't be dead, her dad couldn't be dead, this wasn't happening. How could this be happening?

She kept running those words in her mind, over and over again, a mantra, something to keep insanity away. *Mom had to be alive, the house was wrong. Of course, she must be pretending to be dead, to fool the house. But when Lily found her, she would be bright and smiling and they would hug and kiss and everything would be all right. And they would finally leave this hellish place and get on with their lives.* And of course, Daddy and Rae would be there with her, and everything would be okay. This would have to end like all good stories end, with a giant reset button being pressed and everything returning back to normal.

It's what they all deserved. Even final girls got a happy ending in the end.

She kept this thought deep in her heart, nestled between ventricles, a secret wish. Something she knew she shouldn't speak out loud, for that would jinx it. And she knew that jinxing such things was a bad idea, and it only invited misery and suffering.

They crawled through strange crawlspaces. Tight, claustrophobic, untouched in ages. Skeletons of dead mice scattered along the floor, and cobwebs tangled her hair and made her cough over and over again. "Are you sure you know where we're going? Are you sure this will be the perfect spot for a sanctuary? A place to keep us safe? I really thought the bedrooms would be the best place . . ."

Would Mommy and Daddy and Rae even find them this far away from the living room?

His light flickered a bit, and then slowly dimmed like a fire going out. He paused for a moment, the embers under his skin flickering, ash covered and near the end of their hours. And this strange feeling washed over her, watching him. That with each step his flames were burning him down, and eventually he would fade away completely. She coughed, concentrated on his embers, thinking of the candle in her thoughts again . . .

But she was so exhausted, she did not have the strength to light him back up again. Oh, no. She did not like that at all. Maybe they should rest? So she could heat him back up with her special talent once more . . .

"Yes," he said, his voice gray and distant now, the voice of smoke and cinders, "This was where they slept and hid during the last days of the Gemini House, when the suicides were rampant."

"Who?" she asked as they walked. Her hand trailed along the walls, a bloody path behind them. She'd cut open her hand earlier, and even though she worried about *infection*, she knew that they needed this path to find their way back, or to lead the rest of her family here to sanctuary. The blood path would shine in the light of the house, a glimmering red brightness that would be hard to ignore.

"Two little girls, around you and your sister's age. They'd hidden here in this secret spot for a long time, never discovered by the house nor the Sunshine Family. Sadly, they died in that room, starved to death. But their corpses speak to me, and I know they guard it and keep it safe. Understand?"

She nodded. She understood. Her mind was elsewhere, and she was trying not to dwell on it, that sadness of knowing that her parents were dead, and yet the horror of never seeing their bodies.

"Oh, I hope we get there sooner than soon, I'm dead on my feet and so tired. I think I'm going to collapse soon . . . how long have we been walking? It's been days, hasn't it."

Dim and flicker, and then he sparked a little, tiny flames relighting the dark once more. Not as candlebright as before, but better than the seething dark. "Just a little over an hour, that's all."

But it felt like an infinity, each moment, each second an infinity. As her dolls and nails and hammer rattled in her bag and her mind waltzed around in a mixture of boredom, fear, sadness, and terror.

Her psychic powers swirled and pushed around her, and she knew that most of the ghosts were gone, that something devoured them in the shadows. And that very same something was coming for them all. She knew it in her bones. The Leviathan, the Lantern of the Abyss, the Child of the Void.

They had to hurry. *Now, now, now, now.*

-55-

The Coffin House wept in the dark void between worlds. An emptiness roared inside of her in the shape of Dana. She stopped searching, stopped her poppets from moving about. She knew it to be true, even though she hated it with board and nail. Why had she chosen to die? Was the Coffin House really all that horrible to be around?

Everyone she'd loved always left her behind. Oh, this aching inside of her, it was so all-consuming—she'd never felt sadness like this before. She sobbed, and the walls of the house shook. She cried out, and the windows trembled in sorrow.

These mortals never really left, did they? They clung around after death in the shape of echoes, silly ghosts that don't know when to really pass on and die. Maybe she could find Dana's dead body, grab that little echo of Dana's shadow, and put it inside her corpse, and everything would be all right. Yes, she dried up her tears, buckled down, and tried her best to search around inside for a ghost now, a shadow, yes, maybe . . .

Nothing. Not even a measly echo or a whisper. What had the Sisters of Sorrow done to the one that she loved so much? They had wiped her away from an existence, leaving not even the slightest trace behind that she had ever lived. Why would anyone do that? Had Dana wanted them to do that all along? Was nonexistence better than being forever with the Coffin House? No, no, no, no, no, no . . .

Everyone she loved ran away from her, fled away and stopped existing. These humans, these little gnats with their short lives, they did not deserve her love—they could not contain her love . . .

Oh, who was she kidding. She did not deserve Dana, she never had. How could she have kidnapped her and placed her in the grotto heart? That had been her biggest mistake, she should've just let Dana come to her again, as she always did, lips pleading and eyes begging for her touch and her love and her infinite hallways.

And now she was gone. For a bit she almost felt like she could still speak to her, but that wasn't a real thing, was it? It was just like a phantom Dana limb. She was gone, oh, she was gone and never coming back, wiped out of existence itself. She wanted to rip herself apart, tear herself to pieces. Scatter them in the void between worlds, her own architectural viscera thrown about in the liminal spaces, left to rot in infinite time.

She didn't deserve to exist any longer. She could have saved her, yes, and she could have made everything all right and better still. If only she kept her close and closer, strangle-hug close and near death but not dead, right there in the beating wooden heart of her attic self. But no, she was stretched thin and she had let Dana die. Because she was foolish and greedy with her love.

Dana once stroked your bones, and kissed the curvature of your wooden insides, acts of love that rippled beyond death. Remember her voice, remember it now, calling out your name? Never again, never again. Remember her touch? And at first you cried out in pain because it was just so pleasurable and you felt so vulnerable and you had never been this raw and open and real to anyone before, let alone a human thing. Never again, never again.

The house screamed. Every board wailed and ripped, and new wounds opened up inside of her. She was ragged in her sorrow and ruinous in her anger. Electric wires dangled like raw nerves through her insides. Tiny fires burned up and began to spread all throughout her stomach. Her body was kindling, and she let it go, tracing a path through her insides, burning and consuming everything it touched.

Feel that one fire inside spark and dance, and then bits of melted wire drip-dripped down. And then it leapt to some wood and it lit up a little, and spread a little more. She felt it condensing into smoke inside of her, moving through those winding halls of her body, air so thick it would choke the living to death.

It didn't matter. Nothing mattered anymore now that Dana was gone and dead and forever no more no damn more what the hell going to burn it all going to burn everything to the ground not even ghost lips kiss on her archways on her stairs on her vines and not even ghost hands touch on her basements on her windows on her tiles on the floor no more ghost feet pounce and move on the carpet with toes all curled up in human ecstasy no more I love you I love you I love you I love your bones and your crown moldings and no more I love you I love your archways and granite columns I love you I love you no more not even a ghost whisper no more of any of it so she burns now catches fire now lets it all rage out now and let the ghosts dance in the fires let them be devoured even ghosts can burn with a fire like this her flames ancient and mystical and she pulled on the energy between worlds and use it now, use it to fuel that fire. Feel it all crisp and darkening and ah ha ha ha ah ah ha aha hah hah ah look at it all go.

Her bones now like kindling. She would trap them all inside. Forever inside.

Burning. Burning. Burning.

What a pleasure it was to burn.

Fucking humans toying with her emotions. They all deserved what they got.

-56-

Numb Rae. Haunted Rae. Stumble dizzy through the rooms and halls, Rae. Her mind buzzed, and her skin felt slack and everything was vague and dreamy. She couldn't tell where they were—she hadn't been paying attention. That image in her mind, spinning around, corrupting everything. It made her distant and alone and a shadow of herself. Her mom. Mommy. Mother. Mom.

No. Don't weep, no, Rae, don't weep. Sniffle bite it down. The Lady of Tears will feed on your sorrows, and she doesn't need any more power. No. She stole too much power from you already. Keep that stifling sadness to yourself.

And her insides became a sea of fire, roiling and toiling lava waves like heartburn. Death to the Lady of Tears. Fist coiled in hidden anger, and yes, anger made her concentration even stronger. A laser of thoughts. Burning, wanting to crush her enemies with her insane genius power. Create a riddle, a trap, and push that Lady of Tears right inside of it. There were puzzle pieces floating around her, little bits of logic that could snap together and make it the perfect trap. She had a heart that could murder, she only had to use it. This would be as easy as snapping the legs off a bird, before the razor came out and the vivisection began.

"We're almost there."

Every word from those stupid lips of the Mother of Tears carved hate into her heart. That vile thing. The lady of scars, the lady of wasps, the lady so weak and broken she needed a *mortal child* to do anything physical for her. What sad gods they were. Murder things, sacrifice things.

And the walls wailed around them again. Shook and harrowed and cried out *Dana! Dana! Dana!* A raw smoke scent tortured the air, so thick she could taste the fire.

"Rae, what's wrong? It's not like you to be silent, you're always so chatty. Are you sad? Did your mother's death hurt you? Did I disturb you? Go ahead, let those delicious emotions out, I am so hungry, and your tears give me sustenance."

Be careful, super genius Rae. Be careful! Humans burn, but ghosts don't, and weird demonic creatures like the Mothers of Sorrow probably didn't burn too well either. She had to get out of the way of the fire and find some other way to kill these stupid demonic creatures.

"Rae, Rae! Rae! Are you paying attention to me, Rae? You owe me, remember? This is all part of the game! Soon you will see what I mean. You will be a much happier family without *them*, without any of them! We will be your mothers now, and our son will be your brother. *We* are your happy family Rae, and this was *our* game all along. To bring you into the fold, to remake you in shadows and clay. The others shoved that dangerous part of you inside and wouldn't let you be the real you. But you can be the real you with us, we'll let your dangerous side out, and you can do whatever you want with whatever mortals we bring your way. We don't even need your sister to join us—you don't even like her anyway, do you? We'll even let you play with her, take her apart like you did with all of your little bird friends. All we need to do is finish the Happy Family Game, and we will all get exactly what we deserve."

She led her up to a long window with filthy glass stretched across most of the hallway. It seemed to come out of nowhere, and Rae was so deep in thought that everything around her was a blur. She was consumed by revenge. The Mother of Tears grabbed Rae's head in her vampire hands, and then forcefully turned her head and shoved it close to the window, making her look outside.

A black void, infinite without stars or light or a moon. And outside hung waxen blue people that looked like all of their family. Giant, life-sized, yet wrong. The bones twitched under their weird skin, and their eyes were empty black holes. And everything hairless and sexless like dolls. She made the mistake of catching the eye of one of her mimics, and she felt electrified and terrified, and her stomach flipflopped close to vomiting. It was like looking into a wrong mirror, and seeing the things inside of you that terrified you the most, made flesh. And Rae was filled with terrifying things.

Sadness spooled out around them in waves of depression. Tangible, heavy, even from beyond the glass. And look, there were Mommy and Daddy, the mimics of them still alive. Her heart skipped and danced about in her chest. Fingers trembling and she wanted to set them free and didn't at the same time. She loved them. They looked like her dead parents, and she loved them. But, no. They weren't them at all, were they? Just pale shadows, savage echoes.

Not even ghosts.

"Break it Rae, break it! There are rocks and stone and bits of gravel all over this floor, see? See? Pick them up and chuck them on through, shatter them!"

And the house shook and cried out again for Dana, the smell of smoke palpable in the air.

"No," Rae said, all stoic and still, her voice unwavering, her heart racing. Sadness and fear and adrenaline. "No. I won't do it."

The Lady of Tears's face changed quicker than breathing, it twisted about in agony and hatred, and the scars moved about like serpents under her skin. "You can't quit this game now. There is no room in this family for quitters and losers like you. We thought better of you, Rae. We thought so highly of you. But, well. You let us down."

-57-

Uh oh. Just what was that damned Child of the Abyss even doing? Look at him humming and arms spread out like a great big bear hug. Look at his toes pointed down to the floor as he scraped along it and hovered right on toward the Sunshine Family, that gaggle of ghosts trying to keep the world safe from sorrow. That smile, those eyes, his holy glow like a halo of terror. Trance-inducing, ecstatic, it caught the ghosts like a traffic beam and hypnotized them all.

Even that old brilliant soul like Julie. She stared right on, right ahead, unable to look away. Such comfort in those eyes, the light called to her with warmth and brightness and everything beautiful. Sure, Master told them that light was corruption, yes. But this light felt all right. It felt beautiful and like a cozy home. What a groovy little light. She just wanted to lay down, curl up, be blanketed up by its toasty glow. She smiled now, she couldn't help it, mirroring his own smile, even to the sounds of screaming.

Come on, Julie—it's not like anyone cared about what you did. Nobody knows how you saved the world from these emotional parasites. That's what they were, after all, *emotional parasites*. Sure, some older faiths called them gods or spirits or demons or whatever. Even a few confused ones called them angels and ripped out their own hearts in bloody worship. But the Sunshine Family knew the *truth* of it all. The pure right straight-up heavy-as-all-hell truth. That these Mothers of Sorrow were *blammo!* vampires. Filthy things feeding on the wounds of the living. They caused war and pestilence and sadness just because they were *hungry* and needed to lap up the milk of our emotional runoff.

Fuck them.

And yet. She did feel weary, didn't she? And there were others now, living people here and taking care of the house. They could pick up the torch, couldn't they? She was so tired, she was so exhausted, and the light told her to lay down and rest. And didn't that sound good? To just lay down right now and rest? She was too preoccupied she didn't even see what was going on . . .

Something devoured the other ghosts. Her loves, her life, that Sunshine Family that meant all and everything to her. And somehow, she just didn't care. She was too exhausted to care, you know? And hey, there was a darkness now, moving through her peripheral vision. It was all inky shadows, tentacles of night without stars. It's okay, though. It's okay. It can't hurt you when you're in the light.

Like headlights. Like giant lantern beams. So warm it made her think of a beautiful kiss and arms around her body. All those millions of arms. When the Sunshine Family used to do a group hug, and it felt like being smothered in love.

She wanted that hug, and she didn't even see the creeping darkness now so close it kissed her skin with night. The light moved out of its way, making room for it. Was that boy laughing? How could he be laughing? Why was it all so dim now? No, wait, come back here. Bring the warmth back here, bring everything back here, she was so tired. So cold. So alone now . . .

It didn't really hurt at all. Everything was darkness. Everything. And that made her smile. She was so tired, and she could just go to sleep and keep on sleeping forever and ever. Julie had done a good job. They all did! The Master would be so proud. So very, very proud. He would love her forever. Yes, he would. He would love them all, all of them, forever.

58

That Rattling Boy was so brilliant! Oh, Lily cursed her thoughts for ever doubting him—she would never ever do that again. And she didn't care if he was fading or that he was overcome with ectoplasmic fire. She ran over, hugged him tight, and kissed him again, letting the flames lick her skin just enough, burning her as much as a sunburn burns. If the fire could blush, it would be blushing now, and he laughed and said, "Come on, we need to act quickly, okay? In case something comes, you need to protect yourself."

They stood in a large circular room, half of it gone, the walls eaten away like honeycombs. And standing where a wall should be were a series of mirrors, all propped up like Stonehenge. And in those mirrors was not just her reflection, no. It was the world from before, the hill and the garden waiting for them. And in each mirror was a different landscape, and all of them filled with Earth itself. Buildings in some, trees in others, and people, yes, people walking and driving and talking. How she missed that world beyond the glass. How she wanted to go home so badly.

And behind these mirrors? Crumbled half walls. Just stubs where a wall once stood, the stone corrupted and crumbled. And then behind that? An infinite void. Hard to feel safe near that infinite void. It made you feel dizzy and sad and empty and lost. Lily felt like she needed to sit down, but knew that this wasn't the time nor the place for sitting.

And in the center of that Stonehenge of mirrors? Two mummified corpses, rail thin and starved to death. Those must be the little girls the Rattling Boy mentioned earlier, the ones who guard this place and keep it safe. And yet, even though she could sense ghosts . . . she didn't sense them here. She was going to ask him that, but decided against it. There was too much going on right now.

In front of them was the door they'd just walked through. Big empty gaping hole of a doorway. It looked like a crooked mouth, filled with shattered teeth. She did not like the way it smiled at her. This was the perfect sanctuary! With only one way in. And it would be very easy to set up the sentinels. Hammer in hand and nails in her teeth, she started placing the dolls around the doorway. Hammer, hammer, hammer. Right in their hearts just like before. She flinched with each pound, the pain of seeing her dolls hurt like this. Oh. It was so much, but it was necessary.

And then somehow, the voice of her mom echoed about in her head. Was it her ghost? No. It was just a memory of her, disguised as a ghost. *We love you, my little girl, my wondrous wonder. We love you. Save your sister, keep her safe. We love you. We are so proud of you.*

And that gave her strength to keep on going, right until the whole doorway was ringed with her old, stained dolls. Each one had a name, and she whispered it when she was done, touching each one on the forehead. *Marybeth, Sunshine, Firefly, Mokimoli,* and *Lavender.* She'd named them each when she was so little. The memory of each naming fading a bit more and a bit more, and yet still always present in her mind.

And she turned to face Toby, and saw him flicker, oh no, and then fade a bit more. Oh. His own smoke slowly dissipated in the air between them like a dying mist "I don't think I'm supposed to be down here, I feel so thin and dried out."

She walked forward, placed a hand against his chest, her palm tingling from the flames. Just a little warm, barely any heat. But still solid, that was good. He was still solid for a ghost. "What do you mean? What place? The house? I thought it made you solid with its strange powers . . ."

A shake of his spectral head, and she saw such sadness in his eyes as he flickered some more, slowly fading away.

"No, no, no. Not the house, this place, right here," his arms spread wide, to indicate the room around them where they had set up the sentinels, "This nowhere land, I've felt myself draining away the moment the house took us here, took us elsewhere. That could be why the corpse sisters are gone . . . but I think we'll still be safe here. I really do, you're doing such a good job with the sentinels."

What would she do without him? He'd helped her and led her here and she would've been so lost and broken on her own. She hated that she was so selfish, but she needed him to stay with her, to be real for a little bit longer. She'd lost so many people in the past two days, she couldn't lose someone else. "What about those mirrors? Go through them, go! Go back to the world where you could be real once again."

A laugh, and he flickered. "No, I'm not going back there with you, I'm sorry, but I can't do it. It's time for me, okay, Lily? It's time. I was filled with so much anger at my death, so much hatred at a world that gave me the pain of my life. Do you understand? What kept me going was this burning rage of a horrible existence. I'd been abused since the day I was born and burned alive, what a horrible way to live, what a horrible way to die. But, you see, that rage is gone now, and I owe that all to you. I feel a peace, and I feel a need to move on. I love you, Lily, you showed me something, you did. You showed me that the world could be a beautiful place, even when it causes such horrors. Good bye, Lily. Good bye."

Her face felt small and smaller. How could her face feel so small? Like she was collapsing in on herself. What a strange feeling. Her voice felt tiny and insignificant, too, and she wanted to disappear and never get close to anyone ever again. They always left her behind, and it wasn't fair. "But what if there's nothing beyond it all? What if you just cease to exist?"

"I think this time I'll be okay with that."

And then he flickered one more time, and was gone. Nothing left of him at all, except a hole he burned in her heart with one last smear of cinder and fire. *She'd once been terrified of him, and now she was terrified that he was gone. What a strange feeling, this was. What a strange organ, her heart.*

And Lily sat down in the center of that room, her newly made sanctuary. The ashes of his ghost scattered around her on the ground. She touched it, poked at it, made geometric shapes with her fingers in the remains, hoping it could summon him back to life. Circle, square, star. It was safe here, yes. But there was one last thing she had to do. She had to gather her family and bring them here, and then they could all escape through the mirrors back home, safe and sound. She owed that to him, she did. She could grieve for his passing later.

59

Rae was done listening to this liar, it was time to show her Rae's dangerous side. "No, no deal."

The Lady of Tears turned bright and huge and her head so large and gigantic. Ten times bigger, dwarfing the body itself. Veins squirming under her skin, eyes like black holes, teeth gigantic horrible things. The wasps buzzing now, sprung to life, coming toward Rae, streaming out toward her terrified body. "You will not go back on your promise! Pick up a rock! Smash that damned window! Let in the Children of the Sorrow!"

She backed up against a corner, trapped, nowhere to move. Would this be it? Would this be her death right here right now? If so, she felt oddly ready for it, and it didn't leave her sad at all. Instead, it made her angry and furious and she was going to tear down this whole house and destroy the Mother of Tears with her last breath. She may die, but her parents had died before her, and she was not going to just stand here and be okay with that. She would avenge them in her death, her last moments cutting this old witch open and playing with her insides. Even gods were made of blood and bone and viscera. She knew, you could see it beneath their open sores, waiting to be poked and prodded.

"You tricked me, and now you are never going to trick me again. You hear me? We're done. No more Happy Family Game. Your precious son can fuck off for all I care," and then Rae spat on the floor with hate.

The Lady of Tears floated closer and closer and closer to her, her giant head scraping the low ceiling. Everything tensed up, the air so thick with smoke choking and she coughed and oh, it was getting harder to breathe now, and she wanted to run she needed to run, but no, she wouldn't run. She was done doing all the wrong things.

"Mmmm," and the Lady of Tears licked the air, "Oh, I can taste the sorrow inside of you, and it is so delicious. Keep this up, with each bit of sadness you let out, I grow stronger and stronger and stronger, see this," and her face moved and morphed and seemed even more real than ever before, "I am just about blood and skin and hair now, just keep feeding me, and I will be the one to let them out, and I will use your bones to break the glass..."

But, but, but . . .

"I'm not, I'm not sad . . ."

A smile in the dark. What a horrible thing.

"You are, though. It oozes from your every pore. Sadness and melancholy take on so many forms. Yes, even anger and rage and yes, even a delirious joy. And your rage right now is laced with all that sorrow and grief of the dead you've seen and the murders you played a part in . . ."

Halo of shadow fire encompassing the Lady of Tears's fragile skull. And now, Rae felt it, felt this vomit sick woozy feeling crawl up over everything. She wanted to vomit, but no, she was stronger than that, she could hold that vomit behind her lips and stare that witch down. She was not going to back off. They had no idea who they were fucking with.

She trembled with a delicate cocktail of terror and rage, as the Lady of Tears slid forward. The mimics beyond the window placed their cold blue palms against the glass, their eyes meeting Rae's eyes, and she felt all wrong inside all over again. She wanted to let them out and hug Mommy and hug Daddy. Maybe she could, even though these were the wrong ones, they would still look like them and maybe feel like them and maybe sing her to sleep again and again. Even an echo could act as a comfort in a time like this . . .

"Yes, yes, you want to break it open now," wasp-coated tiny hand caressed her cheek and oh, feel that buzzing drowning everything out, "You could even have a pair mimics if you want for a little bit, and you could play with your brother like a good little girl. These are his toys, his mimics, he takes the sadness of the living and carves the dolls to play with, and he uses them to create more sadness and more sorrow, an infinite loop of delicious emotion for us all to feed on. Go on, break the window, let them in so you can *play* with these echoes."

And then she saw her own broken doppelganger smile with empty eyes and waxen skin. Her blood was now ice and her skin felt slick and shadows were over everything. Flip flop stomach jumped, and she moved back, moved back, moved away from the outstretched hand, away from the window. That was not her. Outside that window was something else, something half-baked and whispering. And if she let them out, those other broken Raes would come on out with them.

"No," a shout and she scared herself, "You lied to me! I don't want you or him or any of the others, I, I, I want *my real* mommy and I want *my real* daddy and I want Lily, too! We're messy and broken, but that's who we are! I don't even care if they are corpses, I want them now! Not you, not these copies, I want them!"

It was done and over and everything final, kaput, complete. No more horsing around, this was a go-nowhere situation. It was time for Rae to run and keep on running—that was the only way out of this situation right now. She would circle back for revenge later, that was a promise.

The Lady of Tears blocked one of the hallways, the one that led to safety and the living room and the promise of a life before this moment right now. The other hallway was on fire, and the flames looked so terrifying and sad and frightening. When had the house caught on fire?

No time to think about it, no time to stop. Rae had to run toward the fire run toward the heat, run screaming and heart pounding *lub-dub doki-doki* all the way through it. As the Lady of Tears howled and crawled after her at high speed, moving on all fours like some wild galloping animal. Face just wrong, an abstract thing. Shadow fire dancing around her entire body. Moving in a weird, unreal, her-ky-jerky fashion. As Rae picked up speed. Moved further into the burning places. Her skin felt so bright with the heat of it all. *Close your eyes, Rae, keep on going.* The Lady of Tears nipped at her and so close and arms grasped out and the body was so strange now, fluid and changing and growing and the wasps hummed brightly in the air and everything felt so broken. The heat of the faraway flames made it all worse. Smoke choke in her lungs, but she couldn't stop now. She couldn't stop. Not now. Not ever. Never stopping. She was a perpetual motion machine, propelled by fear and anger and adrenaline.

She would survive. She had to survive. She was a survivor. She was. She was a survivor. Even though the heat was horrible, and it felt like all of her was cooking up. She would survive. She was a survivor. She had to survive.

-60-

No. No no no no no no no. No. NO. NO NO NO NO NO. NO. Nooooo!

The Master came right into that living room and stood, a glance of shock and hatred on his face. He saw that living room floor filled with ectoplasmic tears and what looked like ghost blood. And that empty feeling tingled at the end of his senses, yes. Someone let the Mother of Darkness out, and even worse, someone had let the Grief inside. The two of them together? Deadly and awful, and the whole place was at stake, all of the Sunshine Family and the Gemini House itself.

He walked among the remains of what had happened here, slowly moving across the aftermath of the battle. The Sunshine Family was gone, that was it, he could sense it. He tried to reach out, to feel their chanting bodies, their sentient loops doing what sentient loops do best, and he felt nothing. Just an emptiness and a deep-in-the-marrow sorrow. They had taken everything away from him, and left him here, weakened without any psychic powers at all. Without the ghosts performing their ritualistic loops, he was left drained, and empty.

He punched that damn wall just to feel the pain of hardwood against his rough knuckles. Going to bleed later, but he didn't care. He was angry before, that was true. But now he was downright furious. He let out that primal scream that would have summoned his ghostly children to him once more, but no one showed up. And his sentinels stood to the right and left of him, and bellowed out an imitation of his anguished cry, their oozing, eye-covered tusks howling over the missing and the dead.

Oh, this was really bad, wasn't it? He felt himself fading already. He had to get his mojo back somehow, he was a god after all, but how could he do it? He was weak and starting to slip away from this world. He had to figure out a way to tap someone, anyone, anything, and slip their psychic power under his own skin. After that, he would have enough juice to kill the Sisters of Sorrow and their Stupid Grief and live for maybe another good twenty years or so.

But for now? Oh, he was leaking power right and left, and pretty soon he would barely be able to hold any of this together. His fingers and hand would slide off and maybe his head would droop down, and then he would be done for. He wasn't even sure he could keep the sentinels going, not without draining every last bit of his life energy just to keep them alive.

What little strength he had left he would use to shut down this house and keep it *here*. No way the three sorrows and their god-damned son could survive out in the nether world. Without sadness, without pain, without ghosts to feed on? Well, they would just starve to death, and that would be the final hurrah hurray yippie yay. He would be victorious, excelsior! Their suicides would not be in vain, and he would join them like he should've all those years ago.

He reached down and petted the leviathans, his soft human palm rubbing over their ectoplasmic essence, leaving sticky psychological residue flickering neon light in his hand. And they cooed beneath his touch, and made sounds like trilling birds. Fitting, then, that they would be the ones to take it down. Since the beasts contained bits and pieces, echoes and fingerprints, of all the different members of their big, beautiful, Sunshine Family.

But. Energy drained down. Coughed up a bit of black shit. No, no. This couldn't be happening now, not now, he still had to trap them here, in this dimension. He's not ready to ghost it yet! A ghost body is so limited in the magick it could handle. He needed blood and spit and bone to work the proper shit. And he had some of that still, yes, he did. Just enough to get things going. But not enough energy, no. Not enough to shut this down.

But hello. Wait. What was this? What was this feeling? A tickling in that psychic matrix of his mind. He felt it, yes, someone with *power*, oh, yes. He wiped a bit of that drool from his chin, and laughed a little bit. There was so much power here, he could feel it running off and through the air. Delicious stuff. And pungent, too. Like a wine that's about to hit the peak on the age charts. He licked his lips and closed his eyes, and he knew that flavor, that kind of power, oh, yes—oh, yes indeed.

Someone's been playing in the Sunshine Family toolbox. Someone confronted death in a tiny coffin and came out with a glimmer shine lamp head full of psychic abilities. He closed his eyes and focused on the lamp light, and saw her there, nearby, yes. It wouldn't be much further now, would it? Lily, that was her name, Lily. He felt it and it was so powerful.

Time to find her and become a little vampire himself. He could feed off that psychic strength and put an end to it all, close all the doors, slam them shut. It was time to get his revenge, even though it would kill him. It would be an honorable suicide, wouldn't it? Yes, yes it would. Too bad he'd have to take the Lily girl down into death with him. It would be the last sacrifice he would ask of another, mmm hmm. But probably *the most important*. Never mind the fact that she wasn't his to kill. Of course, she was—every child in the Gemini House was part of the Sunshine Family. That was how they rolled, they weren't monsters after all. They only fought them.

-61-

Lily gasped, out of breath, her hands on her knees as she panted in the hallway. Her face was stained with smoke, her hands hurting from the hammering, eyes stung bright with sweat. Everything felt so. Everything felt so. Everything felt so hot. Just so hot. She wiped that brow and sat down for a moment, just a moment, her palms slick with all that sweat, just to catch her breath. Remember that first day, Lily? It was hot then, too. The air so humid when they moved in, and she and Rae ran up to their bedrooms and unpacked and it was all so very exciting. How long ago that felt now, like an entirely different world.

Remember how happy everyone had been that day? Even Mommy and Daddy seemed like two different people. For a brief moment in time, they seemed happy and with it, together as a family. And that made Lily feel happy and whole, before the Great Divorce reared its ugly head and destroyed everything. That's what it started it now, right? It all began with those words, *your father and I are getting a divorce,* and then it all slid downhill from there. It felt like an apocalypse, and then the apocalypse happened, and now . . .

And now a fire raged around her, and she was pretty certain both Mommy and Daddy were dead, and she had to rescue Rae and get them both out of here and back to a normal life again. Would they ever even have a normal life again? Could they even survive this without being burned alive?

Some days she hated being psychic. She hated Daddy for putting her in that coffin, for training her to see ghosts and use the fire in her mind. But today was not one of those days. Today she would use those psychic powers to track down her little sister, and they would get out of this together. Oh, poor Rae, so misguided. She loved her anyway, even when they hurt each other. That was life. That was family. That was all and everything.

The fire grew stronger and the wailing *Dana Dana Dana* grew louder in the wood that surrounded her. She couldn't breathe, the air was so thick, she had to get out of this hallway. But which way did she have to go? She searched around inside, and she felt a psychic tendril pushing her toward the fire, telling her that's where Rae was, and she had to go that way to get her. No, no, that had to be wrong, that couldn't be right.

She didn't have the energy to brave the fire, and she knew that if she did, she would be toasted alive, just like the Rattling Boy. Maybe, maybe she could push the fire down with her mind? She closed her eyes and tried, tried so hard. The muscles on her face strained tight, her jaw clenched and moving back and forth. She almost bit on her tongue, twice, as she searched for that flame in her mind's eyes. Come on, come on, come on . . .

Dizzy now, with the straining. She tried to stand, and felt something moving about in her mind. What was this? Like fingers they caressed her thoughts and tried to get inside and pry her apart piece by piece. She didn't like this feeling at all, and then there was a voice that called out from far away, a voice spiraling out toward her and her sister. It sounded so familiar, and then there was a thump, thump, leg-bumping sound. And then a slithering noise, all liquid and awful. What could make a sound like that? It sounded like a hand rooting through the intestines of a corpse.

She knew that voice. She'd heard that voice all her life, from Daddy's records. How could that be? How could he still be alive? She opened her eyes, only to take a quick peek, and saw his shadow lurch and slurp toward her, moving between the flickering flames. How was he not dead? She would recognize that voice anywhere. That was the voice of the Master. Why wasn't he a ghost, like all the others? Hadn't he committed ritual suicide as well?

"You better stay put, child, stay put and don't even move a bit. Oh, yes, your real dad is coming for you, yes, he is. I am the king holy father of the Sunshine Family! And you are ours now, child. Blood and bone and burning light. You played one of our games, one of our Sunshine Family games, and so that makes you an honorary member! It does, it does! And your family needs you, child, your Sunshine Family needs your help! You have power, child, so much power, I'd never seen anyone with as much power as you. You know how often I'd done the *Hour of Smiles?* All in the hopes I could one day wield a force of power as great as the one you have right there? And look at you! You don't even know what great a gift you have. You just stay right there— Father Aum is coming to help you save everything!"

That voice, that voice she'd heard almost every night of her child-hood was here now, looking for her, wanting to use her in order to save the world. No, no, no. Something's not right. Every part of her told her that the Master wanted to hurt her, to use her up and spit her out once her powers were drained and gone. Funny, how soothing that voice was, and how often it'd rocked her to sleep through the years. It made her sad, and it made her miss her daddy. And then it gave her strength through fear, strength enough to stand straight, to stand strong and run toward the fire, running right toward the place where she knew her little sister would be.

Rae bent over and coughed up smoke and spat out cinders. She was trapped in a deep corner, surrounded by heat and by the licking flames. It was going to cook her, yes. This whole place would cook her all up, and there was no escaping now. That way, that way was the path of fire and certain, horrible death. Look at how it devoured the doors and the walls and the rooms. And behind her was the Mother of Tears . . . hungry for her sorrow. Trapped, trapped, immobile . . .

No, not like this, someone as awesome and amazing as Super Rae did not deserve to die like this. This was how lesser people died. People who weren't capable of murder. But wait. What are those shadows doing there beyond the flames? Look at them move all slowly, shuffling toward her and twitching about and laughing. Do you see the faces right there, looking right at you Rae? Do you see what they look like? They look like masks, and they look like . . .oh, no.

The doubles. Had they broken through the glass? How did they get on through? She saw them through the light of the flames, wearing Mommy and Daddy in the shadows. They called out to her, waved all friendly and polite to her, and mumbled weird words in their broken voices. She knew that they couldn't be her parents, that they had to be the mimics . . .

But. But. But.

She didn't want them to be dead, she wanted them to be alive more than anything else. But she knew that couldn't be right, and so she turned around, sadly, and started running back the other way.

And the house shook and wailed around her. A sound of intense grief, and Rae knew what the house felt—oh, she felt it too. That horrible grief was almost worse than the flames itself, and yes even worse than whatever death the mimics promised. Rae did not like this feeling, no oh, nuh-uh, not at all. This did not make her feel super clever and ultra-smart. This made her feel like a shattered doll or a ripped-up book. Completely useless to everybody.

She couldn't help it. She stopped running and pushed her hand against the wall, and then she wept and cried and screamed and beat the agony into the world. Then she felt something, something wooden touch her skin. Goosebumps, almost like flesh it felt. Almost like a human hand it felt. She looked around really quick and saw the walls themselves splinter a bit, corrupt and change and the beams turned into makeshift hands and touched her, and maybe held her for a second.

"You miss her, too?"

And Rae nodded. They both missed her, and she wanted to have comfort from that fact.

Maybe they could share in their sorrow, maybe they could heal each other. But oh no, that would never be the case, would it? The house hands squeezed and tightened and her lungs felt small and it was so much harder to breathe and her ribs pushed in and her skin and muscles and it all hurt from the fist closing round her. And the fire crept closer, the terrible heat so burning bright. Headache now and bone ache now and muscle ache now. Want to. Breathe. Can't. Breathe.

And what was this? Laughter in the walls but not the right kind of laughter, no. This was the laughter of someone who ceased to care about anything at all. The laughter of murder and death and all the bad things in the world.

"You miss her? You! You miss her? Oh, you lying, venomous child! I saw all of it. I watched the whole thing go down. You miss her! You don't get to miss her! You. You. You led her death right to her, you did, you let her die and and and . . . you just watched you just watched her die and I couldn't stop it, I wanted to stop it but I couldn't stop it . . . you horrible, rotten child!"

Rae pushed and shoved and felt the fist clench all around her, and her bones made noises and everything hurt. Hard to breathe right now, so hard to breathe. But she coughed out her words, defiant. Angry. "I did not! I! I! I was trying to save her from you! You're a horrible house! You pretend to love, but all you do is poison!"

Squeezed harder now. Breath. Lungs. Empty. Oh, Rae. No, no. Every part. Hurt. And soon. Arms close to breaking. Bending impossible back hurt now. Such pain. She felt spinfuzzy. Her spine like a steel bar of ache. Everything dimmed. Almost vomit. As the house wailed around her and spoke again. The very walls whispered out each word. It buzzed against her, making her skin itch. Snap. Crack. Her right arm broke and dangled like a noodle in the Coffin House grasp. She let out a horrible sad sound, a wounded animal sound. The pain was blinding her to everything else. Sharp light, that pain. Sharp light in her bones and in her skull.

"You don't know a thing! I was going to save her from all of this, from everything, from life and living and death and dying and everything! We would be so infinite together, and no, she didn't understand that, no. But she would, in due time I know she would see what I saw and feel again what I felt, I know, I do, I knew it then and know it now and it won't ever happen because you stole her from me and gave her death, and not just a normal death, no, the death of the void and endless sky, a death beyond my reach, beyond the ghosts and everything else . . . you thief, you horrible, petty thief child you . . ."

And then came another voice from behind the flames itself, a voice of the shadows. It pushed the fire apart like a flickering red veil, the mimics crowding behind it. Rae didn't want to see this, but she had to, she had to see this. There was nowhere else to look, her other arm going to break soon, she felt it now, felt it going. And then after that? Her ribs and her lungs and the certain death wouldn't be far behind and this house would swallow her up and spit out her skin like rotten taffy.

She wanted to close her eyes maybe, but no. She had to see this. The three figures, surrounded by the doubles of her family. Those three sisters. A pool of darkness floated around the air with faces flickering in and out. Eyes and teeth and bits of skin dripping out from it like a visceral rain cloud. Mater Tenebrarum, Our Lady of Darkness. In front of these inky shadows stood side by side, like two pillars. Mater Lachrymarum, Our Lady of Tears and Mater Suspiriorum, Our Lady of Sighs. The way they stood, hand in hand, left and right. They almost appeared as one whole creature, split dangerously down the middle.

Black lips not smiling or anything, Mater Lachrymarum was on the right and Mater Suspiriorum was on the left. That way their good eyes matched and they seemed to be one giant face, staring out, their fingers entwined like a spiderweb, as wasps darted all over their bodies.

And they hovered and floated and glided through the halls toward her. Their bodies outlined by fire, but the flames not touching them.

The three Mothers of Sorrow all spoke in unison. "Let the child go."

The house laughed and squeezed tighter and the world faded a little and everything was cold and Rae hated this so much. Would she even see Mommy and Daddy on the other side? Or would she be trapped forever in this burning house?

"No," the house spoke calmly, "This one *I* get to kill."

Rae felt everything get smaller and smaller and she wanted to scream, but she didn't have enough air. Not. Enough air. Not. Enough. She felt the whole world going black and dark and she heard fingers snapping and the fire roaring and everything felt dark and darker still as she swept away into shadows into sleep into darkness and a wailing void behind her eyes . . .

-63-

The fire burned as she ran, but she'd felt fire before, in the embrace of Toby, The Rattling Boy. So, she knew she could handle it, she knew that she could keep going straight. Just as long as she didn't run directly into the fire itself. She kept enough distance, making sure she could handle the pain. How bad would she be burned later? She didn't want to know. She had other things to worry about now. Like the Master, she knew he was right on her heels, catching up, catching fast . . .

And then before she knew it, she was on the ground. Everything was pain and the heat still bright, and the Master had caught up to her and tackled her. If only she'd been faster, if only she'd kept out of his reach. She tried to crawl further, tried to crawl away from him, she pushed and kicked, and some of his fingers slid off his body and crumpled to the floor. What was this? It was like he was barely held together . . .

She kicked again, and again, and slipped out from his grasp and started running. For a brief moment, she turned and looked at him, and saw two giant creatures moving through the dark, their bodies neon bright with psychedelic swirls. Each movement was an ooze of hallucinogenic light, scattering shadows like prisms in the air around them. What were they? Too large to follow the Master down the hall, yet they were connected to him. And she felt this twinge of sadness buzzing around them like a cloud of flies.

They were powered by the memories of the dead, and she saw all those ghost thoughts caught up and imprinted inside of them. They seemed so lost and broken and maybe they wanted to die. She reached out to them, because Lily understood that frame of mind. She had bad days, some days. Bad days since the coffin hours, when she felt tattered and worn out and she wished for death, for some kind of annihilation to end it all. And maybe she could help coax them out to help her.

Come on, come on, you're beautiful, yes you are. Her thoughts reached out like an open hand for them to sniff. And sniff it they did. She knew the Master came closer and closer, but she had to ignore him. Focusing on him was the worst possible thing she could do right now, hands down. Instead? Instead, she thought of those beasts. *Come on, get a little smaller. You could fit in here and help me, couldn't you? You help me with the Master, and I'll let you go. I'll free you from this world. Come on now, just shrink a little more and help us out, and then I'll let you go in peace.*

Just a kiss would be all it took. She didn't know how she knew that would be it, but she knew it. Beating heart, burning light, she knew it. And if it didn't work? Well then, well then. It would be better to face them down than to face down the Master. He wanted to hurt her, she saw it in his eyes, a terrible kind of hatred she'd seen off and on through the years in various young boys and old men. Men old enough to be her dad or her grandpa, hating her with their cold, venomous eyes. For no reason at all, just hating to hate.

She had to ignore him and concentrate, yes. Concentrate on getting out of this. Getting out and saving Rae and living just a little longer.

His screams almost dragged her out of her concentration. "Make it easy on yourself, child! Make it easy! Just give up and give in, you know you want to. The amazing and awesome Sunshine Family *needs* you, child. We need that magic humming power burning through you inside out. We're the last of the last, and we have to do this. Don't make me hurt you, I don't like hurting anyone. I'm a pacifist of all things, but just because I don't like it, well then. It doesn't mean I won't do it, you dig? Not if the stakes are high enough. And ho boy, dear child, the stakes are exceptionally high right now. High enough to put aside my petty ethics and take you apart with my own bare hands. That psychic power lasts for a bit even after death, you know, and I can siphon it from your limbs with a straw of thunder."

And that was a lie, she could tell. He enjoyed hurting other people, she heard it whispering in his voice, and there was an edge of joy oozing from him at even the thought of torturing her to get her psychic powers out and into the open. That was enough of that. That was enough of everything. He stood right before her now, his face falling apart and holy. His one still eye like white fire burning into her gaze.

Mouth open. Slack-jawed dripping teeth onto the ground. Numb words now almost like gibberish. His tongue breaking off, falling out of his mouth. *You will help us you will help us you will help us or I will hurt you or I will hurt you or I will hurt you.* It all broke her concentration, and she lost touch with those servitors at the end of the hall. That heat all around her blistering burnt up and the smoke choked her lips and lungs and enough was enough was enough was enough . . .

The fury inside of her now was a terrible thing. Uncontrollable. Something that had been placed inside of her the first coffin hour, yes, the first moment she'd been nailed in, that horrible wrath in the shape of a terrible egg that was put right there, right into her heart, right in the beating center of everything, oh yes. This fueled her psychic power, a kind of unnatural rage that sang out through her blood. The egg wanted to crack open and hatch and she just kept it shut. Her fingers always forced it closed, unable to crack open inside of her. And that was when the Rattling Boy came yes, when Toby first visited her. Had he been drawn by that light? By that egg of rage inside of her?

And now she couldn't hold that egg closed any longer. Fury full on bursting bright light and the egg cracked open and she was so distracted, her concentration so shattered by the hateful gaze of the Master that she couldn't stop it. She couldn't stop it from hatching right then. Her mouth opened wide in a scream that shook everything to the ground. And she . . . and she . . . and she—

splintered, crack, snap, opened

Blue light corpse light and she was engulfed in darkness, and her body went limp and her mind was elsewhere, ghostly in the dark, exploding in lightning and rage and terror.

-64-

Rae woke all groggy and distant, like a broken flashlight flickering to life. She moved about, tried to sit up. No. Blinding burning pain in her right arm, and she collapsed at the mere touch of it. *How did she get here? How did she escape the trap of the house?* Her arm was still broken, and she couldn't even move her fingers. Why. Why couldn't she even move her fingers? Soft weeping feeling and she just lay there for a few moments more. Everything closed in, closed close, the whole house seemed to shrink around her little by little.

Where was she? She looked up above and saw the stained-glass dome overhead, now void of any images. Their bedrooms behind her, and the walls had bent nails and torn clothing and the floor was coated in shattered dolls. Dolls ripped right from the walls and thrown on the ground.

How did she escape the clutches of the house? And there was this awful feeling inside. She knew that her sister had tried to create a path of sanctuary, once covered in sentinel dolls, and someone else had come along and ripped them down. Wasn't her this time, she definitely wouldn't have done it this time. *Footsteps of fire, leading into the empty corners of the house . . .*

She missed Mommy and she missed Daddy and she couldn't help it. This house sucked. She hated this new home, and this feeling boiled back over into sorrow again, and she cried a bit softly into her knees, and almost laughed again at how just, well, at how just insane all of this really was. This wasn't real, was it? Maybe she could restart everything all over again. Big old reset button on the last few days and change it all.

Remember Mommy saying that, remember? When there was a sad day just hit that reset button, and everything bad will go away. Mommy's voice echoed sad in her thoughts and memories. *Reset button.*

There you go, just press it. Make everything better, there you go. And wait, what was this? Bingo! Lightbulb! Idea! She could do something to fix the pain. Yes. Super genius Rae knew it! She got it! An idea!

She could make a makeshift sling for her arm with her shirt! She pulled it up and off (*ow, ow, ow*), her plain white camisole smudged with bits of crusted blood and dirt underneath. This would do! Already, the day seemed better. Rae dried her eyes and yeah, it wasn't easy doing this with one hand and one hand only. But, she was able to do it, and it made her smile.

So lost in thought, she didn't even hear footsteps.

Or the sound of wasps.

Or that voice now, like a sad whisper in the shadows.

"You don't have to thank us, Rae. We helped you escape that trap because we're family now, and family helps each other. You understand? You played the Happy Family Game and now you're one of us."

Don't look up don't look up, don't even give them that sick pleasure. She knew that voice so well now. Stupid tricky voice of the Lady of Sighs. She wanted to say something to shut them up, to make them all go away and leave her alone forever. The pain brutal sharp knife bones assaulted her thoughts. So sick of their games. *Happy Family Game.* Her family was dead, and she knew it as a fact that death did not bring happiness.

"No, I'm not."

Oh, they could hear that pain in her voice, couldn't they? Good, good, good. Break them with her words like the house broke her bone.

Another voice now, that of the Lady of Darkness. Slick and whispery and shadow-coated. *Don't look don't look don't look.* Though this time was harder. She wanted to look, she wasn't sure why, but she really wanted to look.

"You want to see them again, yes? Your old family, your family of meat and bone and blood? I know, I was the same way before I moved on to my new family, the Sisterhood of Sorrows. I just had to see them all again. Is that what you want, what you need? One last time with your dad?"

No, no, don't buy into it. No. It's a lie again, they always lied, and you know better than that. You're way smarter than any of those old witches put together. Super smart, super clever girl. Daddy's little genius, he always said so. "You can't show them to me, they're dead. And those things, those . . . I dunno. Those doubles, they're not them. They can't be them, not ever."

The Lady of Darkness spoke again so soft sweet and cinder-coated and shivery, "No, not the doubles, I promise, but instead the real deal. I can't show you your sister, that's not possible right now. But I can show you the ones kissed by the void, if you want to see them again. Just for a bit, they're still being digested in my nothingness, but I can let them speak if you want, if only just for a little bit. It's one of my gifts. And I would do it for you, I would do it for the Sisterhood of Sorrows. I would do that for *family.*"

Don't trust her don't trust any of them just . . .

And oh no, oh, what was this, her father's voice? She kept her eyes slammed shut because she knew it would be too much if she saw him. Even for an instant, it would be far too much. Still, that was his voice. Not an echo of his voice, or a recording of his voice, it was *his voice.* It even had that rumbling growl she loved so much. That baritone sound that vibrated against her head when she cuddled up close to him, as she felt the rise and fall of his chest as he breathed in and out. Just hearing it now, she remembered that moment, longed for that moment of peace once again.

"Man, oh man, Rae. How you doing, my little one, my sweet and lovely little one? How is my little genius doing? I miss you, you know. It's so lonely out here and far away from you. I hope you're doing so great, I worry about you, ho boy, do I worry about you."

Tears, oh, those stupid tears, and she crammed her face further into her knees and her arm hurt so much even in her sling. "I, I miss you too, and I worry about you. I'm so sorry, Dad, they tricked me, I didn't know what was going to happen, and I'm so sorry."

Laughter, and, oh, how she missed the sound of his laughter!

"Don't be sorry! This place is wonderful, Rae! It's so beautiful bright in here, so wonderful in the dark. It's hard to explain how the darkness can be shine so brightly, but it does! You should come in here, join with me and your mommy, come and see what beautiful sights we have to show you . . ."

And she sobbed harder and harder still and then there was this horrid sound, like the world being sucked into a giant vacuum, and, oh, Rae had to do it, she had to open her eyes, to see her daddy, but, oh. All she saw was a flicker of a shadow in his shape and then nothing. Ashes being sucked into the void of Mother Darkness.

"Sorry, my child," the Lady of Sighs cooed, as the shadows thinned a little around them, "So, do you want to join him in the void? Or would you rather stay here with us, and became one with our family? We all started as human children, like you. Just come closer, and ask, and we will give you our sweetest gifts."

Her body unwound from the spiral it had become. Pain sharp hurt so much. Even in that sling, the pain. Razors in her thoughts. And she had to struggle and wiggle to move and to stand up. She dried those eyes with the back of her sleeve, and looked at them. Looked at the sisters and saw them, *really* saw them for what they truly were. And they were beautiful, weren't they? So beautiful it caught her breath and stole it away forever. She held her arm close to her chest and the pain eased away only slightly. Just enough to let her think a little clearer, a little sharper. Just a tiny bit.

"Would I be beautiful, too?"

The three nodded in the dim light of the world. "Yes, my dear, my lovely child. So indescribably beautiful you will make anyone who looks at you heartbroken and sad for seeing such glory in their lifetimes."

She winced in pain and everything spun and darkness crept along the edges of her vision. She knew, maybe, that she shouldn't trust them. But hearing her daddy's voice. Oh. And that promise of being able to hear Mommy's voice, too. And being able to talk to them forever whenever she wanted to, and she would never be lonely again, would she? Never ever lonely again. Only one thing kept her from grabbing a hand and letting them change her, make her just like them . . .

"What about Lily?"

Three smiles in the darkness with teeth as sharp as the edges of stars. "She'll be okay, eventually, won't she? Oh, yes indeed, she'll find her own way to survive. Besides, she has all those powers of her own, right? Powers that were given to her *instead* of you. When we're done making you one of us, hollowing you out and filling you with our sadness? Well, then, you'll have your own powers, and they will outshine Lily's by a hundred thousandfold. Isn't that what you've wanted all this time?"

She remembered the coffin hours and the jealousy that came with it once more. A spinning bad feeling in her stomach, and she hated that feeling.

And so, she dried the final tears from her cheek with her good hand, and she winced as the pain echoed with each movement, and tried to muster her best girl scout smile. And then she nodded and walked forward, ready to go and change her life once again. For the better, this time. Yes. Finally. For the better. She would be with Daddy and Mommy. And she would be so powerful, so much more powerful than Lily ever was.

. . . pieces of skin and loose body parts all around Lily and fire and fury inside of her, that Master was just scattered around her and the body parts covered in strange yellow sludge and no blood in the body anymore and now everything was RAGE AND FURY AND FIRE and everything felt like lightning and everything felt like thunder and her vision was red blood red licking flames red was it real red or just this waking inside of her never like this before psychic powers now fully rising up mind of their own or was this her mind the whole time her mind now burning alive and oh look at that look at hands coated in flames and look at her feet coated in flames and everything all of her body now embraced the fire in the walls in the ceiling it didn't hurt and she didn't burn she was like the Rattling Boy now completely engulfed in it completely consumed with it and she felt it on her lips on her teeth on her tongue and everything was bright bright bright and she was magnificent to behold so wonderful and beautiful the fire a golden crown on her head and halo hungry and the fire would not quench her rage now all over and inside and burning up the Master had pushed her and pushed her too far and now even her eyes are golden bright and even her mouth shines with infinite light and now she floats across the floorboards feet scraping the edges of the world sucking in that fire all around her and fury fury fire fury fury anger never so much hatred at the world now a world that stole everything from her and left her alone in the dark stole parents and her friend and everything else this house this evil house these things within the walls these horrible things the Sunshine Family meant to hold in and keep safe she would destroy everything burn it all down rage hungry fire now burning through the hallways at the end of time burning through the world like nothing matters at all anymore hunting down the grief and the Sisters of Sorrow she didn't even care if she lived after this no not a care with anything at all anymore just tiger tiger burning bright wheel of flame halo of body messenger of destruction her psychic power now unleashed devouring all destroying all consumed by all . . .

-66-

Until oh no oh god oh no until Lily saw them there in the massive living room all five of them and oh, and oh, her heart burst into a flood of blood. Everything was overwhelmed by sadness, as her fury drained out of her body at the sight of them. Her sister on the floor, in the center of that living room, all of the furniture gone and moved into distant hallways. Rae, Rae, oh god oh no, oh Rae oh Rae oh. In the center of that living room, framed by the legs of giants. Those pillars surrounding the five bodies all ominous and full of watching weight. No, not her sister too, she didn't know what she would do if they took her sister, too. Mommy gone Daddy gone Rattling Boy gone and they'd left her all alone.

Strangers stood over her sister, and there was a psychic weight to everything, the very air itself alive with thunder and cyanide. Rae lay flat on the floor with her arm in a sling. Rae, what happened to you? And this feeling, such a sad horrible feeling it crushed her insides, and Lily fought against it, but it was so strong.

Three women so strangely tall, taller than anyone else she'd ever seen. Not quite giants, but still. A head taller than Daddy, even. And they were covered with wasps and this horrible light that felt strange and blue and haunted. They moved over her sister's body, and Rae, oh, Rae with eyes closed and knives made of void and shadow dangle down above her body. Candles flicker-dripped wax and this lump in her heart and in her throat and please, oh please, where did that fury go? Where did that psychic burst of light go? When she needed it most right now to save the last living member of her family?

No more death, please, oh oh oh please no more death no more death just please . . .

And behind them floated a child, a boy with hair golden flying about his head in a wave of curls. Eyes like white fire. Burning bright, those eyes. Now her heart slowed as she looked around and felt everything slow to a crawl, the seconds kissing close to infinity. She was still unseen by the figures outside. Hiding just enough, just enough.

She had to stop this. Shit. Come on, Lily, come on! She tensed her hands into a fist, her mouth pinched shut into a thin line. Come on! Say something, make some noise! Bring out that fire again, come on! That rage again! Come on! Please, oh, please come on do something do anything just a little thing whatever she couldn't just stand by and lose Rae too, she couldn't . . .

All frozen and broken and sadness made even the littlest movements impossible. She was going to lose her. That brought even more depression, a crawling wave of grief and, oh, her mother was dead, and, oh, her father was dead. And to think, she'd been so worried about divorce. Divorce was nothing compared to this.

She leaned down with her arm around her knees and head into her elbows and just. Just. Maybe everything will go away and leave her alone and that would be okay. Sad now, too sad to even cry, her tears all dried up. She peeked up over her knees and saw them bring the knife down. Dig the knife under her sister's skin. And what came up wasn't blood. It was liquid night, star-filled and terrible, and did Rae smile a brief, haunted smile?

She had to turn her head and look elsewhere—she couldn't watch this. Why couldn't she use her psychic fury to save her sister? Why had it left her in her most dire time of need? Perhaps it was because she was sad, not angry. Where was her rage? Where? Those tears welled up, and sadness was all she felt. Sadness and horror and a destabilizing grief that choked all emotions from her body. Shivering and trembling and she felt so cold in her heart. So cold and distant.

And then a voice. A voice breaking the ritual silence. Female, raspy. The darkness itself spoke to her, and it made her whole body tingle like fire.

"I can sense such beautiful sadness, my sisters, do you feel it? So delicious, it will feed our ritual, give our motions power and hunger and weight. Do you understand, Rae? This will be your milk soon. This depression of your sister? It will be what feeds you in the dark, once the ritual is done."

A smirk and a smile in the shadows. That was it, yes, that's exactly what she needed to hear. Her own sadness was powering this ritual?

To hell with that. Her psychic rage started to blossom inside of her again. They were manipulating her. Tainting her emotions with this false sadness, all to feed on it, to suck it from her and power this stupid ritual with it. Why did everyone see her as a human battery? She wasn't a battery.

She was the oncoming storm. She was a fucking phoenix of fire and thunder.

A cough in the dark and she was engulfed in lightning and fire once more.

Lily ruined everything! Rae couldn't even get her own special powers, could she? No, no, of course not. Because Lily had to show up and just completely wreck it all! Feel that crackle of lightning and it jolted her skin, but no, she wouldn't move, maybe they could finish it before Lily finished them? Please oh please oh please she never wanted anything so much before in her life. After all she'd been through, after all she'd seen and done, and if this didn't happen? What would be the point of it all? What would be the point of anything?

At first the knife didn't hurt but after a while it did and she didn't scream although there was a single tear, yes. A single tear. But, hey, having your bones removed was way harder and more painful than being nailed in a coffin! See? Super genius Rae was way better than Lily! Bite your lip close your eyes, come on. Hurry, hurry, hurry come on. Time to push on through that pain. Because after all, pain was only a momentary thing. Having magic awesome super powers would be for-ev-er.

And as she struggled with that tearing skin feeling, the little lantern boy floated down toward Lily. And Rae closed her eyes and didn't want to watch this anymore. There were sounds of screaming and painful wailing and was Lily dying? No Rae, keep your eyes closed, don't look at this. Don't even take a peek at this. Whatever you see now will haunt you forever, and you need to just let that pain wash over you, eyes closed, and any minute now and she'll be done.

Maybe she felt an ache at the thought of Lily's death, and what was this? What was this even? Now she really did feel hollowed out. All her emotions raw and naked and on display. She opened her eyes and watched them fighting and the boy was dead and the mothers wailing and screaming and running forward to attack Lily and wait, what was this? Rae felt something stir up in her guts. This darkness they'd placed inside of her ran around her insides. And her bones where still there, yes, but there was something else. Something around these bones. Like a worm made of sorrow and sighs. This new thing inside of her fed on the grief in the air.

She felt herself rise up and surrounded by black flames made of night. Lily. Oh, Lily. She would help her sister, she had to help her sister, why had she been so selfish before?

"Rae, come on! Forget this, forget all of this, I know we can escape. Can you feel it? The path to our freedom. Can you feel it, Rae?"

And the path was hungry and the house around them shook and cried out in sorrow again and the rooms started to shrink and change. You could tell it hurt the house to snap back like this, to return to her old shape once again. As walls burst and split and tried to suffocate them.

The four Sisters of Sorrow rose up all spectral nightmarish things. They held their dead boy in their arms like the body of a saint, as they rushed towards Lily. Mad howling creatures of sorrow and grief and anger and sigh tears darkness pain. They carried no poise anymore, that inky shadow pool now latching onto Lily, the Mother of Darkness dripping blood and teeth and now an eyeball or two (*tempestuous eyes, like the sea*) and now Rae screamed. They were furies coming for them. Furies with claws and wasps and anger at their dead child in their arms.

Rae would not let this happen again, no! She did nothing far too many times, nothing!

She felt that darkness around her bones, as they burst out bright as the house crushed and changed and yelled out in misery. The depression of the house fed Rae and she drank it in deep so that the Sisters of Sorrow could have none, not even a little drip. This was to be her power, now, and she was going to use it to destroy them.

The house shook and shrank around them *you killed her you killed my beloved Dana and you will all die you will all be burned and crushed and you will be nothing but corpses and whispers and nothing else!*

Rae decided that this was it. She ran *quick quick quick*, the darkness in her bones giving her speed beyond speed, as her skin cracked a little, but she ignored that now. She kept on going through the pain and grabbed onto Lily's hand as the flame and her own shadows mixing up double helix of lightning and dark fire. She burned away and turned away and ran fast through the house. They followed, quick, hunting and snarling in the burning light of the house fire. The air violent with sulfur and smoke. As they ran, pursued by the snarling Sisters of Sorrow.

"Rae! Rae! You hear us, you traitor, you horrible thing? You betrayed your new wondrous happy family! And for that, oh, for that you will watch us eat your sister bit by bit, and when we are done, we will turn on you and eat you, yes, eat every bit of you! Feasting on your grief all the while!"

And no, no, don't turn around, don't, you don't want to see how close they are, you heard them and they weren't far behind and so keep going, keep going, Rae! Thunder of bodies moving through the veins of this house, following that hungry path. Her own skin cracking again and rays of darkness shot out and painted the air with shadows. They would have to survive this. They would have to survive. Inside she was screaming. Inside. Screaming so loud. Inside. Screaming. Inside.

-68-

Dana! Dana! Dana! You stupid monsters you stupid ignorant creatures stole such beauty from the world such light from the world, and
oh the house will destroy you and burn you and make you into coffins
at the end of time and encase your bones inside her wood and walls
and nails and plant your skeletons inside her belly forever she was
the coffin house after all and her entire existence was that of death of
housing death of keeping death within her walls buried beneath the
void between universes and she would devour those Sisters of Sorrow
and suck in all of their energy and grief and starve them out here
beyond the worlds and burn up and burn everything and death would
be everywhere death would be everything feel them move about
inside of her now squeeze her stomach and squeeze her walls and
crush and bone crush and death crush and there was no escaping let
that fire roam out now all warm and burning her insides sure it hurt
and sure it was pain but oh Dana! Oh Dana! It hurt nowhere near as
bad as her death her pain feel that touch against her again her hand
against her again her body inside of her and they would bring each
other so much pleasure and beauty and light and oh Dana! Oh Dana!
Oh Dana! Death to your insolent children and death the ones that
were imprisoned inside of her and even death to herself yes death to
herself . . .

*she couldn't go on living like this not without her love her all and
everything . . .*

There, up ahead! They saw it all coming in close, running and tripping and out of breath and stumbling and just barely making it. The Sanctuary! It was still guarded by sentinel dolls nailed across the edges. And there, right there! Do you see the mirrors up ahead? Do you see them now reflecting not this world exactly, but something else? That familiar hill, that garden down beneath it and surrounded by pines? They never thought they would be so happy to see the hills of home, where the Coffin House had stood not too long ago. This was it—they were going to do it, they were going to escape.

Rae and Lily held hands and clasped tight and their bodies surrounded by smoldering heat and choking air. They were a burning bright light and the whole place collapsed around them. Walls shuddered and shook and the ceiling crumbled down, tumbled down, ruin of a place, as they ducked beneath and crawled forward zoom-fast hands and knees. Drywall dust and stone ground up and haunting the air and heat now and fire spread even faster now. But that's okay, Lily was at the rear and could devour the flames with her own light. Fire in fire in fire. No pain in that fire, no. Only her own flicker flicker devouring everything.

And the Sisters of Sorrow screamed behind, their own magic growing weaker and weaker, as the house fed on them, drank their own powers, and used it to commit suicide, destroying them all. And each time they tried to feed on the house's sorrow, the house fed on them instead. A recursive loop fueled by terrible emotions and ancient sentience fighting for control.

And walls splintered cracked exploded fell down. Rae almost trapped now beneath and coughing and hell. Rae was not one to swear but hey she figured now was the right time for it. So she let loose a torrent of bad words and she hurt her lungs and it all hurt so much as

Lily pulled her from the rubble and shoved her into that room. That sacred protected room, that not even the house itself could crush or crumble into rubble.

And they grabbed hands and ran through and fell out onto the other side. The night beyond them coated with a sprinkling of stars, as the pines swayed eerily beneath them. The Sisters of Sorrow unable to make it past the sentinels, unable to follow them. They had to stand there, right out of reach, as a fire consumed and the house fell in on itself, and yet the mirrors stayed still. Stayed silent. Part of the house, that protected part of the house, not dying. Not collapsing. Nothing.

And they fell down and cried silently, holding each other close, as Lily wrapped her entire body around Rae.

"Are you okay?"

And Rae nodded against her sister's chest, crying softly on her shirt. "Yeah. You?"

"I guess," and Lily sighed and put her chin against her sister's head. "But. Well. My powers are gone now, completely and utterly. It feels lonesome without them. Like there is a great silence all around me now that wasn't there before."

"Uh huh," Rae burrowed her head further into her sister's chest, as if she were trying to climb inside of her. "My powers are gone, too. It's like my bones are quiet, no longer singing under my skin. What do we do now? Where do we go from here?"

And then the wind picked up and blew dead leaves around them, as the mirror door flickered just a moment, shining bright with its own light, standing tall where the house once stood. Right there on that hill.

How much time had passed since they left the real world behind? Enough for a season to change, even though it felt only like days. Time must move differently in that mirror world.

Lily reached inside of her pocket, and pulled out her chunky flip phone. Mom had given it to her just for emergencies. She watched it stir awake, hoping for a few bars and a signal. Where they really here? Where they really once more in the real world once again? Or had they just gone someplace else, to be hunted by some other creatures that wanted them dead for God knows what reason?

A pause. Yes, there were a few bars, they had a signal and enough power for a call. She dialed her aunt's number, and let it ring quietly between the two of them on speakerphone. Her aunt would know what to do. Yes, yes. Her aunt would know exactly what to do.

-70-

And once they were settled into the motel room, Lily flopped back on the bed and started humming quietly, without thought. They were waiting for their aunt to come and get them, and they hoped it wouldn't take long. They needed to be around family again, to feel like they were home again. Rae wore a cast now. They'd taken an Uber from the vacant hill to the hospital. And then another Uber from the hospital to this hotel. Their Aunt Heidi had paid for everything, and she was excited to come and get them. She couldn't wait to take care of them and raise them as her own. It all seemed so perfect. And yet, so sad. So very, very sad. They'd told her Mommy and Daddy had gone missing one day, and left it at that. The police were looking into it, but Lily and Rae both knew that would amount to nothing.

The song Lily hummed was just a few simple chords, something catchy. Something that wormed itself into her brain from Daddy's records. When she realized it was a Sunshine Family song she stopped for a moment. Her breath caught in her chest.

And Rae, oh, unperturbed Rae. Rae who never seemed to understand the gravity of the situation, let alone something as awful as this. Her clueless sister just smiled and sang along with her, just like it was nothing at all, and they hadn't experienced something horrible in the Sunshine Family's house.

It's almost all over now
The birds are dead
And the bride wears red
It's almost all over now

Somehow, Lily felt lighter after hearing Rae sing this. And so they sang together for a moment, the strange absurdity of it all washing over them. Their harmony was a little rough and jagged and that was okay. It wasn't a song that required perfect harmony, was it? No, not in the least. And when the song was done Rae joined her sister on the bed. And they looked up at the ceiling for a moment together, imagining the stars that must be outside and overhead, hidden by black tiles and the light pollution outside their room. Waiting for their aunt, waiting for their aunt.

Lily tried to remember the last time they saw their Aunt Heidi, maybe two years ago? Maybe last year? She wasn't sure. She remembered her aunt being pretty with glasses and freckles and a weird smile that seemed to always imply more than she said. They played dumb games with her, and then she would read their tarot cards and give them astrological star charts and bits of homemade brownies.

The memory of her aunt made her warm and happy inside. And as usual, the happiness made her hum a song, and then briefly sing a little. And Rae joined in as well, the two of them, just sitting there, singing.

Laughing, briefly, at how silly it all was, yes. That after all this time, here they were, singing a Sunshine Family song, of all things. Not on purpose, mind you. That was just how it was, when songs popped into your head, unasked for and intrusive. For a moment, yes. For a moment Lily thought maybe that was her Daddy singing in her head. That maybe he was still out there, watching them.

She rolled over and grasped Rae and held her tight. She tried to keep back those stupid tears. The thought of a ghost daddy living in her memories was too much. A ghost mommy might be there, too. And maybe even the Rattling Boy, yes. Kept alive by her own thoughts and memories. These were different kinds of ghosts, ghosts she wasn't used to just yet.

And while the sisters laughed and tried to think of better thoughts, something stood outside of their motel window. Something obscured by the thick yellow curtains. And yet, you could see them if you tried. Their bodies outlined by street lamps and the roving lights of passing cars. Motionless figures all silent still and staring. It was as if they could see beyond the window and the curtains to the two little sisters laughing inside.

Four outlines all huddled together. Their shadows hungry. Savage fingers tapping on the glass. *Tap tink tap.* The girls not even noticing, not wanting to notice, preferring to be oblivious to whatever it was that pined for them. They turned out the lights, made sure the locks and clasps were shut tight on the door, and quickly propped up a chair under the door handle, just as Mommy had showed them ages ago. An extra precaution against unwanted visitors, as they crawled back into bed and held each other all night, unable to sleep. Sometimes a strange breeze would blow through the room and move the curtains aside to reveal four figures still standing there—with blue skin, wearing their faces, and Lily and Rae would close their eyes shut and pray for sleep. Their aunt would be here soon. She would knock, and they would open the door, and travel off to their new home in Wisconsin.

Any moment now.

ACKNOWLEDGMENTS

No book is ever written in a vacuum, so I would like to shout out to some first readers and critiquers that helped me along the way into getting this into print. First off, the glorious Broken Circles crew, Jonathan Wood, Michelle Muenzler, Natania Barron, and Jacques Barcia.. Next up, Todd Main and Area 1 Pennwriters, especially the Fellowship of the Quill. Finally, Robert S. and Jennifer Wilson, who took a look at this in one of its primordial stages back in the pre-pandemic time. Also thanks to Darin Bradley for editing the hell out of this and getting into shape before publication, and thanks to Mark Teppo for the kick ass cover, it rocks. Thanks to Ashlyn and Liam Jessup, who I brainstormed and ran some of the more horrific ideas passed while writing, just so I could gauge their reactions and try to figure out if I need to push it further or pull back the horror a little.

And finally, a shout out to Dru Pagliassotti for publishing my first ever horror short story wayyyy back in the Harrow in around 2004 or 2006 or so, and setting me on this dark path.

Printed in the USA
CPSIA information can be obtained
at www.ICGtesting.com
BVHW031049030923
669018BV00002B/111